A Different Summer

Sophia Escajeda

Print ISBN: 979-8-9879169-0-2

EBook ISBN: 979-8-9879169-1-9

Developmental Edit by Makenna Albert

Formatted with Atticus

Warning: This book contains sensitive material relating to child abuse, suicidal and self-harm implications, and language. Please read with caution.

To Ernesto and Ella, for being some of the greatest people I know.

Thank you for always being by my side and supporting me.

Here's our council anime!

— • —

Content Warning

This book contains sensitive material relating to

Child abuse

Suicidal Implications

Self-harm Implications

Language

Please read with caution.

1

THE FINAL BELL RINGS, signaling the end of the day, and the end of my sophomore year. Summer has finally begun. My heart pounds as I put my notebook into my backpack. My eyes scan the classroom. Through the open door, students throw their papers into the air and cheer. Others run through the hallway, trying to get out as fast as they can.

Most of the students have already left, but Rose is still putting things in her bag. Her wavy red hair rests on her shoulders. She turns to face me, and I look away. The letter is in my pocket. I can do it. I know I can. Her notebook lies on the table. I could slip it inside. I start taking the letter out, but I freeze. I can't move. Rose puts the notebook in her bag.

There's still a chance. I still have time. She zips up her backpack and looks at me. "Are you coming?" she asks with a chuckle.

"O-oh, yeah!" I snatch my backpack off my chair. "I'm coming!"

The hallway is empty now. Rose goes to her locker that's across from our classroom. She pulls out the textbook inside. Rose holds the book with one hand and slides her backpack around herself. She unzips her backpack, nearly dropping her textbook.

"Do you want me to grab it?" I ask, staring at the textbook. Her teacher made the class hang onto it longer for their final.

"Yeah, if you don't mind," she replies. I grab the textbook, and Rose holds her backpack open. I place it inside and zip it up. Rose smiles. "You have any plans for the summer?"

"Not really. Play games, hang out with friends, cook, then preseason," I answer.

"Isn't preseason at the end of summer?"

"Well, yeah." Preseason is the marching band's training—or band camp. It always signifies the end of summer. "There's not much I do during summer," I tell Rose.

"Well, there has to be *something* you want to do," Rose says as she slams her locker shut. I don't answer, because what I really want to do depends on her. We walk toward the hallway door that leads to the stairs. My heart's beating fast, and I put my hand in my pocket, feeling the letter once more. I open my mouth, wanting to stop her, wanting to talk to her. Anything.

"Hey, Rose?" I finally say. She turns around with a lovely smile. My mouth runs dry, and my cheeks turn red. I'm tripping over my words when the sentence comes out, "Y-your shoe's untied."

She looks down, and it is untied. "Again? Oh well, I'll fix it later." Before she can finish her sentence, I crouch down to the floor and tie it for her. Her face is light pink when I return. "T-thanks! Um... I have to turn my book in! See you later!" Rose says in a hurry. She runs out the door and down the stairs.

Dammit! I blew it! I walk through the door and go down the stairs, cursing myself for letting the chance fall out of my hands. My friends helped me plan it during fifth period. Maybe they won't ask?

The door opens behind me. "Paco! Wait up!" *Oh no.* I turn around. It's my best friend, Owen. Considering he's the only other kid in the hallway, he absolutely saw what happened. I wait for him to say something. He points to my head. "I just noticed. Your hair's pink again."

"Oh, yeah. I re-dyed it last night."

"Good, because it looked horrible." Owen laughs. "Did not think pink dye would end up looking like that after a few months. That's the worst you've had it."

"In my defense, it was a different brand," I say, reaching the bottom of the stairs. We step into the sun and walk to the right. Curse the band room for being so far from the B hallway. We make it to the band room and cut through it to exit the school. A few seconds of air-conditioning makes me feel better. Although Owen's face is still red when we leave.

Owen leans against the pillar in front of the band room. "Is everyone on their way?" he asks.

"They should be. We agreed to meet here," I answer, joining Owen on the pillar. He takes out his phone, and we stand in silence.

"You completely failed your mission," Owen says. Dammit. I should've known he wasn't going to let that go. I look away, and he continues. "Also, you look like a mess, and Rose is coming this way."

"What?" How did she return her book so fast? I don't stop to think as I snatch Owen's phone out of his hands and go to the camera. I move my fingers through my hair. Not much I can do with curly hair, but it looks better now.

Owen takes his phone back with a smirk. "I lied, it's Sam. Pachi and Yann are behind her." I gulp. *I'm so screwed.*

"You won't believe how fast I ran into the band room this morning," Pachi says, running his hand through his dark hair. "I followed a car through the gate, and it was my math teacher. I'm still shocked I got it up here, and in the front." Pachi's car is a seven-seater with strong air-conditioning, and definitely not a car that belongs to faculty members.

"So, where are we going?" Sam asks. She wipes the sweat off her brown face. "I'm freaking starving."

Yann pulls his hair into a ponytail. His stomach growls. "You guys pick. I'm up for anything."

Pachi shrugs, so I turn to Owen. "Want to get chicken?" I ask.

"Let's get chicken," Owen answers.

"Ooh, you know what I've been craving? Lumpy's. They have some good chicken there." Sam smiles.

Yann scratches his head. "Lumpy's? I haven't been there before."

"What? You've lived here for how long and never been there?" Pachi exclaims.

Yann counts on his fingers. "Three years? I don't know, and you guys have been here longer!"

"Well, Lumpy's it is." Pachi unlocks the car. "Let's get going. They close early."

My friends walk toward the car, but Yann pulls me to the side. "How did it go?" he asks in a soft voice. I nearly facepalm. Of course he would ask! He's the one who brought up the idea, and he's been telling me to confess for weeks! *Okay, I'll tell him that Rose had to leave really fast, and I couldn't give her the letter. He'll believe that, right?*

"I chickened out." *Wait, no!* I keep my hands at my side, praying that he didn't hear me.

Yann stares at me for a few seconds. When I don't respond, he groans. "Are you serious?" I stay still, the embarrassment clear on my face. "Paco!" Yann yells.

"What? What happened?" Sam asks, turning to face us. I don't know how to answer the question. Sam sighs. "You didn't give her the letter, huh?"

"I panicked!" My defense is crumbling, and every excuse I've come up with has gone out the window. "I was going to put it in her notebook so she wouldn't see me, but there wasn't a good time." That's half true. The notebook idea wasn't smart. She would've seen me instantly.

"How long have you liked her now?" Pachi asks.

"Since seventh grade," I mutter, and when he claims he didn't hear me, I say again, "Seventh grade!"

Sam puts a hand on my shoulder and turns me toward her. "Paco, if you do not tell Rose before preseason starts, I will kick your ass."

"Tell me what?"

Shit! I turn around. Rose stands behind me, and I nearly bump into her. She's so close to me. "Hey, Rose," I stammer. "You turned in your book already?"

"My friend took it since she was on her way there. Saved me a trip." She smiles. The silence is thick. My arms are stiff at my side as Rose tilts her head. "Did you need to tell me something?"

My heart races as I reach into my pocket. My hands are clammy, and my face is red. Rose stands there so beautifully, still wondering what I have to say. My hand touches the letter and time freezes. *Just give it to her!* I yell at myself. My arm turns to stone, my mouth runs dry, and no matter what, I can't bring it out. What if she says no? What will I do? Maybe I can give it to her and run. Run fast and far. Or maybe I can hop in the back of Pachi's car and never see the light of day again.

"It's nothing, don't worry." Rose's eyes look to the right after I speak, and I hope my friends aren't showing their disappointment at the chance I just wasted.

Rose looks back at me. The tension between us is still awkward. "Okay then. I'll see you around." Rose waves, and my heart sinks to the bottom of my chest.

"Do you need a ride, Rose?" Pachi's voice cuts the silence. My head turns to look at him. He smiles. "We're heading to Lumpy's. We'll take you home after. You could sit in the back with Paco." *Huh? Pachi, what are you doing?*

My face is red again as Rose chuckles. "I'd love to, but my parents are here already." She looks at me. "Maybe next time?" With that, she walks away. Dammit.

My friends get inside the car. Sam's riding shotgun, Owen's in the third row, and Yann's sitting behind Sam. I sit next to Yann as Pachi starts the car and pulls out of the parking lot. The car is silent as we depart from school. I think they're letting me off the hook. I lean back in my seat and look out the window.

"Dude, what the hell was that?"

My head turns to see Sam glaring at me. "What do you mean?" I ask.

"You had the perfect chance to give it to her!" Pachi answers, looking at me through the rearview mirror. "You were so close! Hell, if she could've come, you could've given it to her then! Imagine that, us at one table and you lovebirds at your own. A diner date!"

"You need to tell her soon. I'm going to do it myself at this point!" Yann says, and I shrink. He then asks, in a serious tone, "What happened? You were so confident during band when we planned it."

"I don't know. Really, I don't," I respond, taking the letter out of my pocket. I wrote the letter in my notebook during class. It's folded nice and neat, complete with the drawing of a heart.

Owen peers over my shoulder from the third row. "Hey, it's okay. There will be other chances. It took me ages to confess to Katie."

"She got tired of waiting and asked you, remember?" Sam counters.

"I was going to tell her that week!" Owen's face has brushes of red as he continues. "My point still stands, but I really think you should do it soon."

I put the letter back in my pocket. "I don't want to tell her over text. It doesn't feel right."

"We could try giving her a letter again," Yann says.

"I've lost count of how many times I tried to give her one. It never works." I keep chickening out. The letters don't seem perfect, and everything goes wrong.

"Maybe you could give her a present?" Pachi suggests.

"What do I do with it if she says no?" I ask. Pachi doesn't know how to answer. He shrugs in defeat.

"Aren't you working at the bakery tomorrow?" Owen asks, and I nod. "Make her a cupcake!" My eyebrows raise. He shrugs. "At least you can eat it if she says no."

"It would be easier than the letter." I don't think I can hide it from her any longer. I've loved her for so long. It was the first day of seventh grade, and she was in a table group with me and Sam. The popular kids bullied me the previous year because of my looks, but Rose wasn't like that. Rose talked to me like I was normal.

I didn't believe in love at first sight, but my crush only grew the more I got to know her. I've almost confessed three times this week by accident. If I don't tell her soon, I might explode. "Okay, I'm doing it. I'm telling her tomorrow." And to get it in my head, I say it one more time.

My friends cheer. The car ride downtown is swift, and we park in front of Lumpy's. Pachi pushes the door open. The diner is bustling with servers, and the smell of french fries makes my mouth water. My eyes trail from the signs on the wall to the empty tables. It's not as packed as I thought.

"Hi there!" the waitress says with a smile. "How many?"

We look at each other. There are only four seats at the small tables. How are we splitting?

The waitress chuckles. "You know what, go ahead. Take the table at the back. There aren't a lot of people coming in today."

I sigh in relief as we hustle to the table. My friends get settled and I take a chair from the table beside us. The waitress comes with our menus, and we order drinks and food. My phone blares with a message.

Paula: Ay Paquito, of course they can come! As long as they're free and bring their own beds, LMAO.

I roll my eyes at the nickname and turn to my friends. "Are you guys going to be free for Paula's party?" Since my sister has a pool now, she throws a party whenever possible. Last time, Owen, Yann, and I stayed up the entire night. Paula almost made us sleep in the hot tub.

"Considering I got fired, I'll be free." Pachi sighs. The poor man was "let go" and still doesn't know why.

"I'm free in ten years," Sam says, sipping her coffee. I'll never understand how she takes it straight black. She looks down with a sigh. "I'll see, cross your fingers."

I frown. "You haven't been there in ages. Paula will pay you to come at this point."

Sam smirks. "Told you I was the favorite."

Sam and I have been friends since preschool. We met on the first day and hit it off immediately. The summers back then were filled with us running around and getting into trouble. From towering pillow forts to water balloon fights that broke two windows. It was just the two of us until sixth grade. There we met Owen, and after a few months in band, we met Pachi. The next year, Yann transferred to our school. We've been inseparable ever since.

"You know who you should invite?" Pachi asks. "Rose. I'm sure she'd love to go." My face turns a deep red, and Pachi bursts out laughing. The waitress returns with our baskets of chicken strips and fries, stopping Pachi from teasing me any further. Yann digs into the food quickly and comes up with a smile. Safe to say he likes it.

A family of four walks in. The three kids are cheering as they race toward the table behind us, not noticing we're here. Their father apologizes for the rush in and walks toward them. The first thing I notice is that he's tall, maybe even six feet, with dark brown skin and eyes. He takes a seat, telling his kids to settle down. I catch the name of the boy with spiky hair, Leo.

The waitress comes by a few moments later, refilling our drinks and taking the orders from behind us. She drops off the bill, and we fight over who's paying. Leo keeps sneaking glances. I lock eyes with him and wave. He hides his face in the menu.

"Are any of you trying out for section leader?" Pachi asks. "We're going to need some good ones."

I look at my friends, and Owen stares at his soda. "I am," he announces, "I doubt I'll make it."

Yann leans forward, shocked. "What do you mean? You're one of the best players we've got!"

In the corner of my eye, Leo's head perks up. "Wait, you guys are in band?" he asks.

We turn to look. "Yeah, we are," I answer with a smile.

Leo's eyes light up. "Do you guys remember us? We were at the Showcase! You know, when you perform with the eighth graders?" Leo points to himself. "I'm Leonardo, but you can call me Leo. This is Lucy and Peter." They look identical to Leo. Tan skin and brown hair, but Lucy has long, wavy hair, and Peter's is short with no spikes. When we shake our heads, Leo says, "The triplets!"

I turn to Owen, who has a much better memory than me. "There were triplets there?"

"I don't remember," Owen answers. He looks at Leo. "What section are you in?"

"I'm a trumpet, Lucy's a flute, and Peter's a clarinet. He can play saxophone too!" Leo points to his brother, who turns away, embarrassed.

"No wonder we don't recognize you. We're all low brass," I respond.

Leo's mouth starts to move, but Lucy speaks first, "Oh, really?"

I nod, and quickly introduce myself before continuing, "Pachi and I are trombones. Owen and Yann are baritones. Sam is a sousaphone."

Leo's smile is wide. "Well, I can say for all of us, we look forward to playing with you! We got in the marching band! You're looking at the incoming freshmen!"

Their father chuckles. "He's pretty excited about band." He looks at me. "I'm Logan. It's a pleasure to meet you." The waitress returns with some fries. The triplets' hands go flying, and Logan laughs. She picks up our bill and brings out the triplets' food.

A few moments later, we gather our things and say goodbye to Logan's family. We pile into Pachi's car and he drives us home. Yann gets dropped off first, mainly because Sam, Owen, and I live on the same street. We pull up to a big house with a white picket fence. Yann's parents are outside, and they wave to us as we leave.

Pachi drops the rest of us off at my house. I unlock the front door, and we go inside. Mom and Dad are still at work and won't be home till later. Paula moved out a few years ago. I grab my friends some drinks, and we sit down on the couch, turning on my Nintendo Switch to play games.

"Are you ready for tomorrow?" Sam smirks.

"No way," I answer.

Owen leans back on the couch, saddened by his death in the game. He shoots me a smile. "She'll say yes. What's not to like? You're a good guy." He grabs his controller as the round ends. "If she doesn't see it, then she's missing out."

I put down the controller after Owen knocks me off the level. That was my last life, so I get up from the couch and walk to the trash can. I press the pedal and pull the letter out of my pocket. Before dropping it in, I open it. I might as well read it one last time.

The letter expresses all my feelings about her. How I fell in love at first sight, and how it's grown the more I've gotten to know her. How I love her kindness, her humor, and just being around her. I wrote more than I thought. My eyes fall on the last sentence. *I love you, Rose.*

I can't throw it away. I'm not shoving my feelings away anymore. I put the letter in my pocket and return to the couch. My friends and

I play more games, and I try to give myself confidence. I can do it. I know I can.

It doesn't help, but I'm ready now. I think.

2

—·—

THE BLOOD RUSHES TO my face the moment I wake up. I had a dream about me and Rose. We were together, dating. She looked so happy. I pulled her close to me and ran my fingers through her soft hair. The moment we kissed, I woke up. The dream keeps popping into my head as I try to get ready. I don't want to get my hopes up. She could still say no, but I can't help it. My heart flutters every time I think about her.

The TV is blaring with the daily news when I come downstairs. My parents sit at the dining table eating breakfast. *"Buenos dias,"* I greet them. Dad nods and Mom smiles. She points to the microwave, letting me know where my food is. After grabbing the bacon and eggs from the microwave, I squeeze behind Dad and sit at the other end of the table. Sometimes, I wonder how we got this table to fit here.

"It's supposed to rain tonight," Dad says, repeating the words on the TV. "Let me know when you're done at the bakery, so I can come and get you. I don't want you driving in this weather."

I nod. I don't want to drive in that rain either. My phone buzzes, showing two notifications. One is a reminder that I have work, and the other is a text from Owen.

Owen: Good luck man, I'm sure she'll say yes.

Me: Thanks, I'll need it.

I'm surprised I even fell asleep last night. I keep going over the plan in my head. Right now, I'll text Rose to invite her to the bakery sometime before we close. I want it to be private. Just us.

Step one: Ask Rose to come to the bakery. I scroll through my contacts and find hers. I can't help but smile at her contact photo.

Me: Good morning!

Rose: Good morning! :)

Me: Are you busy today?

Rose: No, not really. How come?

Me: Can you come to the bakery after I'm done? I need to give you something.

Rose: Yeah! I'll be there.

Me: Okay, see you later.

Step one is complete. I take a deep breath and look at my plate. My eggs are gone. I didn't notice I was eating them. "Everything okay?" Dad asks, realizing the same time as me. "You're eating rather fast."

"I'm okay, just hungry," I answer. Dad takes my plate after I finish the rest of my food. I run upstairs to my room.

My room isn't that messy. Just some clothes on the floor and my blankets falling off my bed. It doesn't matter right now. I have to find that letter. I run to my desk and start searching, finding it in a drawer. I'll give her the letter too. Maybe I'll start with the letter, then slide the cupcake to her.

I walk into the bathroom before going downstairs. I open a container of curl cream and comb it through my pink curls. Paula said it helped with her hair, and I'm hoping it makes mine look better. I don't want to look like a mess in front of Rose.

"You can do this," I say out loud, staring at my reflection. "You can do this."

I run down the stairs as Dad calls me. I say goodbye to Mom and follow Dad outside. The sun beats down on us as we get in the car. Dad turns on the radio, and we drive off. I keep spacing out during the ride, thinking about what I'm going to do. Before I know it, we make it to the bakery. I tell Dad goodbye and go inside.

I push open the wooden doors to the bakery and the bell rings above me. It smells delicious. My cousin Nicole is placing pies and cakes into the glass display. She hasn't seen me yet, too busy trying to get everything ready. I look at the light gray walls covered in family photos. My favorite is the one with the whole family at the grand opening. I was seven at the time. I wanted to cut the ribbon, but they wouldn't let me.

Nicole turns around. Her eyes land on me, and she smiles. She closes the display and comes to hug me. She looks over her shoulder. "*¡Papa, Paco esta aqui!*"

My tío Harvey is cleaning the front counter. He looks up and cheers, dropping the cleaner and running toward me. "There you are!" he says, pulling me into a hug. "Glad to have you back from finals. Business has been well the past few days, and I know we'll have our hands full today. Antonio and Steve should be here soon."

Soon is now, because my cousins walk through the doors. Steve comes to me and ruffles my hair, while Antonio gives me a hug. Tío Harvey smiles. "All right, now that everyone's here, we open in three minutes." Antonio and Steve go to the kitchen, while Nicole and I go behind the counters. Tío Harvey flips the sign, and we're open for business.

Most of the time, I switch between being a cashier and a baker. The main reason I'm a cashier is that I'm quick with people's orders. But honestly, I'd rather be baking. I've been in the kitchen ever since

Mom let me help her cook. The moment she introduced me to baking, I never stopped. I love every part of it. The smells, the tastes, even the mess it makes. If I can, I'm making it my career.

The phone rings, and I answer it as Nicole takes someone's order. "Order for Jacob. One vanilla cake, chocolate frosting, with happy graduation written in orange frosting," I tell my cousins. After getting the details, I hang up the phone and keep taking orders. Time goes on quickly. It's now noon, and we're about to go for lunch.

"This is ridiculous! I want a coconut cream pie!" I turn to my right. Nicole is dealing with an infuriated woman. I peek into the glass display. We're completely out of coconut cream. A lot of the phone calls have been asking for that today. In fact, Nicole said one of the callers sounded like...

"Excuse me!" the woman groans, pushing her way past the person at the door. It's Owen. He shuts the door behind him.

Nicole looks at the clock on the wall and then at Owen. "Could you flip the sign? We're closing for lunch."

"I thought I wouldn't make it in time." Owen sighs, flipping the sign. He walks to the counter. "Mom ordered a pie. Coconut cream."

I ring Owen up for the pie. We talk for a bit before his phone goes off. He pulls it out, and his eyes widen. The color drains from his face as he puts his phone to the side.

"Are you okay?" I ask.

"Yeah, it's just her friends."

My face falls. "Are you kidding? I thought you blocked them all?"

"I thought so too. But they're trying to follow me with their spam accounts. Get this, they're trying to be friendly and everything." He shows me a message from one of the girls. She says how they should let bygones be bygones and all that crap.

My fists clench, and Owen takes away his phone. "No, Paco. You're not confronting them." I raise my hands in defense. "No! Remember when all of you did? You got suspended for a week!"

"Renise started it! She threw hands first!" I say, crossing my arms. "Besides, I wouldn't fight them. I'd talk to them."

"Yeah, talk, huh? Like how you cussed out that one girl that was blaming me?"

"It wasn't your fault. Renise was the asshole, not you. You did so much for her and always treated her well."

Owen takes a deep breath. "I'm grateful you and everyone came to my defense. That will never change. But confronting them won't solve anything." Owen places the phone on the counter. His block list is on the screen. He scrolls down the list. "That was her last friend, and it's set to block any accounts they make. Plus, Renise goes to a different school now. She's not worth it."

Owen's right, but it still pisses me off. Owen's ex was horrible to him during their relationship. They got into a lot of fights. She would insult him for everything. Owen finally broke up with her after a big fight about it. He called me after, and even though he knew he had to, it still hurt.

Renise started spreading rumors about him, but she didn't know Owen recorded their last fight. The recording wasn't even halfway done when I stormed off to find Renise, with Sam and Yann following close behind. Pachi's a year older than us, so he was at the high school. Owen chased us, but we had already found her. When Renise denied it, I took Owen's phone and played that recording at full volume.

Her face turned dark red. She lunged at Owen, and I pushed her back. Sam and Yann jumped in after Renise shoved me against the wall. It was the biggest fight of the school year. We were suspended and banned from going on the end-of-the-year trip. This was in eighth grade.

"You and Katie reacted the same way when I told you," Owen says, breaking the brief silence. "You wanted to beat her ass."

"Yeah. She said all these horrible things to you. And she tried to play the victim when we exposed her."

Owen puts his phone in his pocket. "I'm just glad it's over. Katie's helped me through it a lot."

"How are you two doing? You've been going out for a year now, right?"

"Yeah, yeah." He smiles. "I'm so much happier with her, I can't explain it. It's nice, knowing she loves me for me." I can tell he's gushing over her when he snaps back into the conversation. "Enough about me! It's the big day. Are you ready?"

"N-no, not really," I stutter. "I need to start making it."

"You'll be fine. Did you find all the ingredients, or whatever you need for it?"

"Yeah. The batch of chocolate cupcakes is almost done. She loves chocolate."

The bell chimes as the door swings open. Steve walks in carrying bags of food. He mumbles under his breath in Spanish, cursing the idiotic drivers he met on the road. I laugh at his words, and Owen stands there, confused. I forget he doesn't know Spanish. So many times, Pachi, Sam, and I have had full conversations in Spanish with Yann and Owen sitting there, confused.

"*¡Buenos tardes, Owen!*" Steve says. Owen waves back, relieved he can understand that.

Owen looks at the clock and grabs the pie. "I should head out. The pie's for my brother's birthday, and Mom's probably wondering where it is. You let me know how it goes, okay?"

I chuckle. "Yeah, I will. Tell him happy birthday for me. I'll see you later."

Owen nods, waves goodbye, and walks out the door. I grab my food from Steve and devour it. I go into the kitchen after throwing away my garbage.

The cupcakes are done, and I take out one of them. I put it on a rack to cool and start grabbing the decorations. I have the design in my head. Red frosting with sprinkles, and a heart-shaped cookie placed on top. I ice the cookie with pink frosting. After it settles, I write with white icing the question that's bursting out of my chest. *Will you be my girlfriend?* The writing fits, but it looks a little squished. It's still legible though.

As I finish pouring sprinkles on the cupcake, Steve calls my name. "Paco, we open in five. Want to work in the kitchen?"

"Yeah, sure," I answer. I take a deep breath and grab the cookie. I slowly lower it on top of the cupcake. Thankfully, it stays as I back away from it. I take a photo and send it to Owen.

Owen: Damn, that looks good!

I put the cupcake into a small white box and set it off to the side. Steve takes my spot at the counter. The orders come in, and I run around the kitchen packing pastries, frosting cupcakes, and writing phrases on other cakes.

Time at the bakery can't go any slower. I keep looking at the clock, hoping it will go faster. As time goes on, people come in less. It's an hour before closing, so I text Rose and ask her to come. The bakery is quiet, only filled with the sounds of my family's chatter and music in the background. Then, the occasional pitter-patter on the roof turns into roaring raindrops crashing down.

"Holy cow! It's raining cats and dogs out there!" Steve exclaims as he looks out the window. The rain comes down hard and fast. Steve groans. "It's the first week of June! It wasn't like this in the morning!"

Nicole finishes sweeping and walks over. "That's California for you, droughts and crazy-ass weather."

"Hey Tío, is it all right if we take off? I have a shift tomorrow morning," Antonio asks.

Tío Harvey stops wiping the tables. "I'm sure no one else is coming, not in this weather!" He whistles, watching the rain come down. "Thank you for all your help. Let me know when you get home, okay?"

I say goodbye to Antonio and Steve. They run to their cars to avoid the rain. Nicole looks at me. "Do you need a ride, Paquito?"

"Oh yeah, thank you. Could we stay for a bit? I'm waiting for some-one." I look at my phone. No response. I send another text, just in case.

"Is it a girl?" Tío asks. I don't respond, but the color on my face answers the question. Tío laughs. "Sure, I don't mind. Who knows, there might be someone with a pie craving this late. We can stay till closing time, and I'll tell your dad we're taking you home."

A few more minutes pass, and I'm starting to get antsy. I'm still waiting at the table, looking at the door, then back down at my phone. It's not long before I'm refreshing the chat between me and Rose.

Me: You still coming? - Delivered 24 minutes ago.

Me: Rose? I can't stay for much longer. - Delivered 15 minutes ago.

Me: It's okay if you can't come, just tell me. - Delivered 10 min-utes ago.

Me: Rose? Are you okay? - Delivered 5 minutes ago.

Me: Hello? - Delivered 3 minutes ago.

The minutes ago keep getting longer and longer. I try to call her, but it goes straight to voicemail. So, I wait, and wait, and wait. The clock strikes nine, and it's closing time. I can't stay any longer. I freeze as I listen to the clock ring out. She isn't coming, and that can only mean one thing.

Rose stood me up.

As the words escape my mouth, I slump in my seat. Why? Why would she? I reread our messages, and she said she was coming. Why would she just...

No. This isn't like Rose. She wouldn't do this. Rose would tell me. Maybe something happened to her. No, that's even worse. I'd rather she be okay and stand me up than anything else.

Tío Harvey put his hands on my shoulders, offering his sorrows in his own way. I do my best to suck in the tears threatening to roll down my face. "Come on, *mijo*. Let's go home."

Nicole locks the bakery while Tío runs to unlock his car. We get inside, and despite being in the rain for a short time, we're all soaked. The little white box is damp, barely hit by the rain. I stare at it. Out of all the ways I thought tonight could have gone, this was not one of them. I was more prepared for her to say no than this. Hell, I preferred it. I know Owen said I could eat it if she said no, but it doesn't feel right. It'll make me feel worse.

"Tío? Could you take me somewhere real quick?" I ask.

A few minutes later, we arrive at Rose's house. All I'm going to do is leave the box here and go home. The house is two-story, and a room on the second floor is lit up. The room has pink floral curtains, ones that Rose has told me about. That room is Rose's. She's okay, thank God.

She really stood me up then.

I knock on the front door. Her mother answers it, looking confused. I must look weird. A random kid holding a box, soaked from the rain. "Can I help you?" she asks, crossing her arms.

"Hi, could you give this to Rose, please?" I ask, handing her the box. Rose's mom takes it, nods, and shuts the door. I walk back to the car with the rain hiding my tears.

I'm shivering when I get inside. Nicole tosses me a jacket and turns up the heater. "Home?" she asks.

"Yeah, thank you."

We arrive at my house, and I watch from the porch as they drive away. Mom's waiting for me inside, and Dad's already asleep. "Hello, *mijo.*" Mom says, kissing the top of my head. "How was your day?"

"It was good," I answer. Mom crosses her arms. She doesn't believe me. I sigh. "I'll tell you tomorrow."

I say goodnight to Mom and head upstairs to my room. I change into my pajamas, throwing my clothes onto the floor. My mind is blank as I fall back on my bed. Dammit, dammit, dammit! My hands land on my face as I try to stop the tears from falling. Out of all the ways tonight could've gone, why this one?

I get up from my bed and grab the shorts I wore today. I dig into my pocket and find the letter. My hands shake. I want to crush it, rip it into little pieces, and never think of it again. The paper crinkles and I stop at the sound. No matter what, I can't get rid of it. I can't tear it up, I can't throw it away. I'm holding the letter over the trash can, and no matter what, I can't let it fall.

A loud bang interrupts my thoughts. I face the window above my bed. The tree shakes with the wind. It must've been a branch. I step away from the trash can and place the letter on my desk. I walk over to my bed. The tears break through as I turn off the light and get under the covers. Rose has every right to reject me. It's okay if she doesn't feel the same. I just wish she would've told me instead of this.

My hand reaches over to my nightstand. I fumble around until I finally grab my phone. I scroll through the contact list and find Owen. The phone rings, and the one time I hope he's not, he's asleep. I listen to his voicemail play out and wait for the beep.

"Hey, I'm home. I... dammit." I groan. I take a deep breath before saying the next sentence. "Rose stood me up."

3

"WHAT DO YOU MEAN she stood you up?"

"She stood me up!" I repeat to my friends. I stomp into the kitchen and start putting away the food I took out of the fridge. "I waited at the bakery until we closed, and she never showed. I didn't get a text or anything."

"What the hell?" Sam questions. "Is it that hard to say no?"

"What did you do with the cupcake?" Owen asks.

I walk over to the couch, holding a plate of snacks I prepared. I place it on the coffee table and sit on the couch. "I've given her rides before, so I know where she lives. I gave the cupcake to her mom, but I still haven't heard anything." I put my head in my hands. "Dammit."

Owen places a hand on my back. "I'm sorry, man. She's missing out."

"Don't worry, the right one will come around. At least she knows now," Pachi says as he turns on the TV.

The front door swings open once more. It's Yann. He smiles. "Sorry I'm late! Paco, how did it go?" Yann shuts the door behind him and stares at us. "Why is it so sad in here? What happened?"

"She stood him up!" Sam shouts from the couch.

Yann's jaw drops fast. "She what? No, you're joking!" His face falls when I nod. "She did? What the hell!"

I take out my phone and go to my messages with Rose. I sigh. "I don't know what happened. She hasn't read my texts either."

"I don't understand!" Yann fists his hair, flabbergasted. "Why would she say no? She likes you! It's obvious!"

"It's more obvious that she doesn't."

"Let me see," Yann says, motioning to my phone.

"There's nothing there. She still hasn't..." I look down at my phone and watch as the word delivered changes to read. My eyes widen. "She just read them."

"She what?" The five of us gather around my phone. The text bubble on Rose's side pops up. After a few seconds, it disappears.

"What was that about?" Pachi asks.

"She realized she messed up, that's what." Sam walks back to the couch and sits. "If she's not willing to give you an answer, then don't bother with her."

I shake my head and walk back to the kitchen. I open the fridge, letting the cold air hit my face. My eyes scan the inside. Once, twice, three times. Nothing is registering. I blink a few times before scanning the fridge for a fourth time. It's a little after eleven, I can make everyone brunch. There are enough eggs in the container, and we still have bacon.

"You all right, man?" Owen asks. He stands on my left, also looking into the fridge.

"Yeah, I'm fine. Are you hungry?" Owen shakes his head. I turn to my friends, and I'm met with the same reaction. I sigh. "I'll be fine, don't worry about me. And Sam, I know you didn't eat."

Sam looks away. "Yeah, if you don't mind."

Owen pats my shoulder as he steals a piece of cheese from the fridge. "We'll do something later to get your mind off it," he says, patting my shoulder once more before heading back to the couch.

The silence is awkward as I start cooking. My friends turn on my Switch and play games. Sam helps me in the kitchen, not wanting me to cook alone, I guess. I don't hear her reasoning. I keep spacing out.

"*¿Estas bien?*" Sam asks as I flip the egg in the pan. She's chopping an avocado next to me. The chopping stops as she waits for my answer.

"*Si, no te preocupes para me, por favor,*" I reply.

"You're a terrible liar," Sam groans. "I'm worried about you."

"I'm okay. I can't do anything about it. If she doesn't feel the same, it's okay. As long as she's happy." I take the egg out of the pan and place it on Sam's sandwich.

Sam sits at the counter, topping her breakfast sandwich off with bacon and avocado after drowning the egg in hot sauce. She takes a toothpick from the cabinet and sticks it into her sandwich, placing a green olive on the other end. I don't understand her taste buds even after all these years.

"No!" Owen shouts from the couch. Yann laughs. They're playing a racing game. Pachi speeds past them, ending the race. He throws his hands back and laughs, while Owen and Yann demand a rematch.

Knock knock knock!

I put down the pan I'm washing and rush to the door. My eyes go wide, it's Rose. I trip over my words, "R-Rose? What... what are you doing here?" Sam says something, but everyone shushes her.

Rose twiddles her thumbs. "I'm sorry I didn't come last night. I get it if you're upset, but please, let me explain." I nod. She takes a deep breath. "I got into an argument with my parents, and they grounded me because of it. I was in the middle of texting you I couldn't come when Mom snatched the phone out of my hands. She wouldn't let me check to see if it sent, and I saw your texts this morning."

My mouth hangs open. I should've known it was something. Rose has mentioned multiple times how strict her parents can be. At least she told me why she didn't show. Although, I don't get why she came all this way.

"The cupcake was yummy, by the way." She smiles. "So was the cookie..." she mumbles.

"I didn't think you got it." I chuckle. Rose looks down, and her cheeks are bright red. I blink, then I blink again. She squirms, her face turning red even more. She saw the message. Holy hell, she saw the message.

My face turns red. "You saw?" Rose nods, and I gulp. "What's your answer?" My mouth is dry, and my heart is beating so fast I think it'll burst out of my chest.

"Yes." My eyes widen more, and she giggles. I'm a stammering mess as I ask if she's serious. "Yes, I want to be your girlfriend." The way she assures me makes my heart pound faster.

A car horn rudely interrupts us. We turn to look. It's Rose's parents. They're in the car and becoming impatient. "I have to go. I'll call later, okay?" Rose says as she turns to me, smiling sweetly.

"Y-yeah! That'd be nice." I can't hide my excitement anymore. I feel like I'm on top of the world. Rose likes me! She actually likes me! Me!

Rose looks at her parents, then back at me. She steps on her tiptoes and plants a kiss on my cheek. She runs down the porch steps, smiling and waving at me. With one hand, I wave back. I shut the door after she drives off, my hand still on my cheek. I can't stop smiling, and I shout, "She said yes!"

My friends cheer. "I told you she likes you!" Yann says, "How do you feel?"

"What do you think? He's pinker than his hair!" Sam laughs. "Congrats, Paquito."

I roll my eyes and go to sit on the couch. Yann passes me a controller, and Pachi looks at the kitchen. "Hey Paco, the door is open," he says.

I stand to see the back door cracked open. As I step toward it, the door flies open and hits the wall. I'm confused. I haven't gone outside at all, and Dad always locks the doors. When I reach the door, I mess with the lock. It's hard to turn, making a scraping noise whenever I try.

I step outside and look around the backyard. There's nothing out of the ordinary except the broken fence in the back. Dammit, the wind must've broken it off. I have to pick it up.

"Hey! Who took a bite out of my sandwich?" Sam shouts.

"Are you sure it wasn't you?" I ask from outside.

"I already bit it." I go back inside. Sam's holding up her sandwich. There are two bite marks, one on each side. The yolk from the over-easy egg pours out onto her plate. "My olive's gone too, and I like eating that last."

Thud!

"Dammit!" someone says, but I don't recognize the voice. Oh hell, is someone in my house? The thud came from the laundry room. Normally, I'd assume it's the washing machine, but I haven't started a load yet.

"Sam, pass me something," I whisper. Sam puts the frying pan in my hand. It still smells like oil and eggs, but it's something. I equip it like a bat and approach the door, ready to swing. The door flies open, and someone pushes me to the floor. The frying pan falls out of my hand as I hit the cold tile floor.

I jump up and look around. Sam's blocking the back door, and Owen runs to block the front, barely beating whoever tackled me. Pachi's still trying to process what the hell just happened as he jumps from the couch.

The intruder is a young girl, with wavy brown hair and tattered clothes. There's no way she's older than us. She slowly backs into the kitchen. Yann's approaching her like a predator going after prey. Any sudden moves and we'll have front-row seats for a boxing match. The girl turns around. She's only steps away from me and Sam.

"Oh no," she mutters. Her eyes dart around the room. She runs toward Yann, shoving past him and making a break for the stairs. She slams one of the doors.

I run up the stairs. My bedroom door is the only one closed. I grab the handle and push my body against the door. I don't have a lock, so she can't lock it. After a few seconds, I get the door open. The girl backs away from the door and runs to my window.

"The window's locked!" I shout. In response, she slams her body against it. "No! Stop that!" I jump onto my bed and grab her.

"Let me go!" she cries, trying to wiggle out of my grip. She leans forward and slams her head back into my face.

"Dammit!" I fall onto my bed. My eyes water and I feel my nose. It's not bleeding, but damn, that hurt. As I slide off my bed, I look around. My friends are blocking the door. We've trapped the intruder. Going to my room was a dead end.

"You have three minutes to explain before I call the police," I say. I'm met with silence. "What's your name?"

"Not your business," the girl spits. I look at her arms. The bandages that cover her left arm are falling off, revealing a burn mark. There's a bruise on her tan face. Her dark brown eyes are bloodshot, but look so familiar, like I've seen them before.

"Do I know you?" I question.

"What? No," she answers, offended that I asked.

"What happened to your arm? And your face?" Yann asks softly. He points to her arm. "Have you put lotion on it? It'll help with the burn."

She steps away from Yann, her right hand gripping her left arm. She winces, and the rest of the bandage comes off. The burn looks bad. If she doesn't treat it, it'll leave a nasty scar.

"Okay, let's go downstairs. I'll replace the bandage, then you can answer my questions," I say. She stares at me.

I walk down the stairs and into the bathroom. Mom stashes first aid kits all over the house. Band-Aids, ointment, anti-itch, whatever you can think of. Yann grabs the lotion and gives it to her. Neither of us wants to overstep. After she puts on the lotion, she sits on the barstool. We wrap her arm in a bandage. There's not much we can do about her bruise.

"That's better," I say, zipping up the first aid kit. The girl stares at her arm. She slowly looks at me but doesn't say anything. I sigh. "Let's try this again. What's your name?"

"Olive," she answers.

"Okay. Olive, why did you break into my house?"

Olive swings her legs. "I was hungry, and her sandwich looked good."

"Not cool," Sam grumbles. She cuts the sandwich in half, sliding Olive the half she took a bite out of. Sam takes her half and continues to eat it.

"How did you get in?" I ask, and Olive shrugs. "Answer me."

"The door was unlocked. And before you ask, I didn't break the fence. It was like that when I got here last night." Olive's eyes widen, and she looks down.

"Last night? You were here all night?" I question. Is that what that loud noise I heard was?

Olive doesn't look at me. "Why do you care? I didn't steal anything."

"You broke into my house, of course I care. Why did you come here, anyway?" Olive looks away and crosses her arms with a huff. I sigh. "Okay, fine. Your three minutes are up."

Olive scoffs. "You're not going to call them, are you?"

My voice shakes. "Yes, I am." Chills run down my spine as I put my phone on speaker. Olive's eyes widen as it rings.

Owen looks down at his pocket. He sticks his hand inside to shut off the vibration. I called him instead, hoping it'll be enough for Olive to talk. Thankfully, he's out of Olive's view, and she can't see him.

Olive digs her nails into her arm as she listens to the ringing. I look at my friends. Worry fills their faces as they put the pieces together. Owen's voicemail is going to play if Olive doesn't crack. I'm surprised she hasn't caught on already. 911 answers immediately.

"Fine!" Olive shouts. "I'll tell you, just hang up the phone." Phew, just made it.

Olive slides off the barstool and walks to the couch, stomping the entire way there. "I got into a fight with my mom, and ran away from home," she tells us as she plops onto the couch. "I'll go back later. I just don't want to be home right now."

"What did you guys fight about?" Sam asks.

"Doesn't matter. It was my fault," Olive answers sharply, crossing her arms.

"Did you get those from your mom?" Owen questions, eyeing her wounds.

Olive's head whips around. "N-no! What the hell? She may be a prick, b-but she wouldn't do that on purpose."

My eyes widen. "Do what on purpose?"

"Stop with the questions!" Olive rises from the couch. "I already told you what you need to know. Now, if you excuse me, I'm going home." Olive pushes past us and walks to the back door.

"Wait," I say. My body's moving on its own, trying to stop her. She turns around, her eyes like a lost puppy, and my heart sinks. "You can stay here for a bit. At least until my parents get home."

"Why?" she asks.

"Because..." I stammer, "I think you need to."

"I don't need to. But..." Olive pauses, and she sighs. "I don't want to go home yet."

"If you don't want to go home, maybe you can stay with a relative? A cousin maybe?" Yann suggests.

"That's it," Pachi says out of the blue. I turn to him, confused. "That's why you recognize her. She looks just like the kids from Lumpy's."

I look at Olive and try to remember the triplets from two days ago. They have the same tan skin and deep brown eyes. Olive's brown hair matches Lucy's as well, and their faces look the same. "Holy shit, you're right," I finally answer Pachi.

Pachi pulls out his phone and goes to Instagram. "Lucy's a flute, Leo's a trumpet, and Peter's a clarinet. We can find them from the showcase photos."

I take out my phone and look for people I know in those sections. I find the trumpet section leader's account and tap the photo from the showcase. It's covered in black nametags. After tapping a few, I find a username with Leo in it.

Me: Hey, this is Paco. We met a few days ago. Could you come over? I think we have your cousin here. Here's the address.

Leo: Cousin? Did they say their name? We don't have a lot of cousins.

Me: She said her name is Olive.

Leo doesn't respond. His text bubble pops up and then disappears. Then pops again, then stops. It's like that for a few minutes.

Leo: We'll be there in five.

As we wait for the triplets to arrive, I make some more food. Olive tears it up. She keeps getting more and eats it so fast. When I tell her to slow down so she doesn't get sick, she looks ashamed. The tension is tight, and nothing's settling it. Finally, the doorbell rings. I run to open it.

Leo dashes inside. "Where is she?" he asks. I step to the side, letting the rest of the kids come in. Leo's eyes land on Olive, who is walking to the couch. She turns to look at him, and Leo freezes. "Peter... are you seeing this?" he asks.

Peter comes closer. "What the?" He turns to his sister. "Lucy, could you stand by her?"

Lucy walks to Olive and stands next to her. They're identical. The only difference is Lucy is a few inches taller.

Peter looks at Leo with his jaw on the floor. "Do you think?"

"I-it can't be," Lucy stammers. "There's no way, right?"

"Your name's actually Olive?" Leo asks. Olive nods, confusion written on her face. Leo takes a deep breath. "When's your birthday?"

"Why do you want to know?" she answers harshly.

Leo's voice is shaky. "Please. Please, just tell me."

The begging tone in Leo's voice causes Olive to freeze. She sighs. "January 18th. I'm fourteen."

Leo steps back with a gasp. The triplets' faces span through a sea of emotions. Their eyes widen, their jaws drop, then...

"Olive!" Leo screams and runs to her. He pulls her into a tight embrace, and he's laughing like a little kid. His siblings follow behind, their faces full of happiness. They surround Olive, pulling her into a group hug.

Olive, however, is not a hugger. She struggles to get her arms free from the triplets' tight grips. "What are you? What's going on?" She breaks out of the hug and steps back. She stares at Leo, and her eyes widen. Her hand goes up slowly, pointing at Leo. "Are you?"

"It's you. God, it's really you," Leo's voice cracks. He holds his arms to his side, and Olive steps closer.

"You know each other?" The words that come out leave my mouth dry.

The triplets and Olive look at each other. Lucy steps forward. "We weren't lying when we said we were triplets, but..."

"But?"

"We're not triplets," Leo pauses. "We're sextuplets."

4

"Sextuplets?!"

The four of them nod. My jaw hits the floor. I figured they have some relation to Olive, but sextuplets? "Are you serious?" I ask, just to hear it again.

"Yeah, we are." To my surprise, Olive answers me. She's not as happy as her siblings. While they have wide smiles on their faces and joy in their eyes, Olive doesn't. She holds her arms close to herself, standing away from them.

"After we turned two, our mom disappeared with three of us," Leo says, turning to Olive. "Olive was one of them."

"And Theodore and Christina," Olive mutters. Leo's head perks up.

Disappeared? I'm about to ask Leo what he means when he turns to me and my friends. "Can you give us a minute?" he asks. I can only nod. My friends and I walk into the backyard, leaving the four of them alone.

The backyard is spacious. Mom spends a lot of time making it look nice. In the left corner of the backyard is Mom's garden. I rush to check on it. It looks okay, and I sigh in relief. Looks like Olive was the only one who got in the backyard last night. I prop up the fence that fell over and go to the outside table.

Pachi passes me a water bottle as I sit down. "She really got in through the fence?" he asks.

"Yeah. It fell with the storm last night. Dad should be able to fix it," I answer, taking a sip of my water before continuing. "At least an animal didn't follow Olive inside."

"I wonder how she got through the night. It was pouring," Yann says.

"Maybe she slept under the table," Sam suggests, looking down. "It gives you some coverage."

I sigh. "Ran away from home, only to find lost siblings. Sextuplets, holy shit."

Owen nods. "That's something you don't see every day."

I look at my friends. "Did any of you hear what I did? Their mom... disappeared with three of them?"

"That's what he said," Yann answers. "I thought I heard wrong too."

Silence falls between us. The birds stop chirping, and so does the chatter inside the house. Sam leans back in her seat. She's closest to the door. Her eyebrows raise and her eyes widen.

"What?" Yann whispers. "What is it?"

"They're arguing," Sam responds. She holds out her hand, telling us to be quiet.

"That's not what happened." Olive's voice cuts the silence. Her words come out bitter. "You're lying to me."

"It's the truth, Olive!" Lucy stammers. "We were in the news for a month! The police couldn't find you!"

I can't hear anything else. Sam turns around. A few seconds later, she stands and stomps to the door. I run to her and grab her hand, shaking my head. *Not yet.* We won't be much help. Sam backs away from the door. The two of us stand there, listening to the conversation.

Everything goes out the window when Olive yells. Chairs scramble and scrape as we rush inside the house. Olive's standing away from her siblings. Lucy steps toward her slowly, like she's approaching a cat that's ready to run at any moment.

"Olive, we're not lying," Peter says. "It's the whole reason Mom and Dad got divorced. Mom wasn't treating us right, and she—!"

"Dad was the horrible one! Not Mom!" Olive cuts him off.

"Dad always took care of us! Mom was horrible! Hell, she's the one that took you away from us!" If Leo wasn't crying earlier, he is now. Tears run down his face and Leo takes a sharp breath. "Olive, please, we just want to take you home."

"I already have one!"

"That's not your home!" Leo's cry echoes throughout the house. Olive takes a step back, holding her hands in front of her. Leo gasps. He reaches his hand out to her, but he stops. He grabs at his hair, turns around, and runs for the back door.

"Leo!" Peter cries.

"Hey! Wait!" I reach for Leo's arm, but he slips through, disappearing into the backyard. I glance at the kids. Peter sits down on the couch with Lucy, while Olive looks away.

I usher my friends over to the laundry room. The way the layout is, the kids can't see us over here. We crowd around the entrance. "What do we do?" I ask.

"What *can* we do?" Pachi whispers. "It's not really our business."

"I know, but we can't leave them like this." I poke my head around the corner. Lucy and Peter are still on the couch. They're staring down at the ground. Olive looks at them as she slowly sits on the other couch. She wraps her arms around herself. Biting her lip, she turns away from them.

"I'll talk to Leo," I announce. "I want to check on him."

"I'll talk to Olive," Sam says.

I walk into the backyard and find Leo sitting at the table. He picks at his nails, not noticing me come outside. When I come closer to him, he stops moving. He clutches his knees, still not looking at me as I sit in the chair next to him.

"Do you want to talk about it?" I ask, skipping the are you okay. There's no point in asking. He's absolutely not okay.

Leo looks up from his hands. "I've wanted this moment for so long. So damn long." He leans back. "Every birthday, every star in the sky, I'd wish that they would come home, for us to find them. And it's here! It's finally happening, but Olive doesn't want it. She doesn't want to come home."

Leo rubs his eyes. "I don't even know why! We tried to tell her the truth, that Mom was horrible, but she doesn't believe us. She keeps defending Mom! I don't know what she told Olive, but it's making her not want to come home."

"Olive mentioned she was going to go back home," I say. Leo turns toward me. "That was her original plan."

"Why would she run away if she was going to go back?"

"You said she was defending her. Maybe that's why."

"That doesn't make any sense! None of this makes sense!" Leo gets up from his seat. He paces back and forth, his hands flying all over. "The police said she was dead! They stopped answering Dad's calls and never updated us again, no matter how much he tried to pry. If she was alive this whole time, why did they lie to us? Why did they stop looking?"

"I don't know why, Leo, but she's alive." I'm not sure what to say to him, but I hope that helps.

Leo stops walking. He stands up straight and takes a deep breath. "Yeah, you're right. That's all that matters." Leo walks to the door. He wipes his face and glances at me. "I'm heading back inside. Thanks... for this."

I follow Leo back inside. Yann's waiting for me in the kitchen. Owen and Sam are sitting on the couch with Olive, while Pachi sits with Lucy and Peter.

"How's it going?" I ask Yann.

Yann shrugs. "I'm not sure. Sam talked to her for a bit, but she hasn't said anything about her mom."

"Anything about Theodore and Christina?" Leo asks.

"Not really." Yann looks at Olive before continuing. "Why don't you try talking to her?"

Leo frowns. "I don't think she wants to talk to me. I made her upset."

"If I had siblings, I'd want to make up with them as soon as possible. It's worth a shot," Yann says. Leo nods and walks to Olive.

Yann pulls me away. He lowers his voice. "Olive isn't cracking. But she said something about her mom. I didn't want Leo to hear it though."

"Didn't Lucy and Peter hear it? There wouldn't be a point."

"They had to answer a call from their dad. He's on his way home from work, got off early." Yann looks over his shoulder for a second. "Olive confirmed she got the burn from her mom. She didn't tell us what happened, but she said it was an accident. I don't know about you, but I'm calling bullshit."

"I had a feeling too," I answer, looking at the couch. Leo's talking to Olive now. He does a small bow, apologizing for getting upset with her. Olive stares at him, and judging by Leo's face, she accepted it.

"Owen stepped in after she said that," Yann says. "I hate saying it, but when it comes to that, he knows what to say. Olive's not liking it though."

I look over at the triplets. Lucy and Peter move to sit near Olive. She looks down at the ground until they start talking. There aren't any questions about Theodore or Christina, or anything about their mom. They talk about other things. Games, memes, food, anything and everything. Olive leans toward them, captivated by the stories they tell her. It's working. She tells us things about her. She knows how to swim, ride a bike, and she can cook eggs. Olive only talks when it's relevant, listening to her siblings most of the time.

"I can teach you how to play chess! It's fun!" Peter beams.

"Have we mentioned he's a bit of a nerd?" Lucy asks. It gets a chuckle out of Olive. "He runs a chess club at school."

"Ran, you mean. Unfortunately, I don't think there's one at Pitt."

Olive blinks. "What even is chess? It sounds old." Peter's jaw drops in disbelief while Leo and Lucy laugh. "Don't old people play it or something?" Olive asks with a smirk.

Peter turns red. "It's not like that! It's a very fun strategy game where—!"

Olive jumps up from the couch. She dashes through the kitchen, turns to the left, and slams a door. I go after her, recovering from the secondary whiplash. There are only three doors by the kitchen: the back door, the laundry room, and the bathroom. She's not in the backyard, and the laundry room door is open.

"Olive? You okay in there?" I knock on the bathroom door. It creaks open. Olive stands next to the toilet. Her face is pale as she looks down. Confused, I walk inside. Her phone is in the toilet. My face wrinkles in disgust. I open the cabinet under the sink and grab a pair of tongs.

"Is everything okay?" Lucy steps into view. She stares at the tongs. "Why do you keep a pair of tongs in the bathroom?"

I pull out Olive's phone from the toilet with the tongs, showing it to Lucy. "Because this has happened more than once," I say, quickly putting the phone onto a few pieces of toilet paper. I wrap my finger in another piece and tap the phone to see if it works. It does, and a notification pops on the screen. *Three missed calls from Mom.* Another notification pops up. *Updating location.*

"Crap!" Olive snatches her phone off the counter, her fingers tapping rapidly on the screen. She puts her phone back down, and it vibrates. Over and over.

"Please wash your hands." Lucy shivers.

"What was that?" I ask Olive.

"I turned off my location," Olive says as she douses her hands in soap. "Mom's pissed, as you can see."

"She knows where you are?" I question.

"I'm not sure." Olive grabs the disinfectant on the counter and sprays her phone. She wipes it down, doing her best not to answer her mom's army of calls and texts. The vibrating stops. Olive taps the screen a few times and holds out the phone in front of her.

"You have three new messages. Message one, left at 12:34 pm."

"Olive! Turn your location back on, right now!" the voice demands. Footsteps come toward the bathroom. "This is going too far. This rebellion, whatever you call it, has to stop. Come home tonight, or you're grounded, and you won't get dinner either!" The voicemail ends as Owen pokes his head around the door.

"Message two, left at 12:36 pm."

I hear heavy breathing immediately, and it hitches. "S-so I'm the bad guy now, huh?" Olive flinches and the voice on the phone shakes. "After everything I—!" Olive turns off the voicemail and throws her phone on the floor. She takes a step back, her body trembling.

"You'd better change your plans. You're not going back to her," Owen says.

Olive scoffs and picks up her phone. "I'll be fine. I pissed her off after all." Olive looks at her phone, her hands still shaking. "Wow, and she turned her location off. Oh no, I'm *so* scared."

"Are Theodore and Christina on it too?" Lucy asks.

"No, just me. I've tried to run before, and I've pissed her off one too many times."

Lucy frowns. "How are we going to find them now?"

"Maybe we should call the cops. They could help us," Owen suggests. I look at him, and he sighs. "I mean, what else could we do?"

Olive rolls her eyes. "I've been missing for twelve years. The police will only make it worse. If Mom finds out they know she'll leave me behind."

"Leave you behind? What do you mean?" I ask.

"Dammit," Olive mutters. I stare at her, and she sighs. "We're moving out of the state. We were supposed to leave Sunday, but I don't know anymore. She's scared of the police, and if they find out about me, she'll leave me behind."

"What?" Leo yells. He runs to us and looks at Olive. She nods, and he groans. "No cops. We can't risk it."

"What do we do then?" Peter asks. I step out of the bathroom to see the triplets in the kitchen.

"We'll figure it out. It'll be okay," I say. The triplets look at me, something I can only describe as small bits of hope in their eyes.

The doorbell ringing cuts the tension short. Leo turns to Olive. "Are you sure you don't want to come? I can get Dad on board. It'll be okay." Olive shakes her head. Leo sighs and pulls her into a hug. "Just let us know when."

I rush to the door as the triplets say goodbye. Sam takes Olive out of sight. I open the door. I look up at Logan. Yep, definitely six feet. His hair is wavy, with curls popping out. I didn't notice at first, but the kids have his eyes. Logan holds out his hand. "What was your name again? I didn't catch it at Lumpy's."

"I'm Paco," I say, shaking his hand. "Nice to meet you again."

"Ah! You're Jackie and Alejandro's kid! No wonder you looked familiar." Logan smiles. I nod, surprised. "I went to high school with your mother. Tell them I said hello." He looks at his kids. "Hope they weren't much trouble." He laughs.

I smile as the kids walk out the door. "You have nice kids," I tell him. I wonder if Olive is close enough to hear him.

"They're my pride and joy." Logan smiles. "Thanks for keeping an eye on them. Have a nice day!" The triplets and Logan disappear down the steps.

I shut the door, sighing in relief that he was quick with the visit. I feel bad lying to his face. Well, it's not exactly a lie, but I still feel bad. I could ask Mom about him, but as much as we hate the cops, she won't hesitate to call them for this.

Olive comes around the corner, her hands cupped together. "Paco, right?" she asks, and I nod. "Can I ask something?"

"Yeah, what is it?"

"Can we play on the TV?" Olive points to my Switch. I nod, and she smiles. My eyes widen. I think that's the first time I've seen her smile.

"You guys can set it up. I'll finish cleaning." I walk back to the bathroom and grab the tongs off the counter. I turn the water on and wash the tongs.

Through the mirror, I watch Owen walk into the bathroom and lean against the wall. "Do you at least have a plan?" he asks, looking at the ground.

"Not really," I respond. I place the tongs on the counter and turn to face him. "But I can't stand on the side."

Owen crosses his arms, hands gripping his skin. His body tenses and struggles to stand up straight. "Are you okay?" I ask.

"Worried about her," he answers. "I see a lot of myself in her, maybe too much. But she wouldn't listen to what I was telling her. I don't blame her. Shit's hard to hear."

"Did she say anything at all?"

"From the bit she's told us about her mom, she's extremely manipulative, and those voicemails proved it. Plus, she's doing the same shit Renise was. Insults, backhand comments, and I don't believe that story about the burns."

"We'll talk to her more and help her realize it. That's all we can do." *Optimistic, just be optimistic,* I tell myself. I turn to Owen. "I'll try talking to her." *She reminds me of my younger self.*

"Thanks, I think she'll listen to you." Owen turns around with a sigh. "Let's go show her how great games are."

We leave the bathroom and go to the living room. Pachi leans over Olive's shoulder, trying to teach her the controls. Sam waves, inviting us to the couch. The silence is awkward.

Olive stares at the TV. "Are you winning?" I ask her.

"Surprisingly, yes," Yann answers. His hands grip the controller tightly, fighting for his life. I'm in shock. They're playing a fighting game that Yann's amazing at. I still haven't been able to beat him, and Olive is ahead by one win. His fingers mash on the buttons, and he knocks Olive out.

"You got lucky." Olive scoffs. I struggle to hold in my laughter. Yann can get super competitive during games, especially if he's losing.

"Oh, you are on!" Yann says, with fire in his eyes.

The intense battle begins. It's neck and neck through the entire round. Yann acts like he's in the game. His body moves left and right as if he's dodging actual punches. Olive inches closer and closer to the screen. Both of them are sweating. Finally, the game calls for the finishing move, and Olive's character hits the floor. Yann throws his hands in the air, and Olive slumps in her seat.

"You did good! We can rematch if you want," Yann says, trying to wipe the smirk off his face.

"No, it's okay." Olive gives me the controller. "Your turn."

I stare at the controller in my hands. There has to be some way I can get her to open up. She's not as tense as she was earlier. I look at Olive. "Where are you staying tonight? I don't think you should go home."

Olive stiffens. *Dammit, too upfront.* She shrugs. "I don't know."

"You can stay with me," Sam says. "The top bunk's free. My sister doesn't come home for a couple of weeks."

"You have a sister?" Olive asks.

"Yeah, two actually. One younger, one older."

"Do you guys get along?"

"Yeah," Sam says with a smile. We look at each other. This is our chance. If we can find anything out about Olive and her siblings, it's now. Sam takes a deep breath before continuing. "My dad passed a little over a year ago, so Mom's been working a lot. Clarissa's at college, and Ruby's only four. Mom tries, but she can't do it all by herself. I help wherever I can. Clarissa calls often, making sure I'm okay. It's taken a bit, but we're okay now. It's nice having her to lean on."

Olive pats Sam's shoulder, not saying anything. She looks at us and makes eye contact with Pachi, waiting for him to speak.

Pachi chuckles. "I'm the oldest of four. Two brothers and one sister. We live with our parents in a small house. It's tough, but we make it work. We even have game nights."

Olive looks at Yann, and he shrugs. "Don't look at me. I'm an only child."

"That sounds better than mine." Olive laughs.

"How so?" I ask.

Olive rolls her eyes. "It's just Mom and my siblings. Mom works a lot, but she homeschools us too. It sucks, and it doesn't help that I fall behind every week because of chores. Theodore cooks, Christina sews and cleans, and I do everything else." Olive puts her hands in the air. "Olive, take out the trash. Olive, come with me to the store. Olive this, Olive that." Her hands fly around, mimicking her mother's many demands.

"She can be a prick. She always gets mad at me for everything. Oh, you're doing this wrong! Why can't you be more like your siblings? You're just like your father! And get this." Olive sits up and chuckles. "After an argument, she comes into my room and tells me how much she loves me. She says that one minute, then the next yells at me about how she should've taken Leonardo, or Peter, or Lucy instead of me." Olive leans back. "I think one time she said I should've died in the hospital," she mutters, but all of us hear her.

"Your mom's a bitch," Sam says, cutting the tension. Olive shoots up from the couch and glares at her. "If she truly loved you, she wouldn't treat you like that."

"I agree," Owen says. "Like I said earlier, my ex would do the same thing. It was a very toxic relationship—"

"That's different," Olive cuts him off. "It just is. She's my mom. She's doing her best, and I always cause trouble." She turns away from Owen. Yann pats Owen's back, assuring him it's okay.

"She shouldn't treat you like that regardless," I tell her. Olive doesn't say anything. "No one should ever treat you like that. It's not right."

"It's not her fault." Olive looks away. "I cause so many problems. I kind of deserve it."

"Well, how about you come with me?" Sam says. "You can hang out at my house for as long as you want, see how you feel after."

"You mean it?" Olive asks.

Sam smiles. "Of course. We can go now to get everything ready. Mom won't mind. Friends stay over all the time."

"Friends?" Olive says, puzzled.

"Yeah, friends."

Olive smiles and jumps up from the couch. I walk them to the door. They say goodbye and disappear down the street to Sam's house. It's nice to live on the same street.

"What the hell is her mom's problem?" Pachi asks after I close the door.

"I wouldn't even call her a mom," Yann says. "You can't treat your kids like that."

"And did you hear what Olive said? About the hospital?" I frown. "That's messed up."

Owen sighs. "It's a good thing she went with Sam. Mrs. Sanchez is nice. Maybe she'll help Olive realize it."

"I think what you told her helped," I say. "She's going to think about it, whether she wants to or not."

"I hope." Owen looks down. "I didn't expect her to believe me. I didn't either when I saw the signs, but still."

She'll be okay. I think to myself. I sit down on the couch to join my friends in another round of video games. Sam will take care of her. She was there for me when I was completely alone, and I know she'll be there for Olive. Hopefully, she'll help Olive open up, and maybe we can find out what else happened. Even better, maybe she'll want to go with her dad.

I really hope so.

5

As MESSED UP AS it sounds, I'm relieved we aren't going to call the police. I'm sure someone there could help, but after what they did to my dad, I'd rather not deal with them. Even so, I get why we can't call them. If she takes off with Theodore and Christina, who knows where they'll end up? This is the closest Logan and the triplets have gotten to getting them back. It's not a risk worth taking.

I get a call from Pachi in the morning. He asks me to come with him to the new antique store downtown. Since Pachi got fired, he's been looking for jobs, and the antique store is hiring. Pachi picks me up a few minutes later, and we drive downtown. After finding parking, we walk to the antique store.

Pachi grabs his resume with a groan. "This'll be my third application."

"Hey, someone will call back. Don't worry. At least you have some experience," I say.

Pachi looks down at the ground. "No one wants to hire a seventeen-year-old. Everywhere wants me to be eighteen."

"If you want, you can work with me at the bakery."

Pachi smiles. "Thanks. I'll see."

Pachi pushes the door open and heads straight to the counter. The store smells like leather and dust. There are metal signs all over the store walls and an old oven near the back. Boxes of old knickknacks and glass bottles are on the floor, and rows of tables with more boxes on top are at the front. I flip through a box of records, pulling out one that Mom will like.

There's a bin of newspapers a few tables down. Curiosity gets the better of me, and I flip through them. One of them says Stockton, California. That's not far from here. I've been there a few times for band festivals. I take out the newspaper and read the headline.

Three children kidnapped, a father's plea.

You're kidding me.

I pull out the newspaper as fast as I can. It's dated twelve years ago. I skim through it after shaking off the dust. It's the kidnapping of Olive and her siblings. My stomach turns, and my eyes land on one of the paragraphs.

Diane Page took Theodore, Christina, and Olive (age two), and fled away in a gray minivan. The police found the minivan about ten miles from Logan's house. The keys were still in the ignition. The three car seats were empty, but the stroller that was inside was missing. Please keep an eye out for...

I reach the end of the page and flip it over. I'm met with a photo of a woman. She has dark brown hair, brown eyes, and unusually pale skin. She looks sick in the photo. The bags under her eyes are heavy, and speaking of eyes, hers look dead. It sends shivers down my spine.

Diane Page's mugshot, when she was arrested on DUI charges last year.

"Paco, you ready?" Pachi asks from the counter.

I fold the newspaper and walk to the counter. "How much for the newspapers?" I ask. There isn't a price on the box.

The man shrugs. "Eh, it's on the house. I doubt those will sell. You have to pay for the record though."

Pachi and I leave the store, my eyes are still on the newspaper. "What's interesting about this?" Pachi asks, taking it out of my hands. His eyes widen as he skims the headline. "Holy shit!"

"It has a mugshot of her," I say. "She was—"

"Arrested for DUI? That's not good at all." Pachi reads a little more. "Paco, look who wrote it." He points to a name on the paper, Gerald Torre.

"That's Yann's dad!" I exclaim. Yann's dad is a journalist. Sometimes we see him on the news. I forgot Yann and his family lived in Stockton before moving here. I turn to Pachi. "Maybe he knows something."

"I hope. Remember that yard sale they had last week? They were cleaning out a bunch of stuff, and Yann's dad was talking about donating his old stuff."

"You don't think he donated anything about their mom, do you?"

"Let's go find out," Pachi says, unlocking the car.

Mr. Torre is in the driveway working on his car. His rolled-up sleeves keep slipping down as he digs around the hood of the car. The poor thing is always breaking down. He mumbles under his breath, stopping when we come closer. He smells like oil, and the glasses on his face are threatening to fall.

"Oh, hello!" Mr. Torre smiles, pushing his glasses up. "What brings you here?"

"Is Yann home?" I ask. Might as well fill Yann in about everything.

"Yes, he's home. He went in the gym a few..." Mr. Torre looks at his watch. His eyes widen. "Honey? Did Yann come inside yet?"

"No, I didn't see him come in." Mrs. Torre shouts from inside.

"Blast that boy," Mr. Torre groans. "Mind if you get him? He's been in there for a while now."

We nod and go inside. I stop by the kitchen, grabbing two water bottles out of the fridge. This happens a lot. Yann's been boxing since he was a kid. As he got older, he started working out more. He enjoys it and ends up working out longer than he intends to. He always pushes himself past his limits, and he never has enough water.

Yann's dog, Lobo, follows us from the living room. He's a mix of a husky and German shepherd. Lobo pokes my leg with his snout and looks at me, begging for pets. I rub his head as I open the back door.

The gym is in a shed in the backyard. Mr. Torre made it for his wife, but Yann uses it more than her. I knock on the door. The only response is loud music blasting. I push the door open, very grateful that Yann never locks it.

Yann's hand comes slamming into the red boxing bag in front of him. He rears his arm back, preparing for another punch, when he stops. He looks confused as he turns toward us. Lobo runs to him and starts sniffing him like crazy.

Yann takes off his gloves. "Could you at least come in? It's hot as hell out there." He tosses his gloves to the side and pets Lobo, who flops to the floor. His tail wags as Yann scratches his belly.

Pachi shuts the door as I toss Yann a water bottle. "Your dad said you've been in here for a while," I tell him.

Yann catches the water bottle. "It hasn't been that long, has it?" He looks at the clock and opens the water bottle. "Damn. Well, what's up?"

"We went to that antique store downtown. Paco found this in one of the bins," Pachi answers, handing Yann the newspaper and the second water bottle.

Yann sits down on the weight bench and reads the paper. "This is one my dad wrote. I never doubted them, but seeing it here just…" Yann turns the page. His eyes go wide as saucers. "Holy shit! That's their mom!"

"Do you think your dad knows something?" I ask.

"He might, we can ask." Yann gets up and we follow him to the front yard.

Mr. Torre is still working on the car when we come outside. Yann lets his dad mumble before calling for him. Mr. Torre gets up from the car. "Do you have anything on the stories you reported?" Yann asks.

"That depends. Which one is it? Some of my newspapers got donated by accident."

"The Page sextuplets." Yann hands him the paper. His dad's hands clench the paper tightly. "The one where—"

"I definitely do, and I don't know how this got donated." Mr. Torre gives the paper back to Yann and reaches for a dirty towel. He sighs. "I'll meet you in my office. I need to clean up."

We go back inside and follow Yann up the stairs. He leads us to the back of the hallway and opens a door. The office is crammed with filing cabinets, and a bookshelf takes up one of the walls. Pachi trips on a box as he steps inside. The office must be the smallest room in the house. Mr. Torre's desk is shoved into the corner, piled with papers.

Mr. Torre joins us a few minutes later. He goes to his desk and pulls open a drawer. He grabs a key and opens a filing cabinet. "Everything should be in here. It was the case I reported the most. I followed it for a while, but there weren't any updates." He lets out a long sigh. "It's a shame. I know their father."

"You do?" The words fly out of my mouth faster than I can process. Pachi and Yann stare at me. I swallow. "How is he?"

Mr. Torre sits in his chair. "Better than he was, I tell you. If she managed to take all of them with her, he would've lost himself. He's wanted to be a father for as long as I can remember. The three that were with him kept him alive, gave him hope. I have to catch up with him soon. I think the kids just finished middle school." Mr. Torre rubs his eyes. "Might I ask why you're so curious about this?"

"We met the triplets and Logan a few days ago," I answer quickly. "We didn't know they were sextuplets and wanted to know what happened." I'm not really lying, but I'm sweating like crazy.

Mr. Torre doesn't speak at first. He stares off into the distance, holding his chin. "Well, Logan didn't tell me much, but this is what I know. They started fighting a lot during the last months of Diane's pregnancy, and the fighting only worsened after their birth. Logan took a lot of hours off so he could take care of the kids. Diane never returned to work, so they lost a bit of money. I don't know what the breaking point was, but they divorced before the kids turned two."

"Why would she take the kids?" Pachi asks.

"I can't say. The police stopped searching after a year, and they never came up with a clear motive. Everyone except Logan gave up hope." The room falls into a sad silence. Mr. Torre sighs. "You boys might as well stay for lunch. It'll be ready soon." We nod, and Mr. Torre leaves us in his office.

We get to work. Yann sits at his dad's desk and gets on the computer. Pachi and I go through the filing cabinet. It's not long before we run out of evidence. We only learn bits and pieces. Texts between

Logan and Diane were leaked, showing their rocky marriage. We find their missing posters. The kids were so small. They used a different photo for Diane's poster, and she looks different compared to her mugshot. She looks happier.

Pachi is sitting on the floor, flipping through the few articles we found about the kidnapping. He turns around. "Any luck, Yann?"

"No, I can't find anything that hasn't been said." Yann turns to face us. "What exactly are we looking for, anyway?"

"Anything about their mom and siblings. Any hint of where they can be," I answer.

"If she's been missing for twelve years, we're not going to find anything. She's gone under the radar." Pachi groans.

I shrug. "There must be something we can do."

Pachi sighs. "I think we should call the cops." Chills run down my body and Pachi looks at me. "I know. I know you don't want to deal with them. I don't either, but what else can we do?"

My brain digs around for an explanation and the words fight to escape my mouth. "We can't." I wheeze out. "If their mom finds out the cops know, she'll take the kids and run. We can't risk it."

"I know, but think about it. We're dealing with a mother who kidnapped her kids and who the hell knows what she's done to them? If she comes after us and something happens, the police will be our only option. I don't want that either, but we should tell someone in case something happens." Pachi looks at me as he leans against the wall. "I'm sorry. I don't want anyone getting hurt."

I grip my arm and turn away. "You're right. I know you're right, but..." The color drains from my face as I shiver. "I don't trust them at all. They might make things worse."

Pachi looks down and sighs. "We need to think things through then, or tell someone we can trust that won't tell the cops."

Yann groans. "Who can we tell? No one would let us help without involving the cops."

"Logan." My friends look at me. "He's the only one we can tell."

"Olive's not ready to meet him yet. We'd be breaking his heart." Yann frowns.

"We have to get Olive to open up," I say. "We need to figure out why she doesn't want to go with Logan. There has to be something holding her back."

"Maybe you can. She seems fine with you."

"You think?"

"Yeah, I don't know how to explain it," Yann says.

"You two did patch her up, no questions asked," Pachi mentions.

"I guess, but do you think it's enough?" It's one thing to feel alone, it's another when you have no one to trust. I don't know if she trusts me at all.

"Either you or Sam. Olive was talking to you two the most. That's all we can do right now." Yann gets up from the chair with a sigh. "Let's clean up. We'll regroup tomorrow. That way we can talk to Olive too."

Pachi's eyes widen. He takes out his phone and looks at the date. "Wait, we can't. Graduation's tomorrow."

"I forgot about that." I take out my phone. "Well, I'll text the group chat what's going on. We'll figure it out."

Me: Yann's dad knows Logan. We found out a bit, but not much. We can talk about it after graduation.

Our phones ring a few seconds later.

Incoming FaceTime: The Council.

I answer my phone while Pachi and Yann huddle around me. No point in using their phones when the three of us are right here. Owen and Sam pop onto the screen.

"So, what happened?" Sam asks.

Pachi raises an eyebrow. "Did you not read the text?"

"No, I did. But I have to go straight home after graduation. I won't be able to hang out after. Mom has to run errands, and I don't want Olive home alone."

"How's Olive doing?" I ask.

"She's sound asleep." Sam looks away for a second. "She had a horrible nightmare last night. She mentioned something about her mom, but won't tell me anything else."

Owen looks at the camera. "Has she talked to you at all?"

Sam frowns. "A bit, but she still won't say anything about her mom. She'll talk about Theodore and Christina, but not their mom." Sam sighs and looks at the camera. "What did you guys learn?"

"The mom's name is Diane Page. She's been arrested too." Pachi pulls out the newspaper I found downtown. He holds up her photo to the camera. "Apparently, she and Logan had a rocky marriage."

Owen scratches his head. "Something still doesn't add up. Why would she even take the kids in the first place?"

I grab one of the articles we found and read the paragraph out loud. "Logan and Diane finalized their divorce two months before the kidnapping. The kids were kidnapped on January 23rd, five days after their second birthday and the day that Logan and Diane were supposed to go to court for custody."

Owen frowns. "So, she kidnapped them because she was going to lose custody? Why would she only take three of them?"

I look through the paper again. "There were only three car seats in her car, so she couldn't fit all of them. But I don't get how she got them out without making any noise."

"They found her car abandoned, right?" Yann questions, and I nod. He continues. "Where did she go with three toddlers? And if she's been in Pittsburg this whole time, how has she not been found?"

"Maybe they moved?" Pachi suggests. "Stockton's an hour from here. They should have found her."

Sam sighs. "We'd have to ask Olive. But I still don't know if—"

"Sam?" a voice cries. Sam's eyes go wide. "Sam!"

Sam's footsteps stomp on the floor. A door creaks open. "I'm here! What—?" The screen readjusts. It's just Owen and us on the call now. We sit in silence, waiting for Sam to rejoin.

Sam: We're okay, Olive had a nightmare. I'll call later.

We're still on the call when we get the message. Owen sighs. "Olive didn't tell us much, but she said something. It was a punishment she got when she was twelve."

"What happened?" I ask.

"She went outside to say hi to the mailman, and Diane got so pissed that after the man left, she dragged Olive back inside and locked her in her room. She stayed in there the entire night."

My jaw drops. "Jesus, she should've talked to her about strangers, not that!"

"That's what I said. Olive wouldn't listen. She kept saying it was her fault. She even gets nightmares about it." Owen sighs. He leans back in his chair.

I frown. "Hey, if it's too hard talking about it with Olive, you don't have to."

Owen blinks, then he lets out a chuckle. "I'm fine, don't worry. If talking to her about it helps, then I'll do it."

Owen ends the call a few minutes later, realizing his phone is dying. We get up from the floor and clean up the papers. Yann grabs a folder from his dad's desk and places all the papers relating to the sextuplets inside. Now we won't have to dig for the papers if we need them again. Yann leaves it on his dad's desk for now. We clean for a few more minutes, and the room looks cleaner than when we came in.

We move to Yann's room and start playing on his console. I get up to go to the bathroom a few minutes later. It's a lie. I just need to be alone. I sit on the edge of the tub, pulling out the newspaper I hid in my pocket. I read the entire article, even the paragraph I didn't want to read earlier.

Diane, please come home. I don't know what you're trying to do, but please bring them home. I know we're not together anymore, but you're the mother of my children, and I still care about you. Please come home. If not for me, then for the kids. They don't deserve this. They don't deserve to be separated. Please.

I carefully fold the newspaper back up and put it in my pocket. I sit on the edge of the tub for a few minutes. My heart feels like it's going to explode. I can't believe this. How could someone do this to their own kids? How could a mother just... I can't comprehend it. If my mother did that to me, I don't know what I'd do.

I have a loving family. Great parents, a good relationship with my sister, but Olive doesn't. I don't think she's ever had. I can't imagine what she feels like right now. She must feel so alone.

The knock on the door scares me so badly that I slip into the tub. "Paco?" It's Yann behind the door. "You okay?"

Shit, how long have I been gone? "Y-yeah! I'm fine!" I flush the toilet to distract him and turn on the sink, splashing water on my face. I don't know if I've been crying, and I don't want them to ask.

"Well, hurry up! I'm about to kick Yann's ass in this game!" Pachi shouts, and Yann laughs.

"I'll be out in a minute!" I answer. Their footsteps walk away, and I'm alone again.

I was bullied throughout elementary school, and it didn't stop until sixth grade. During that time, Sam was my only friend, at least until I met everyone else. Sam had my back since the beginning, and she was the only one I could trust during that time. She was the only one who was there for me.

If I can help Olive not feel so alone, help her trust a bit more, then maybe she'll feel better. Maybe she'll want to go home. If being that person helps her, then I'm going to do all that I can. I just hope it's enough.

I leave the bathroom with my mind made up. I'm going to help Olive and her siblings get home, no matter what.

6

— • —

Graduation is always a long day, and this year, it's a mess. Usually, it takes place at a venue out of town, but somehow our spot got booted. The school's running around trying to get everything ready. There's no time to split up the graduations properly, so the football stadium is going to be jam-packed.

It makes things easier for the band. We perform at graduation. Instead of coming early and loading all the instruments onto the buses and trailers, we can set them up in the band room and walk to the stadium. I still show up late. I rush to put my instrument together and catch up with the rest of the band.

We're separated by sections, and I find Pachi with the other trombones. He scolds me when I get to him. "Where were you? Did you forget what today was?"

"My alarm didn't go off," I respond. I run my hands over my hair, and Pachi laughs. "Did you bring the five bucks?" I smirk.

Pachi rolls his eyes. "Did *you* bring the five bucks? I'm shedding no tears today."

"You cried at band senior night," I remind him.

"No proof," Pachi counters, even though we know it's a lie.

We arrive at the football stadium. There's a small platform on the 50-yard line with hundreds of chairs in front of it. Our set of chairs is nearby, just off to the left. We quickly get into our seats.

The way graduation works is that we perform the entrance song while the seniors get to their seats. After some speeches, they excuse band seniors to play a song with us. Then the seniors walk the stage. We play one more song as everyone leaves, allowing any band seniors to come play one last time.

The entrance song is long. We loop it over and over until all the seniors get to their seats. Finally, we're cued to stop playing. Now we wait. I look around to find everyone else. Pachi is sitting next to me. Hopefully, graduation won't be boring now, and he won't be able to lie about our bet. Pachi spots Owen and Yann further down the row. Sam's in the last row. She has her headphones on, already watching a show.

Pachi's on the verge of falling asleep and I'm texting Rose. I want to take her out on a date, but I don't know where. Not only that, whenever I'm free, she's busy. When she's free, I have work. I wait for her to respond with if she's free tomorrow.

Rose: I can't. I have to tutor tomorrow. :(

Me: We'll figure it out.

Time moves quickly. Before I know it, the seniors are coming our way. We play a song, the crowd cheers, and the seniors return to their seats. A few minutes later, the seniors start walking the stage. Pachi cheers for his friends, and I wait for a tear to roll down his face. In the corner of my eye, my phone flashes on the music stand. The unknown number changes, showing the caller ID.

Incoming call: Olive Page.

What? How did Olive get my number? I look back at Sam. Her eyes are still on her phone. What's going on? Why is Olive calling me?

"Hello?" I answer.

"Paco? Is that you? Sam left me some numbers to call."

"Yeah, it's me." I lower my voice, "Olive, is everything okay? Why are you calling?"

"I think my mom found me."

My heart falls to the pit of my stomach. How? How did she find her? Olive's location is off, and no one else knows. My stomach curls as I remember the date. Olive said they were supposed to leave on Sunday, today. What if Diane was waiting for today? Has she known where Olive's been this whole time?

"A-are you sure it's her?" I ask.

"She's been going up and down the street, and it looks like her car. It's a gray Honda Civic." Olive pauses. "I can get a better look."

"Olive, no. That's not a good—!"

"Shit!" A loud bang, and then the sound of window blinds flying around. "It's her. Christina's in the backseat." The blinds sound like they settle back into place. "What do I do?"

"Stay out of sight," I say. "She doesn't know exactly where you are if she's going up and down the street. Don't look through the windows. If you could see Christina, she could see you." My heart pounds against my chest like a drum. My eyes flicker between Pachi and the ground. He looks at me for a second and raises his eyebrow. I give him a thumbs up. *I'm fine.*

Pachi looks at the stage. Olive hasn't said anything in a while, and I can't hear her breathing anymore. Chills run down my spine. "Olive?" No response. "Olive!" Shit! Why isn't she answering? I place my free hand on my knee, holding it down to stop the bouncing. Nothing good ever comes from panicking. I look at my phone, checking if she's still on the line. She is.

"Hey, what's wrong?" Pachi places a hand on my shoulder, snapping me out of my thoughts. His eyes look down at my leg for a second, then back at me. "Paco?"

"Diane found her." The words send more shivers down my spine.

Pachi's eyes widen. He snatches the phone out of my hand and takes headphones out of his pocket. He plugs them in and passes me an earbud. "Olive, it's Pachi. What's going on?" No response. He calls out her name again.

"Mom found me," Finally, she answers. "She's been going up and down the street for ten minutes."

"Are you absolutely sure it's her?" Pachi asks.

"Christina's in the backseat." The blinds rustle again. "Theodore's in the front."

Pachi mutes the call and looks at me. "How the hell did she find her? Isn't her location off?" he whispers.

"Unless it shows where her last location was, I have no idea. Sam and I live on the same street."

"Her cars stopping," Olive says.

Pachi unmutes us. "Stopping where?"

"Across the street. She's looking at her phone." There's a loud vibration. The default ringtone is so loud that it hurts our ears. Olive's voice fades with the noise. All at once, it stops.

"Olive? Are you there?" Pachi asks.

"I'm fine! She was calling my phone."

"What is she doing right now?" I ask.

"Yelling at Christina for trying to get out of the car. I think I can crack the window open to hear what she's saying."

"Olive, wait!" I say, but it's too late. The window slides open.

"She's so pissed. It's almost funny how much." Olive chuckles. "Ah, poor Christina. She hates getting yelled at." Olive pauses and sucks in a sharp breath. "Uh oh. Oh crap! She saw me! Christina saw me!"

Pachi and I look at each other, the same look of fear in our eyes. There's nothing we can do from here. Our eyes land on the line of seniors. There's only ten left. After we play, we have to put the chairs and stands away. It doesn't matter how quickly we move. We can't do anything.

"Hello? Are you two still there?" Olive whisper-shouts into the phone.

"Are you sure she saw you?" Pachi questions.

"Yes. Her eyes went wide, and she immediately told Mom. I got behind the door before she saw me, I hope."

The crowd around us cheers as the principal speaks. Pachi takes off the earbud he's wearing and shoves my phone back into my hands. He picks up his trombone, eyes on our director. Pachi's always been the louder player. He can play for both of us. The crowd cheers again, the seniors move their tassels, and music blasts through the stadium's speakers.

I pick up my trombone and hold it up. Seniors run through the crowd, racing to get back to the band before we start playing. I can fake my playing. We'll be okay.

"Olive, can you hear me?" I question. I don't know where the mic on Pachi's headphones is.

"Yeah. I can hear you." Olive sounds like she's crying. "W-what do I do? Mom's coming up to the house!"

"Hide. Lock yourself in Mrs. Sanchez's room. And grab something to defend yourself!"

Olive stomps up the stairs and shuts a door behind her. The band starts to play, and I move my trombone slide. "Are you okay?" I try not to yell into the phone.

"She's at the front door," Olive cries. "She's at the front door." Olive's breathing gets faster. "I don't want to see her. I don't want to see her."

"You won't. She can't get—"

"She opened the door!" I stop breathing. Olive's voice lowers. "She's calling for me! Oh, god!"

"Did you lock the door?"

"Yes! I even pushed stuff against it." Olive sniffles. "Don't hang up. Please, don't hang up."

"I'm not going anywhere."

"No. No! My phone's dying!" Olive's breathing even faster. "She's near the stairs!"

My body freezes when Olive goes quiet. "Olive? Olive!"

The call drops.

God, no. No...

I take off the earbud and start playing my trombone. The song's nearly over, and I only get a few notes out. Our director cuts us off, and we're released to go home. I slump into my seat. How did Diane get inside? How did she even find her? I'm praying for Olive to be okay as we put the chairs and stands on their racks. I can't even call back. The calls go straight to voicemail.

"What happened?" Pachi asks.

"Her phone died, and Diane's inside." I look straight ahead. Owen and Yann are walking toward us, but Sam isn't with them.

Wait... SAM!

"Has Sam left yet?" I question.

Owen shrugs, but Yann nods. "I saw her heading back to the band room. Why, what's up?"

I take out my phone and dial Sam's number as fast as I can. I hope she hasn't left yet. She has the setting on her phone where calls go straight to voicemail if she's —

"Hey this is Sam! I can't reach the phone right now..."

Dammit! She's driving already! How did she get out of here so fast?

"What's going on?" Yann asks.

"Diane found Olive." That's all that comes out of my mouth. We look at each other, then make a beeline for the band room. We run out of the stadium, run past the gym, and don't stop until we reach the parking lot. When we get there, Sam's dusty orange truck is leaving the parking lot.

"Dammit!" I groan. "How the hell did she leave so fast?"

"The calls are going straight to voicemail." Yann groans. "What do we do?"

Owen points to a car. "Paco, your mom's here." I turn to look. Mom's car pulls into the parking lot. To my surprise, she's by herself.

"I'll call later. Let me know if you get a hold of Sam!" I tell my friends before running to the band room to put my trombone in its case. By the time I come out, Mom's car is closer to the front. She pops the trunk, and I put my trombone inside. I sit in the front seat.

"Is everything okay, Ma?" I ask. It's rare for Mom and Dad to not pick me up together.

Mom looks at the steering wheel. She takes deep, slow breaths. Every passing second makes me worry more. She sits up and looks at me. "Someone broke into our house."

My brain stutters. What did she say? Our neighborhood is so nice! I've never heard of anyone getting robbed where we live. And how the hell did they get in? Dad always makes sure the doors are locked before we leave. Every door. The back, the front, the garage, he always checks.

"What? When?" I question.

"I'm not sure. After we dropped you off, we went to church, then ran some errands. We came home to it like that," Mom answers. "Dad's home with the police now. He's okay, but I don't want to leave him alone."

The flashing lights outside my house shake me to my core. I don't like it, not one bit. I step outside the car and stand there, completely still. The scenes from that night go through my head. Am I breathing? I think I am? I shake my head. I can do this. I'm sixteen now, I'm not eleven. I can walk into my own damn house and not worry about the cops.

"*No los mires,*" my mother whispers. "Don't look at them. Keep walking."

I keep my eyes on the ground and walk up the porch steps. Where's Dad? Mom said he's okay, but I can't find him. Chills run down my spine the longer I look for him. Where's Dad? Where is he? I call for him as I walk around the house, ignoring the damage on the floor. He comes around the corner, and I crash into him.

"*Ay, mijo,* watch where you're walking." I wrap my arms around him. Dad sighs and pats my head. "I'm fine, don't worry. They haven't done anything to me. They're not going to." An officer walks toward Dad and I let him go. The two of them start speaking in Spanish. Even though Dad knows English well, it's easier for him to talk in Spanish. Whenever he has something important to tell me, it's always in Spanish.

I finally see how much of a mess the house is. The couch cushions are overturned, picture frames are crooked and on the floor. Our kitchen cabinets are open, along with the fridge. The fridge itself is empty. There's no food at all.

I go upstairs to my room and push the door open. My blankets are stripped off my bed, my closet is empty, and my clothes are scattered around the room. Whatever was under my desk is across the room. I leave and check Paula's old room. The covers are on the floor, and the closet doors are wide open. My parents' room is in the same condition. Covers, floor. Closet, open. The room, a wreck.

I don't understand. My family doesn't have much. The most valuable items we have are electronics. My Switch is still downstairs, and my computer is here too.

My phone buzzes with two new notifications.

Pachi: Sam texted. She'll call you in a bit.

Oh, thank God. She's okay. I text him thanks, then read the second notification.

Pachi Martinez sent you $5.00.

I forgot about that stupid bet. I send the five dollars back and text him to forget about the bet. We have bigger things to worry about.

I start making my bed. I have to untangle my blankets and put them back on one by one. Now is not a good time to have a lot of blankets on your bed. I can't help it, it's hard to sleep without them.

My phone rings, and I grab the FaceTime call immediately. "Sam! Are you okay?" Seeing her face on the screen makes me want to cry tears of relief.

"I'm—Holy shit!" she says when I answer. "What the hell happened?"

"Someone broke into our house." I sit on my half-made bed. "It's a mess, but that's not important. Where's Olive? Is she okay?"

"Mom said someone broke into our house too. She came home as they were approaching the stairs. It scared the shit out of them, and they ran off. Mom found Olive hiding in her closet." Sam pauses. "She was terrified. Stayed curled up in a ball until I got home."

I sigh in relief. I stand and put my phone on my nightstand. "Did your mom see who it was?" I grab my blankets and start to untangle them.

"Yeah, it was some woman. Late thirties, short blonde hair, about five-eight." Blonde hair? Diane's was brown in the mugshot.

"Did Olive say who it was?"

"No, she hasn't spoken yet. She's downstairs with Mom and Ruby." Sam looks at the camera with eyebrows raised. "Also, why were you guys calling me so much?"

"Diane's the one who broke in." Sam's eyes go wide. "Olive called during graduation. Diane was going up and down the street and she saw her."

Sam shudders and looks away. "Oh, god. No wonder she hasn't said anything."

As I spread out one of my blankets, a piece of paper flies out. It floats back down, and I grab it. The writing on the paper is small and messy, like it's been written in a rush.

Olive, please let me know if you're okay. Here's my number in case you can't use your phone. Signed at the bottom is a name, Theodore.

Holy shit. It was Diane. Diane broke into my house. But how did she get in? And how did she find out that Olive was here?

"Sam," I say. She looks at me, confused. I flatten the paper as best as I can and hold it up to the camera.

Her eyes squint as she reads, before widening again. "What? She broke into your house too?"

"It had to be her," I say, flipping my camera. I show her the few blankets on the floor and my empty closet. "All the bedrooms look like this. Whoever did this was looking for something... or someone."

"How the hell did she find you? And how did she get in?" Sam questions. "I've had that door lecture from your dad I don't know how many times!"

"I have no idea. The front door is fine, and none of the windows were broken." I clutch my hair. "The back door isn't fixed, but still, she wouldn't have been able to get in. Unless..." My eyes widen, and so do Sam's.

"The fence," we say at the same time.

I hang up the call—promising to call back later—and run down the stairs. The cops are finally gone. Mom is picking up the mess in the living room, and Dad is at the back door with his toolbox. He mumbles under his breath in Spanish, blaming his procrastination.

I walk past Dad and go into the backyard. There it is. That damn broken fence. It's taken quite a beating. I prop the fence up and the wind howls. Another piece of the fence falls off. I march over to it with a groan. I prop the fence up and look back at the house. This is the same spot I was in on Friday, the day I found Olive.

Diane didn't get through the fence that Olive did, she broke down a different part. She knew Olive was at my house.

I stare at the piece of paper I found earlier. Why would Theodore leave this? Did he escape too? Is this a trap? I still don't know how Diane found my house or figured out that Olive was here.

I pull my phone out of my pocket and go to my contacts. I scroll through them until I find Rose. She's the only person I want to think about right now.

"Hi, Paco!" Rose's voice rolls rocks off my shoulders, and I let out a sigh of relief. "Whoa, are you okay?"

"Not really. Someone broke into my house and Sam's." I sigh. "I'm sorry for calling. I just wanted to hear your voice."

"Are you guys okay?"

"Yeah, Sam's okay. The robber stole all our food, and we just went to the store." I groan. "I don't know what to do. She trashed the house and went after Olive—" I slam my hand over my mouth. *Oh no.*

"Olive? Who's Olive?" Rose asks. I'm screwed. There's no excuse that I can use.

"Promise not to tell anyone?" I ask.

"Of course."

"Olive broke into my house on Friday," I say. I tell Rose everything. The burn and the bruise she came with, her mother's voicemails, and how we found her siblings. I sigh. "Leo's so stressed about it. I don't blame him, but..."

"Wait, Leo? Leo Page?" she asks. I say yes, and she gasps. "You're kidding. I tutor him in math. We have a lesson tomorrow at noon."

My eyes widen. I wonder if she would've found out regardless. *Stay optimistic.* I tell myself. *It'll be okay.* I find my words. "Do you think you can update him for me? It'll help to have someone to talk to. He's stressed we can't tell his dad yet."

"I will. Oh! Will you be home tomorrow? I want to drop something off before I go tutor him."

"Sure, I'll be home all day."

"Is there anything else I can do?"

I sigh. "I feel better already just talking to you. This whole break-in has me stressed."

Rose giggles. "I'm glad you're feeling better. I'll see you tomorrow then. Goodnight, honey."

I smile. "Goodnight, *mi amor.*"

I look at my phone after she hangs up. My mind is torn. I'm relieved Rose knows. I can talk to her and not worry about anything slipping. But now I'm *worried* that she knows. What if Diane goes after her? I shake my head. There's no way that Diane can find out about her. I won't let that happen.

I go back to the main problem. How did Diane find me? The tracking app is the only reason I can come up with, but is there something else? I look at the paper again and sigh. There's only one person I can ask who might have an answer.

I need to call Theodore. If anyone knows anything, it's him.

7

— · —

THIS IS A BAD *idea.* I think to myself for the fifth time. I'm not Olive, and I doubt I'll do a good impression of her. Not only that, I hate lying to Mom and Dad.

Dad's still working on the back door when I come inside from the backyard. Mom is sitting at the dining table on her computer. I peer over her shoulder. She's looking at security systems and cameras. Our eyes flicker between the options, and we wince looking at the high prices. I put an arm around her, trying my best to comfort her.

"We'll look at it later, Ma." I slowly push the computer away from her. She turns toward me and pulls me into a tight embrace.

Mom's phone rings. She lets me go to answer it. It's Mrs. Sanchez. Mom sighs. "You should go to bed, *mijo.* It's very late."

"You too, Mama." I give her another hug. "*Te amo mucho.*"

"*Te amo mas. Buenas noches.*"

Mom answers her phone after I go upstairs. "Carmen, I don't know what to do." I peer around the corner. Mom's looking at the laptop with heavy bags under her eyes. My dad puts his tools down and walks to her, putting his arms around her. Mom talks to Mrs. Sanchez in Spanish and tells her about the missing food and what a mess the robber made.

Mom sighs. "*Paco esta bien. No quiero estresarlo.*" I frown, and Mom continues. "Something's been stressing him lately. I don't want this to make it worse." *I'll be okay, Mom. We'll be okay.*

I go to my room and finish making my bed. I don't bother with my closet. The mountain of shirts and jackets can wait until tomorrow. I change, get into bed, and stare at the ceiling. I toss and turn for a few minutes. Worry fills my mind. What's going to happen to Olive now? She can't stay at Sam's house, not if Diane knows she's there. Although, I doubt she'll go back, not after the scare Mrs. Sanchez gave her, but I don't know.

Something taps my window. I turn to my side, trying to ignore it. The taps start again, but harder and stronger. I groan. That old tree and its weak branches. It's not fun waking up in the middle of the night and thinking someone's at my window. I look out the window to ease that worry.

Owen is sitting on the roof. I blink once, then twice. Owen waves and I nearly fall out of bed. What the hell is he doing here so late? The one time I'm not going to check, someone is at my window! I fumble out of the blankets and unlock the window.

"Owen? What are you doing here?" I ask. Owen closes the window behind him and sits crisscrossed on my bed. He must've left in a hurry. He's wearing his round brown glasses instead of contacts.

"I couldn't sleep." Owen pushes away his glasses and rubs his eyes. "Sam told me what happened. I figured you'd be up. You guys all right?"

"Yeah. No one was home when it happened, but Mom's stressing out. Diane stole our food, and my parents don't get paid till next week."

"Is Olive okay?"

"Yeah. Diane didn't find her, but she wouldn't come out until Sam was home." I sigh. I should tell him that Rose knows. "I called Rose after I got home, and let it slip about Olive. But I found this on my bed." I grab the note on my nightstand and give it to Owen.

Owen shrugs. "I trust Rose, but this?" His eyes go back and forth over the paper, and he frowns. "Have you called it?"

"No, not yet."

"You should run it by Olive in the morning." Owen gets off the bed and walks toward the door. "I'll be right back, and I'll head home after."

I sigh. "Owen, just stay. It's already late."

He shakes his head. "No, it's okay. I'm only a few houses down."

"You're an insomniac. I have the pullout bed for a reason."

Owen smiles. "Thanks, man. Be back in a bit."

I reach under my bed for the handle and pull out the bed. I stare at the note while waiting for Owen to come back. It's a little past ten. Is Theodore even awake? A hundred thoughts race through my head. That number's now memorized like the back of my hand. Diane was able to find my house. Will she try again?

You know what?

Screw it.

I dial the number into my phone and listen to it ring. One ring, two rings, three rings. Then...

"H-hello?" The voice that answers me is timid. "Olive?" It's him. Although, he doesn't sound sleepy.

"I found your note." As I say that, Owen returns from the bathroom. He glances at my phone and the look on my face. He groans and facepalms. I take my phone off my ear and turn up the volume. It's not on speaker, but it's loud enough for Owen to hear.

"Is it really you? You sound different on the phone," Theodore says in a shaky voice.

"Yeah, it's me," I answer, trying to make my voice higher. Owen makes a face. I shrug.

The relief in Theodore's voice hurts. "Oh, thank God! I was so worried. You weren't answering my texts or anything." His words come out so fast that they catch me off-guard. "I even stole Mom's phone to see if I could find you that way, but your location was off."

"How did you find me then?" My impression of Olive slips. *Shit.*

Silence falls, and the air turns cold. I'm sweating bullets when Theodore finally answers, "You're not Olive." *Fuck.* "Where's my sister? Who are you?"

"S-she's okay. She's safe." Jesus, this was a bad idea. "My name is Paco. I'm a friend of hers, and I'm helping her out."

"Where is she right now?"

"She's safe. I can't tell you where, but she's safe."

"Is she still in that house?" Theodore asks. Chills run down my spine. "I know she's in there, but Mom never found her. And I'm not asking for the reason you think I am."

"What do you mean?" I question.

"I don't want Olive coming home."

My eyes widen. He doesn't? Why not? I mean, I guess that's good for us, but they're siblings. And Diane's been after her since she left.

"You... you don't?"

"No." Theodore's voice is cold yet shaky. "Mom's lost it. She's pissed that Olive hasn't come home. She's getting mad over every little thing." He lowers his voice to a mumble. "Taking it out on us too."

Owen and I look at each other, our faces filled with worry. I remember the bruise on Olive's face when I met her. She denied it, and all of us thought about it, but I was hoping it wasn't true. "Are you okay?" I ask.

"I'm fine. It's Christina and Olive I'm worried about. By the way, how's that burn on Olive's arm? Is it healing okay?" Theodore asks with a sigh. "I tried to fix it as best I could, but I don't know if it was enough."

"We rebandaged and put lotion on it. It looked really bad if I'm honest. How did it happen?"

"Olive won't be happy if I tell you," Theodore says. Olive must be stubborn with him too. There are a few seconds of silence before he speaks. "Okay, I need to get onto the main reason for wanting to call. Are you willing to help?"

"Yes," I answer immediately.

"Okay. I've been trying to convince Mom to take me to the grocery store. I'm running out of things to cook."

"Did you take our food?"

"Yes, I'm sorry. I didn't have a choice. We haven't had a decent meal in days. But that food won't last for long." Theodore pauses. "When I convince Mom to take me to the store, Olive can come get anything she needs. And if I can convince Christina, she can go with you."

"What do you mean?"

"I want Christina to go with you guys. She can't stay here." Theodore takes a deep breath. "Mom's completely lost it. Well, she's hit before, and she's been drinking for as long as I can remember, but this is different. It's like she doesn't care anymore."

Tears threaten to fall from my eyes, and I wonder how he's staying so *calm* about this. "Are you okay?" I ask.

"She won't stop yelling, she won't stop hitting, she won't stop drinking. She won't listen to us at all. I don't know what to do anymore." Theodore chokes on a sob. "I'm happy Olive got out. I just wish I was with her."

"Then run." I say, almost begging him. "Run right now."

"I can't leave Christie behind. I'm scared of what she'll do."

"Who? Your mom?"

"No, Christina. She's tried before." My heart falls to the pit of my stomach and my blood turns cold. Owen's eyes widen. Theodore sobs. "It was a few months ago, but—"

"You don't have to explain, I know." I pause. "What about you? We can't leave you behind."

"I'll figure something out," Theodore says. The air thickens, and he takes another deep breath. "W-will you tell Olive I love her? Please? I don't know if she's mad at me, but in case we're too late, I want her to know."

"Of course I will, but what do you mean, too late?"

"I…" Silence. That's all we hear for a minute. Theodore's breath hitches. "Shit! It's Mom! I have to go!"

"Theodore? Theodore!" I don't get an answer. The call hangs up, and we're left in silence.

The silence holds as Owen cocoons himself in a blanket and flops onto the pullout bed. "You couldn't wait until morning?" he asks.

"I didn't think he'd answer. It's past ten," I respond, still looking at my phone.

Owen sighs. "We'll tell Olive in the morning and go from there."

I can only nod. Are the kids going to be okay? Are we able to wait that long? So many thoughts race through my head. What if Diane does something else? What if Theodore *can't* convince Christina? What if... what if?

"Hey." Owen's voice snaps me back to reality. "I'm worried too, but we can't do anything rash."

"I know. I know." I sigh. "But we can't... I can't..."

"If we do dumb shit, people will get involved." People mean police in this situation, and he knows I hate they very thought of them. "If they get involved, then it's game over."

"Then we're screwed."

"We will be screwed." Owen pulls the covers over himself and turns onto his side. "There's nothing we can do right now. Let's try to get some sleep." Yeah, try.

I send Sam a text about what happened. She'll bring Olive at nine. I'm surprised she's still awake. I put my phone on my nightstand and get back in bed. I turn on my side, doing my best to push the worrying thoughts out of my head.

Ding dong!

The doorbell rouses me from my sleep, and the sun comes through my window. I groan and flip onto my side to fall back asleep. Whoever's at the door does not care about my sleep and keeps ringing the doorbell.

"Paco." Owen groans. His voice is hoarse, and he's still half asleep. "Go open the door." Owen throws his pillow at me, landing on my face. "This is your house. You answer the door."

I sit up with a groan and throw the pillow back at Owen. "What time is it?"

Owen looks at his phone. "It's nine."

Nine, nine, why is that familiar? I grab my phone off my nightstand and look at the notifications.

Missed Call: Sam.

Oh crap! Olive!

I fling off the covers and run down the stairs. The doorbell is still ringing when I open the door. Thank God that Mom and Dad are at work, otherwise, that wouldn't be a good conversation. Olive walks inside, and I watch Sam drive off.

"Did you just wake up?" Olive asks.

"Yeah, sorry."

Olive walks to the couch and sits. I sit next to her. She looks around the quiet house. "Are you the only one home?"

"Pretty much," I answer, and Olive relaxes. "Owen's here though. He came by last night, but he's still asleep." Olive tenses back up. "How are things at Sam's?"

"All right. Yesterday wasn't, but other than that, it's been good." There's some awkward tension between us, but not like when we first met. Olive sighs. "It's a bit weird not being the youngest. Theodore and Christina are both older than me."

"Oh, really? You're the youngest?"

"Yeah. I think out of all of us. I don't know about Leonardo and the others. Mom doesn't like talking about them." She's addressing Leo by name, but she doesn't call him Leo. Olive sighs. "Sam said you wanted to talk to me. What's it about?"

I pull the small note out of my pajama pocket. "Your mom broke into my house too, and Theodore left this." Olive's eyebrows raise when I mention her brother's name. "I called last night. It's him. Not only that, my girlfriend also knows. I said your name on accident and couldn't cover it."

Olive's eyes go wide. She turns a bit pale. "Y-you what?" Olive scoots back. "O-okay, first thing, why would you call Theodore?"

"I wanted to know how they found you, and I wanted to know if they were okay."

"If they're okay?" Olive rises from the couch and points toward the backyard. "I'm sure they're *fine* without me! You shouldn't have called!"

"Theodore's been worried sick about you! He was crying the whole time, wanting to know if you were okay! He begged me to you that he loves you."

Olive's hands move frantically, like she doesn't know what to do with them. "I thought you were on my side!" She points a shaky finger at me. "You promised no one would find out, and you told someone! You promised that everything would be okay!"

"And it will be!" I jump up from the couch, and Olive steps back. She holds her arms in front of her body, blocking herself from me. *Protecting* herself from me. Fear is in her eyes and her body is trembling. I step away. God, what have I done? I take a breath. "I'm sorry, Olive. I didn't mean to hurt you like this."

"Of course you didn't! That's what they always say!"

Footsteps dash down the stairs. Owen steps forward, adjusting his glasses. "What's with all the yelling? Are you okay?"

Olive doesn't look at him. She looks into my eyes. "I trusted you." Olive's words are like knives in my chest. Her cries twist them, pushing them further into me. "I *trusted* you."

"I'm sorry, Olive. I'm so sorry."

"I thought you weren't like her. I thought you cared."

I can't say anything. I can apologize over and over, and assure her countless times that I do care, but it won't fix this. Nothing will fix this. Any chance of her opening up, any chance we had of her feeling safe, that's ruined now. I ruined everything.

Olive turns around, arms stiffly at her side. "I should've known." Olive marches to the front door. I go after her but linger behind. I scared her once, and I don't want to again.

"Olive, you have every reason to hate me right now." The words fly out of me. She turns her head, acknowledging me, but still facing the door. "But please know that I never meant to hurt you. I just wanted to help. I'm sorry. Please, don't leave."

"I can't leave even if I wanted to, so leave me alone."

I go out into the backyard without another word. Owen follows me, taking a seat at the table. We sit in silence. Time passes by, but seconds feel like minutes, and minutes feel like hours. I pick at the skin on my hands, yelling at myself in my head. *I shouldn't have done this. I should've waited.*

"Don't beat yourself up," Owen says with a sigh.

I look at him. "How can I not? I've ruined everything. I didn't even think about how she'd react."

"You couldn't have known."

"I should've."

The front door creaks open a few seconds later. I jump up from my seat and run inside, crashing into Olive. What's she doing near the back door? And if she's here, then who opened the front door? I step in front of Olive and look forward. I sigh in relief. It's Paula.

"*Ay Paquito*, I was so worried." Paula runs and embraces me. She towers over me even without heels. Her hands hold my face, turning me toward her. "Mom told me what happened. Are you okay?"

"I'm fine. I wasn't home when it happened."

Paula lets go of me. Her eyes scan the house. "Well, at least nothing's broken. Did Dad fix the back door?" Paula pushes me aside, revealing Olive. Her eyes go wide. "Layla? What are you doing here?"

Olive's jaw drops, and she steps back. I stand in front of her. "Who's Layla?" I ask Paula.

"She's my co-worker's daughter. She's been missing for three, four days now. She looks exactly like her!"

I look at Olive. Her mouth hangs open, and she groans. "Paula, my real name is Olive. And I'm begging you not to tell Mom. I don't want to see her!"

"Your mom is freaking out. It's like she's gone mad."

"That's the thing. She has gone mad, and I'm not going back to her." My eyes widen at her statement. She glances at me with daggers in her eyes. Olive turns back to Paula. "I'm a missing sextuplet."

"Sextuplets? I knew you were a triplet, but sextuplets?" Olive nods. Paula raises her eyebrows. "Well, what are you doing here?"

Olive looks at me, not saying anything. Paula glares and sweat trickles down my face. She grabs my hand and guides me out the front door. The two of us stand on the porch. We watch a few cars drive by. Paula leans over the porch railing as I wait for whatever lecture she's planning to give me.

Paula turns to face me. "Do Mom and Dad know?" I shake my head. She groans. "What were you thinking?"

Only one sentence comes out of my mouth. "Please don't tell Mom."

"Okay, fine. But I'm calling the damn cops." Paula frowns when my jaw drops. "You're sixteen, Paco! You can't be doing this!"

I grab Paula's arms. "You can't call the cops! They'll only make things worse!" I look down at my hands and let go. *Breathe. Breathe.* "I-I'm sorry. It's just... if Diane finds out the cops are after her, she'll leave and take Theodore and Christina without a second thought."

Paula's head turns. "Diane? Who's Diane?"

"Their mother," I answer.

"No, her name is..." Paula pauses. Her eyes move from side to side. She takes out her phone and hunts through her gallery, stopping on a photo of her and a blonde-haired woman. "She told me her name was Susan Rodgers. And that she left a toxic relationship with her triplets: Layla, Maddie, and Ezra."

I scratch at my neck. "Well, we got the fake names. That's something. What else did she say?"

"She's struggling to find a stable job, and her youngest triplet keeps giving her a hard time. She homeschools them too, but absolutely hates it. Susan..." Paula shakes her head. "Diane wanted to enroll them into Pitt. But when I saw her last Thursday, she said she had changed her mind, and that they were moving."

"Did she say where?"

"No, she hadn't decided where yet. They were supposed to leave Sunday, but with Layla—I mean—Olive running away, she changed the date. Her last shift is the day of the fireworks."

"Fireworks? What do you mean? Wait, where *do* you work?"

"I'm a bartender at the yacht club. The city's going all out for the Fourth of July this year. There's going to be a whole fair downtown by the marina. The yacht club's going to be open to the public too." Paula looks at her watch. "It's in about three weeks."

"So we have until then to save them."

Paula sighs. "I'll keep an eye on her and let you know if anything changes. But Paquito, I swear to God, if you do anything dumb, I *will* tell Mom."

"I won't, I promise."

I follow Paula back inside the house. Owen turns on the Switch and plays with Olive, hoping to calm her down. Paula and I go into the backyard and fix the fence boards. We get the one Olive broke back on, but the one Diane demolished... we duct tape it to the fence. It looks horrible, but it's staying up.

About an hour later, Paula leaves the house to get all of us breakfast. She laughs before closing the front door. "You have a visitor, Paquito!"

A visitor? My phone vibrates and I take it out to read.

Rose: Hi, honey! I'm here!

The doorbell rings after I read that text. I run to answer it, but Olive beats me to the door. "Who are you?" Olive asks.

"I'm Rose," she says with a smile. "Are you Olive?"

Olive steps back from the door. Rose's eyes widen and she gasps. "Oh, no. I'm so sorry, I didn't mean to scare you. I promise I won't tell anyone. I want to help."

"Help? Why would you want to help me?"

"You don't deserve this. You're just a kid." Rose looks over Olive's shoulder for a second. "May I come in?"

Olive steps to the side, and I run to Rose. She's holding grocery bags in her hands. I look inside and my eyes go wide. It's a bunch of food. Fruit, vegetables, eggs, and there's a small pack of meat.

"Rose, how... how much was this?" I question.

"I'm not telling you! They stole your food, and I wanted to help. I know it's not much, but I hope it helps a bit." Rose places the bags in my hands. I can't even process it.

Olive turns to me with her jaw clenched. "You didn't tell me he stole your food. You said he left that note and that was it. You didn't mention anything about food." Olive pauses. "What else are you hiding from me?"

"I'm not hiding anything," I say. "Please, if you let me explain, I'll tell you."

"What is there to explain? You lied to me. You told someone even though you promised you wouldn't." She jabs her finger at Rose.

"Olive, he said your name by accident. He didn't mean to," Rose says, "and I won't tell anyone."

Olive folds her arms and glares. "Why should I trust you?"

"Your brother does." Olive's eyes widen. Her arms fall to her side as Rose continues, "I'm his tutor. He always tells me how he wishes you were home, and this is before I knew about you. They love you, Olive, they always have." Rose looks at her phone. "I'm going to be late for his lesson."

Olive doesn't speak at first. "Tell him I said hi."

Rose nods. Before she leaves, she scribbles her number onto a piece of paper and gives it to Olive. After putting the bags on the counter, I walk Rose to the door and to her bike parked on the curb.

"You don't trust the police with this, do you?" Rose looks up at me with worry in her eyes.

"Yeah, I don't. I think they'll do more harm than good," I admit.

Rose frowns. "I don't blame you. I wouldn't trust them either if I went through what you did."

I sigh. "Shit still gives me nightmares, and it happened in sixth grade."

One night, a cop from another town pulled us over. He thought Dad was drunk driving, but he didn't have a single glass. The cop asked him questions, and even though Dad complied, he moved too fast and the cop slammed him to the ground. Mom ran to him, but the cop stopped her. Paula stayed with me in the car and tried to block me from seeing, but it was too late. They fired the cop and Dad won the case, but I haven't trusted the police since.

"You were eleven. Of course it would give you nightmares. But you can't do anything stupid." Rose pulls me into a hug. "Keep me updated, okay? And if you need anything at all, I'm here. Be careful."

"I will, and thank you for the food," I tell her. "I haven't eaten."

"Of course, and one more thing. Are you free next Tuesday?" I nod, and Rose's face lights up. "You and me, ice cream, around noon?"

My cheeks turn red. "Yeah, that sounds nice." Rose jumps for joy, and before she leaves, I plant a kiss on her cheek. Her face turns red as she bikes away.

Olive is staring at Rose's number when I come back inside. "I don't get it. Why would she want to help me? She barely knows me."

"She knows you deserve better," Owen says.

Olive folds the paper and puts it in her pocket. She looks at me. The fear has faded from her eyes. "What did Theodore say?"

I look down. "He said your mom's lost it. She's been taking it out on them. Theodore says it's like she doesn't care anymore."

"What does that mean?"

"She keeps drinking, she keeps yelling, and she won't listen. Theodore's really worried."

Olive pauses. "How do I know you're telling the truth?"

"I was there too. I heard the whole call," Owen answers. "Theodore sounded desperate. He wants us to take Christina."

Olive gulps. "Christina? Why? What's wrong?"

"Theodore's worried about her. He wants to leave, but he can't leave her behind. He doesn't want her to..." I trail off, but by the look in Olive's eyes, she understands what I mean. I continue, "He wants you to come back to get what you need, and to take Christina with you."

"Christina loves Mom more than anything. That'll take a lot of convincing, and she's always been the favorite." Olive takes out her phone. The lock screen is a photo of her and Sam. She unlocks it and goes to her texts.

There are hundreds of unread text messages. Most of them are from her mother, but a good chunk is from Theodore. Her finger hovers over the conversation with her brother. Olive sighs, slowly sitting on the couch. "Is it that bad?" Olive taps the conversation and reads the most recent text.

Theodore: Please let me know if you're safe. I love you.

"What do we do?" Olive asks. "Has he said anything since you called?"

I shake my head. "No, nothing. Your mom caught him. He might be waiting it out."

Owen rubs his chin. "How will we get there, anyway?" He looks at me. "Do you think you'll have the car?"

I shrug. "It depends. If Mom needs it, I won't. It's her car, after all. Maybe we can bike?"

"I don't have one," Olive mentions.

"Well, walking won't be so bad," I say.

"What happens if Mom shows up?"

"Then we run like hell," I answer, and Olive scoffs. "No, I mean it. We'll keep you safe."

"I don't believe you."

I sigh. "Olive, I know I messed up. I know you're angry with me. But we will keep you safe, I promise."

Olive doesn't speak, and every passing second makes my chest hurt. There are daggers in her eyes when she looks at me. "I need more than that. A promise isn't enough."

The air thickens. I take a deep breath. "I swear on my life that you'll be safe."

Olive nods. "Okay, one last chance. Don't fuck it up."

8

— • —

When I came to work today, Tío told me to go home. He said I looked sick. So, I'm at home, staring at the ceiling, lying in my bed. It's been three days since Diane broke into my house, and I swear I keep seeing a car going up and down the street. I never catch the model, but every time I see the car, it's gray. I keep my baseball bat by my bed now.

I snatch my keys and lock the door. I walk down the sidewalk until I reach Sam's house. Her mom answers the door with a smile and lets me know Sam is in her room. We've been friends for so long that it's normal to show up randomly. The house is still the same. The family photos near the entrance, Cuba's flag hanging in the kitchen, and the house is warm. It feels safe. I reach the top of the stairs and knock on Sam's door before entering.

"Oh, hey!" Sam says when she sees me. She's sitting at her desk on her laptop. "I thought you had work today?" she asks, taking off her headphones.

"I got there and Tío told me to go home." I look around her room. Olive's stuff is on the top bunk, but she's nowhere in sight. "Where's Olive?"

"She's with Ruby in the backyard. You might be able to see her out there." Sam points to the window. Sure enough, Olive's pushing Sam's four-year-old sister on the swings. "What's up?" Sam asks.

"Do you mind if I hang out here for a bit? I don't want to be home alone."

Sam's smile falters. "Yeah, of course. Are you feeling okay?"

"Just tired," I answer, sitting on her bed. Sam spins around in her chair to face me. She places a hand on my forehead. A fever is the first thing I get.

"You don't feel hot," she says, taking her hand off my head. "What's wrong?"

"It's nothing," I answer. I don't want to make a fuss.

"Do you want to take a nap here?" I shrug, but Sam continues, "I'll be quiet, just sleep. You have a bunch of bags." I touch under my eyes, wondering if I can feel them.

"You don't mind?"

Sam puts her headphones back on. "We've been having sleepovers since we were four. I don't care."

Sam goes back to her computer as I lay down. I flip to my side and close my eyes. A few minutes later, I flip over. Then again, again, and again. I groan into Sam's pillow.

"Okay, something is really bothering you." Sam tosses her headphones on her desk. "What is it?"

"I'm fine," I groan, words muffled by the pillow.

"You suck at lying." My head turns. Sam leans closer. I get up from her pillow to face her. Sam glares at me, eyes squinted and eyebrows raised. She points a finger in my face. "You're stressing about something."

I roll my eyes and push her finger back. "No, Sam. Really, I'm fine." She's right on the money, but I don't want to admit it. I've never been good at handling stress.

She doesn't say anything, but I know she doesn't believe me. Her eyes are burning into me, and it's very uncomfortable. She's too good at intimidating. I sigh in defeat. "I'm worried about Theodore and Christina. I just... have a bad feeling they're in trouble."

Sam leans back in her chair, arms crossed tightly. Considering her silence, Olive hasn't told her about the phone call. Oh crap. I haven't even told everyone about the phone call, or about Rose knowing. Only Owen knows. I've been so caught up with work that I forgot to tell everyone.

Sam clears her throat. "Olive said you told Rose?" Ah, there it is. Maybe she did tell her.

"Yeah, I'm sorry. I'll text everyone she knows later." I hang my head in shame. "Is Olive still mad?"

"Not really."

It shocks me, but I don't let Sam see. "How's she doing?" I ask.

"She's all right. She's not as quiet as before, and she's talking a bit more." Sam reads my expression and continues. "Mostly stuff about her siblings. Christina's favorite food is pizza, and she snores. Theodore's the one who always stands up for them. Whenever their mom does shit, he's always there."

"Has Olive mentioned anything else about them?"

Sam shakes her head. "Not really, just what I said." Well, I guess she hasn't told her. Should I? No, Olive should. She got mad at me for calling Theodore, and I don't want to break whatever trust she has left in me. Sam sighs. "We have to wait until she's ready to talk."

"I know, it just sucks."

Sam reaches for a book on her desk. "I gave Olive my old sketchbook since she's been drawing a lot, and she's really good at it." Sam flips the pages, landing on a drawing of Ruby. It's incredibly detailed, from the brown baby curls to her light brown skin.

I flip the page. This picture has five figures in it. Sam is one of them. One has dark brown hair, another has pale skin, and the last one is tan. But what shocks me the most is the figure next to Sam has sienna skin, and pink curly hair.

"Hey, Sam! Are you awake?" Olive shouts from downstairs. The back door closes and Ruby giggles.

"Yeah, what's up?" Sam gets up from her chair. Footsteps fly up the stairs and Ruby comes charging in. She runs past Sam and straight into me.

"Hi!" Ruby smiles and hugs me tightly.

Olive climbs up the stairs and reaches the doorway. Each time I see her, she looks different from when we met. Her hair is brushed, her clothes aren't ripped, and the bandage is gone. The burn mark has scarred, but it looks a lot better than it did before. Olive backs away and tilts her head. "What are you doing here?" she asks. Her eyes land on the sketchbook, and I quickly put it on Sam's desk.

"Came to visit," I answer. Olive doesn't budge, and I get up. "I was about to head home, just wanted to say hi." Sam stares at me, and Ruby whines. "It's nice seeing you, Olive."

"Where are you going?" Olive stands in the doorway.

"Home?" I take a step to the right. Olive follows.

"You can stay." I don't move, and Olive sighs. "Don't look at me like that. Just stay."

"I didn't want to make you uncomfortable, that's all." My stomach is doing flips as I sit on Sam's bed.

Sam, Ruby, and Olive play with stuffed animals while I try to take a nap. I turn to face the wall, but someone's eyes burn into my back.

A few minutes later, I flip back over. I'm not going to be able to sleep like this.

"You look tired," Olive says bluntly.

I sit up with a yawn. "I've only had three hours of sleep."

Olive looks at Sam. "Oh, I forgot. Your mom was wondering what you want to get for dinner."

Sam thinks for a moment. "You pick. What do you want to eat?"

"I don't know," Olive answers. "What can we get?"

"Anything." Olive's eyes light up, and Sam shakes her head. "Not steak. That's a lot of money." Olive pouts.

"I've been wanting pizza really bad," Olive admits.

Sam smiles. "All right, go tell her then. Paco, you're staying for dinner. We're getting wings too."

"Are they hot?" I ask.

"Absolutely." Perfect. Nothing better than hot wings and pizza.

Olive runs out of the room to tell Mrs. Sanchez the dinner request. Ruby follows her down, and Sam and I go too. However, before leaving the room, Sam calls my name. I turn to look at her. "If something's bothering you, tell me. I don't care what it is," she says.

"I will, and don't worry. I'm okay."

We go down the stairs and find Mrs. Sanchez putting photos on the wall. Olive gasps and holds one up. "You look like a princess!" It's a photo of Sam at her quinceañera. Her dress and tiara were forest green.

Before Sam can answer, Mrs. Sanchez swoops her up. "Isn't she pretty? *¡Mi hija bonita!*" She gushes over Sam in Spanish, and I can't help but laugh at Sam's reaction. Mrs. Sanchez puts Sam down. "Okay, I'm off to get the pizza." She plants a kiss on Sam's and Ruby's heads before leaving.

Olive grabs another photo. Her eyes squint. "You look... distinguishable," she says, looking at me.

"Huh?" Olive passes me the photo. It's the one where Sam and I were dancing.

"That's one of my favorite photos." Sam puts an arm around me. "What do you think? You looked all spiffy for once!" I roll my eyes, and Sam smiles. "I'll always be grateful for that dance."

"What dance?" Olive asks.

I look at Sam, but she's already on it. "It was supposed to be the dance with my father, but he passed already. He left me a video to watch on my quince. The music played, and I couldn't move." Sam pauses and looks at me. "Paco picked me up and got me through it."

"You're there for me, I'm there for you," I tell her.

"Me too?" Olive asks quietly. She turns a bit pale and looks at the ground.

"Yeah, of course." Olive's eyes light up, and she smiles.

Ruby steps in front of us. She looks back and forth and smiles wickedly. She raises her hand and smacks my arm. "You're it!" Ruby runs away laughing. She opens the back door and dashes outside with Olive and Sam following.

The backyard is huge. Ruby and Olive are in different corners. Sam's the closest to me, so I chase her. I corner her by the picnic table. She's on one side, and I'm on the other. Sam's fast, but I think I'm faster.

Sam fakes left and runs to the right. I dive and tag her on her leg before hitting the ground. "Dammit!" Sam yells. She looks around. "Olive! You're next!"

Olive runs around the backyard before making a dash into the house. A few seconds later, there's a loud crash.

"Olive?" I grab Ruby and hustle inside the house. We find Olive on the floor in the kitchen, picking up pieces of glass on the floor.

"I'm sorry! I tripped! I tried to catch it, but it hit the floor." Tears fall down her face as she picks up another piece. I struggle to keep Ruby from escaping my arms. She doesn't have shoes on, having kicked them off while we were outside.

"Don't worry about it. We have a bunch of glasses." Sam gets down on the floor with Olive and starts picking up pieces.

"You're not mad?" Olive sniffles.

"No, are you hurt? Did the glass cut you?" Olive shakes her head. Sam takes the pieces out of Olive's hand and puts them in the trash can. "Don't worry about it. I'll tell Mom when she gets home, she won't be mad." Sam walks to the hall closet and pulls out a vacuum.

"Are you sure? It looks expensive."

"No, it was a cheap glass. She won't care."

The front door swings open. Mrs. Sanchez eyes the vacuum and sighs. "All right, what broke?"

"I broke a glass. I'm sorry, I-I'll get you a new one," Olive says quickly. She looks at her shoes, arms stiff by her side. Mrs. Sanchez sighs, and Olive shrinks.

"*Ay mija,* don't worry. As long as you're not hurt." Mrs. Sanchez puts the pizza boxes down on the counter and calls us to eat.

Olive's the last one to get pizza. She apologizes over and over, but Mrs. Sanchez gives her the same response. She shoves a plate into Olive's hands and guides her to the couch. They have a dining table, but Sam's family always eats together on the couch.

As I grab a container of ranch, Olive glares at me. "First you're eating it with pineapple, and now ranch?"

I laugh. "Don't knock it till you try it. The flavors are dancing in my mouth."

Sam mumbles in Spanish while Olive nearly spits out her water. "Never say that again," Olive says. She opens a container of ranch and dips her pizza into it. A few seconds later, she takes the container for herself.

"Olive," Mrs. Sanchez says as she sits down with her plate. "How about you hang out with your cousins tomorrow? You guys should go somewhere. I know you don't quite get along, but it would be nice to do so, don't you think?"

Cousins? I guess that's the story they told Mrs. Sanchez. Olive shrugs. "I don't know."

"Hey, I think it'll be good. You'll get to know them more," I say, taking a bite out of my pizza.

"We'll go somewhere fun." Sam smiles.

Olive sighs. "Okay, okay. Sure, let's do it."

Sam turns to me. "You tell the kids. We can meet here at twelve."

"Where would we go, anyway?" I ask.

Sam looks at Olive. "You have a spot in mind?" Olive shakes her head. Sam puts a hand on her chin and thinks. She perks up. "I know where we're going."

"Paco's in the front. He's older," Sam announces. Olive stares at her, giving puppy eyes. Sam looks away. "Don't look at me like that. You know it's true." I slide past them and get into the passenger seat. Olive waits until the triplets get inside, then squeezes into the seat.

"Be glad Paco's not driving!" Sam shouts over the complaints in the back. The tuplets are packed together like sardines. Olive presses herself against the window, even though there's a bit of space between her and Peter. "If you think my truck is bad, be glad it's not Paco's!"

"What's wrong with my car?" I question.

Sam smirks. "The Accord? It's small! They'd be more cramped than in here!" I glare at her, and Sam's smirk grows. "Plus, you're a bad driver."

"I am a good driver," I state, putting on my seat belt. Sam chuckles and starts the car. As she pulls out from the driveway, the stereo blasts whatever song she puts on. It's a song I sent her. "Told you it's a good song," I say, and Sam laughs.

"So, where are we going?" Olive asks.

"Buchanan," Sam answers. The triplets get excited, but Olive looks confused.

"You've been there before, right, Ol?" Leo asks.

Olive glares at him, but she sighs. "No, what is it?"

"It's a park, and it has swings!"

Her gaze softens. "It sounds fun." She's still awkward around them. She holds her arms close to herself, but turns to look at them.

"*¿Ella ha dicho algo sobre ellos?*" I ask Sam, hoping that Olive has started talking about her siblings. I look at the tuplets. Peter's trying to keep up a conversation with Olive. She only answers in short sentences.

"*Nada.*" Nothing. Dammit. I hope this helps her feel better around them.

We don't butt into the conversation much. I look back. The triplets are trying to get Olive to talk more. She's listening at least. That has to be progress.

A few minutes later, we arrive at Buchanan Park. The tuplets race out of the car. Peter and Lucy run down to the grass. Leo looks at Olive, waiting for her to say something.

"They do have swings," Olive mutters in awe.

"Leo!" Peter yells. "Did you bring the ball?"

Leo grabs his bag from the backseat. He opens it up, revealing a soccer ball and some cones. Peter jumps up and down, telling us to throw the ball.

"I can't throw!" Leo yells as he closes the door.

I take the ball out of his hands and throw it down the hill. It goes far but ends up short. Damn, I know I throw farther than that.

Sam whistles. "No wonder you're a pitcher."

Leo looks at Olive. "Be careful going down the hill. Peter tripped once." Olive steps slowly. Leo stays near her the entire time. We make it to the bottom without losing our balance.

Leo runs to catch up to his siblings. Olive looks at us. "Mom won't find me here, right?" Olive asks, staring at me mostly.

"We'll keep a lookout. If she comes, she won't get you. I swear," I answer. Olive nods, satisfied with my response. We walk with her to the triplets.

Stars appear in Lucy's eyes. "Ooh! We have enough for a team! Two on two with goalies!" Lucy points to me and Sam. "You two can be the goalies! What do you say, Olive? Sisters vs brothers?"

Olive stays silent for a moment. "Sure."

A game of rock-paper-scissors later and I'm the goalie for Team Brothers. Leo gets the ball first, and he is fast. Lucy chases him up and down the field. Olive and Peter are waiting near the goals we made with cones. Leo's running with the ball to Olive. Olive shimmies back and forth, trying to stop him. Leo goes for the goal. Sam grabs it and throws the ball to Lucy.

Peter runs for it, leaving me without protection. Ah, well, at least they're having fun. The tuplets fight over the ball. The ball flies into the air, hits the ground, and now Olive's rushing toward me at full speed. Oh crap. Oh crap! Has she always been this fast? She's leaving Leo in the dust! She flanks left and kicks the ball hard. I catch it, but the force sends me falling back. I drop the ball and it goes past the cones. Dammit!

"Yeah!" Olive jumps up and down and cheers. I hold my chest as I sit up.

Lucy runs to her sister and scoops her up. She swings Olive around, laughing and cheering. "We make a pretty good team, huh?"

Olive smiles. "Yeah, we do."

Peter's about to take the ball to the center when he stops. He looks behind him and yells, "Race you to the swings!" We look over at the empty playground. Buchanan Park only has two swings. The tuplets hightail over there. Sam and I grab the soccer equipment and sit on the grass next to the swings.

Olive and Peter make it to the swings first. They both get on, and within a few seconds, Peter is soaring through the air. Olive pushes herself back and forth, but her legs aren't moving at all. "I don't know how to swing," Olive mumbles.

"Have you been to a park before?" Lucy asks.

"Not in years. Mom says we're too old." Olive frowns.

Leo steps closer to her. "Want me to push you? You don't have to go as high as Peter, he's a bit reckless." Olive nods, and Leo can't help but smile as he goes behind her.

Olive pushes herself back, and Leo tells her what to do with her legs. Tuck in, let out, tuck in, let out. His hand is holding onto her back lightly. When she finally gets the hang of it, he lets go. Olive's soaring. She's as high as Peter.

It's going great until Olive looks down.

"Holy shit! Holy shit!" The swing jerks, no longer going straight. Sam and I scramble to our feet and run to them. I stand in front of Olive, and Sam goes behind her.

"Look at the trees!" Lucy yells, "Look at the trees!"

"I'm going to fall!" Olive cries. Her hands are gripping the chains for dear life.

"Remember! Back, tucked in. Forward, legs out!" Leo shouts.

Olive glares. "How is that going to help?"

Peter stutters, trying to find the right words. "Focus on something other than the ground!"

Olive's head goes back and forth, but the swing moves even more. "Okay! Okay!" Leo yells. "Keep your legs out, don't tuck them in. You should start slowing down!"

"Are you sure?"

"Yes! You'll be okay!"

Olive closes her eyes and stiffens. I stay in front of her swing, light on my feet in case the worst happens. The passing seconds are filled with panic until the swing slows down. Once it slows down enough, Olive jumps off, and I catch her before she hits the ground.

"That was..." Olive gasps for air. "Awesome!"

"You liked it?" Peter asks, his swing slowing to a stop.

"Yeah!" Olive's still catching her breath. "Let's go again!"

Before anyone can move, the familiar song causes all our heads to turn. The triplets run off, but Olive only stares. It doesn't take much convincing once she realizes it's ice cream. Sam and I dig into our pockets for our wallets and run to catch up. The ice cream truck pulls over. At the other end of the park, more kids notice. Two run to their parents, begging and pointing.

"What do you guys want?" I pull out some cash and Olive stares at it. As I wait for them to pick, I order a cookie sandwich, and Sam asks for a Crunch bar.

Leo points to one that's red and green. Peter asks for a Drumstick, and Lucy wants a strawberry bar. Olive stares at all the options, but her eyes keep floating back to Leo's ice cream. She licks her lips for a second.

"You want the one Leo has?" I ask, and Olive flinches. I must've scared her. She shakes her head and points to an ice cream sandwich. "Olive, you can get whatever one you want."

"It doesn't matter?" she questions, and I reassure her once more. Olive looks at the list one more time, then asks for the one Leo got.

The ice cream man comes back empty-handed. "I'm so sorry! That was my last one!" Olive's smile falls. She looks at the list of options again.

Leo puts the wooden stick inside his cup. He hands it to Olive. Her eyes widen, and she reaches her hands out. But she stops, her arms fall stiffly at her side, and she shakes her head.

"Take it," Leo insists. "I can get another one."

"You sure?" Olive asks.

Leo holds it out to her again, and Olive finally accepts the ice cream. Leo walks to the truck and asks for a Drumstick.

Olive flips the stick around and digs in. Her eyes go wide. She takes another bite, and another, and another. The smile on her face is huge.

It's the biggest I've ever seen her smile. Stars are in her eyes as we walk to the picnic tables scattered throughout the park.

"Ah! Brain freeze!" Olive groans.

"Don't eat it so fast!" Peter says.

"But it's so good! I don't even remember the last time I had this one!" Olive takes another bite, then puts her hand back on her head. "Mom said this one was a waste of money, and I haven't had it since. Oh, I've missed it so much."

We sit at a picnic table and eat our ice cream. Olive takes her sketchbook out of a bag Sam gave her, along with some pencils and pens. Her hand glides up and down with the pencils. The triplets pay no attention, sharing stories and cracking jokes. The picture fills with color as time passes.

Leo crumbles the wrapping together into a little ball. He looks at Olive. "What do you want to do next, Ol?" Olive doesn't respond, not even to the nickname. Her hand flies across the paper with a pen, dark ink following behind. "Olive?" Leo calls out again, his voice a bit louder. "Olive?"

The sudden loudness causes Olive to sit up straight. She slides the sketchbook across the table and hides it under her bag. Her pencils fall onto the table, and she shoves the pen into her pocket. She looks at Leo. "W-what's up?"

"Are you okay?" Leo asks in a softer voice.

Olive nods quickly. "Y-yeah, I'm fine." Leo tilts his head, and Olive looks away. She takes a shaky breath. "I'm sorry I wasn't paying attention. I was... drawing."

"Can I see?" Leo asks.

Olive turns to him. Her jaw hangs open, and she fumbles for words. "You... want to see my drawings?"

"Yeah! Why wouldn't I?" Olive blinks a few times before revealing her sketchbook. She flips to a page and hands it to Leo. His face lights up. "This is so cool!"

Lucy and Peter get up from their seats and look over Leo's shoulder. I peek over the table. It's the drawing of Ruby I saw yesterday. Olive flips the page to another drawing and mentions it's her own characters. The triplets point to each character, saying how amazing they look. But it doesn't look like the picture she was drawing before Leo scared her.

I turn to Olive. "Was that the one you were working on?"

Olive looks down. "You noticed? No, it's not finished yet," she whispers.

Olive takes the sketchbook again and turns a few pages. She hands it back to them. The triplets stare in awe at the drawing, but I stare at the one on the back. It's of the triplets. Leo's holding a soccer ball, and Peter stands next to him. Lucy's waving and smiling, with braces on her teeth. I blink. Braces? I look at Lucy. She laughs loudly, showing her braces. How have I not noticed before?

"These look amazing!" Leo smiles and hands the sketchbook back.

Olive frowns. "All my good ones are at the house. Mom got me these watercolor paints for my birthday, and I did so many paintings with them." She sighs. "I wish I still had them."

"What happened to them?" Sam asks.

"Mom destroyed them because I didn't do my chores. I spent the whole day drawing and completely forgot to do them." Olive looks down sadly. "I can't help it. It's calming, and I can tune out Mom's demands." She chuckles.

"Let's get you some more!" Lucy says, and Olive's eyes widen. "A welcome home gift!"

"No. They're fifty-seven bucks." The triplets' faces fall. Olive smiles sadly. "It's fine, really. Besides, you already got me the ice cream." She looks at her brother. "Thank you, Leo."

Leo's eyes widen. His eyes brim with tears, yet he still smiles. "I'm glad you like it."

I collect our trash and go to throw it away. My phone buzzes with a text from Rose.

Rose: I know it's not until Tuesday, but I'm so excited about our date! I can't wait to see you!

I'm really going on a date with Rose. I'm so excited. I wonder what she'll wear. She's beautiful in every way so it doesn't matter... Wait, what am *I* going to wear? Formal? Casual? I need to make a good impression! What's today... Thursday? Okay, I still have time, but I don't know what to do! And the letter, I still have to give her the letter! Wait... where is the letter?

God, I'm a mess.

9

WHEN MY DAD STARTED dating my mom, he brought her twenty-one roses on their first date. In my dad's family, it's a sign of love, loyalty, and devotion. Mom pressed the flowers, and she keeps them in her scrapbook. It's filled with photos and letters from my dad, and eventually photos of me and Paula. Mom gushes over him as we go to the store. Rose and I haven't been dating long, but I want her to know that it's only her. Plus, she likes flowers. I pick orange roses.

Owen and Sam nearly break down my door when I tell them I'm back from the store. They run up the stairs and rip open my closet. Sam tosses shirts left and right, with Owen saying yes or no. Within ten minutes, my entire closet is on the floor.

"So, why is this necessary?" I question, pointing to the piles on the floor. "I'm going to have to redo my entire closet when I get back!"

"Because we've been waiting too long for this!" Sam says. She throws Owen another shirt. It's plaid. Owen throws it into the *hell no* pile. "Not only that, you have no fashion sense."

"You're one to talk. You're picking horrible shirts!" Owen counters. He hops over the piles and stands next to Sam. He looks through the remaining shirts on the hangers. I knew I should've gone to the store. The only times I remembered I had to go was when I was at work.

"Do I need to dress up?" I ask. "We're just going for ice cream."

Sam glares at me. "You literally called the group chat last night, panicking about not having anything nice to wear," Sam says, and I turn red.

Owen pulls something out of the closet. It's the white polo shirt I wear for concert band. Owen gives the shirt to Sam and pulls my dress pants out as well. They hold the clothes up to me. Well, at least I'll look decent. They put the clothes in my hands and leave the room so I can change. As I put on my shirt, I see something hanging in the back of the closet. Dad's old suit jacket, and it matches. I grab it without a second thought and put it on.

I look in the mirror. The jacket hides most of my body. I don't look that bad! I cross my arms. The jacket strains against them, not budging at all. I grimace and squeeze my arms. What size is this thing? I look in the mirror again. I'll suck it up. It makes me look better.

The letter for Rose is on my desk. It didn't get lost during the chaos of my friends and Diane breaking in. I put it in my pocket and walk down the stairs, where my mom and friends are waiting for me.

"*Ay, mi guapo hijo,*" Mom says when I reach the bottom. She kisses my head.

Sam and Owen look at me. "Are you sure you want to wear that jacket?" Sam asks. "It's summer. You'll melt."

"I'll be all right," I tell her.

I say goodbye to my friends and get in the car. Sam and Owen text me while I'm on the way there, telling me not to be nervous. They'll come visit me after I get home. Mom drops me off at Rose's house. As I knock on the front door, I get a text.

Theodore: We're ready. Come tomorrow at noon.

Oh, thank God. It's been over a week since I called him. I hope he's okay. It took a long time for him to respond. I forward his text to Owen and Olive after texting Theodore that I'll be there.

Olive: Is he okay? What about Christina?

Me: I don't know, he hasn't answered.

Owen: Let's give him some time. He still might be hiding from your mom.

The front door opens before I can send another text. Her mom is behind it. Damn. I mean, it's fine. She's just... intimidating. "Can I help you?" she asks.

"H-hi, I'm Paco. I'm here to pick up Rose." I hold out the flowers. "These are for her."

Rose's mom takes the flowers out of my hands and walks to the kitchen counter. "So, you're the one she was talking about. Come in, she's still getting ready. You're here early."

"I like being early," I say, following her inside.

"You're the same boy that came with the cupcake, correct?" she asks, putting the flowers in a vase. I nod. Rose's mom puts a hand on her head. "I'm sorry about that. Something came up and she couldn't go. I hope you got her text message."

"I didn't."

"A-anyway." She motions to the couch. "Please, take a seat."

I sit on the couch. Rose's father is across from me in a recliner. "So, Paco, have you lived in Pittsburg all your life?" he asks, looking away from his tablet.

"Yes, I have. Born and raised."

"That's nice," he says, putting his tablet to the side. "Do you go to Pitt?"

"Yeah, I'll be a junior next year. I'm in the band too."

Rose's dad smiles. "Oh, how great! Rose is in choir. Have you heard her sing?"

"Yeah! She sounds amazing!" My cheeks turn red as I think about her. She has a beautiful voice.

"What else do you do?" his wife asks in the same stern tone she greeted me with. She gives him a cup of coffee and sits with her own.

"I work at my family's bakery. I have more shifts when marching band is done. It takes up a lot of time, so I don't work as much doing it."

"The Cortez Bakery? That's your family's?"

"Yeah. My tío built the business from the ground up."

Rose's dad smiles. "That's lovely. You guys make delicious pies."

"Thank you, um…" I'm not sure what to call him. Rose has two last names. I have two last names, too, but I always go by the first one, Cortez. The last time I assumed someone's last name, they cussed me out in Spanish.

"Mr. Serrano." He chuckles.

Mrs. Serrano clears her throat. "So, where's your family from?"

"Pittsburg," I answer, a little confused.

"Oh, no. Rose mentioned that you have family from Mexico. I was wondering what part."

Hell, I didn't expect that. I have told Rose, and I'm sure she meant well, but why would her mom ask out of the blue? I hope she's just curious. I swallow. "My father and his family are from Torreón. He came here at eighteen, and my tíos came after. Mom was born here, but her parents came before she was." They came illegally, but I keep that to myself.

Mrs. Serrano nods, her mouth forming a small smile. "How nice. I have some relatives in Mexico as well." Oh, that's why she asked. I get it, but it still feels awkward. Why does this feel awkward? I look at the clock on the wall, getting uncomfortable with each passing second. *Don't ask any more questions. Please don't ask anymore.*

"Do you do anything else other than marching band, Paco?" she asks.

Maybe I'm overthinking this; they seem nice. I sit up. "I'm in the jazz band and the baseball team."

"Any hobbies?" Mr. Serrano butts in with a smile.

"I like cooking, and also—!"

"How are your grades?" Mrs. Serrano interrupts.

"I-I'm sorry?" I stutter.

"How are your grades?" she asks again. Her husband gives her a look, but she doesn't budge. She stares at me, waiting for my reply.

"I'm not sure why you're asking all these questions," I tell her. "I'm on the honor roll, and I get the award right before Rose's." Rose gets the highest award, the Principal's Honor Roll. She gets that award every time, even achieving that rank in middle school. "Why does it matter what my grades are?"

Mrs. Serrano's eyes widen. "Oh, no. I was just wondering."

"Why are you asking me all these questions?" I finally ask. "Is this an interrogation? It's starting to feel like one." Their jaws drop. Oh no. I said that out loud. *Recover! Say something!* "I-It's making me uncomfortable."

Mrs. Serrano shakes her head quickly. "No, of course not. I just want to know if you're honest."

"I don't have any reason to lie to you." There's a pause, and I bite the bullet. "Do you just... not like me?" I've been wondering that since I walked through the door.

Mr. Serrano assures me he does, and his wife frowns. "Don't feel like that. It's just..." Her face drops, and she sips her coffee. Tears swell her eyes. Oh no, did I upset her that badly?

Stomping footsteps catch our attention and we turn toward the stairs. Rose is wearing a pink floral dress with a matching bag and shoes. I turn bright red. I want to tell her so many things. How beautiful she looks, how excited I am to be with her, but I'm speechless. I grab the flowers from the table and give them to her. I tell her the meaning of them, and she smiles widely.

"Are you getting along?" Rose asks as she puts down the flowers. There's something cold about the way she said it.

"Yes, sweetie. Just making small talk," Mrs. Serrano says, looking away. Hints of guilt are written on her face.

"Okay, well, we'll be going now." Rose grabs my hand and leads me out the door. Rose waves to her parents and closes the door behind her. We walk down the sidewalk and I move her away from the road.

We're in silence for a few more seconds before Rose groans. "I can't believe they questioning you like that! I'm so sorry. I don't know what was up with Mom."

"Oh, it's okay," I answer, but I want to know why she was.

"I'm guessing it's because you're my first boyfriend, but still!" First? I'm her first boyfriend? It's embarrassing how much my cheeks turn red. "It's not like I'm going to do something stupid!" she says toward her house.

"Are you okay, *mi amor*?"

"Yeah, it's just..." Rose groans again. "Mom gave me a whole lecture about dating. The whole nine yards. I know she means well, but I wish she wouldn't worry so much." Rose slides her hand into mine. I hold it tight, and her face turns pink.

We walk down the sidewalk, pointing at whatever dogs we see and talking about whatever comes to mind. It's only been a few minutes, but I'm sweating. The suit jacket squeezes on my body. It's suffocating.

Rose looks at me and tugs at the suit jacket. "Aren't you hot in that?" She takes off the small backpack she's wearing and opens it. "I brought a bag. You can put it in here."

"Oh, I'm okay. I've worn jackets warmer in this heat before. I'll be okay." The last time I wore a thick hoodie during summer was in eighth grade. It got too hot, and I finally lost a little weight. Not enough though.

Rose tugs at the jacket again. "You look miserable in it."

I sigh and take off the jacket. "I thought it would make me presentable."

"You shouldn't make yourself uncomfortable to impress my parents, or me!" she adds that last part in a rush. Rose stuffs the jacket into her bag. "It won't change how I feel."

I smile and look around. "Where are we going? The only ice cream I know is on Railroad."

"Who says we can't chase an ice cream truck? Besides, I want to get..." Rose stops in her tracks and smiles. "Yes, it's here! Come on, let's get tacos!"

Rose pulls my hand and we run to the taco truck parked at the gas station. I've had it a few times, it's delicious. Rose must love it though, judging by the way she orders once we get there. After telling her what I want—three *carne asada* tacos—she hands the lady some money from her bag.

"Hey! Wait! Let me pay, Rose!" I hold up some money, but Rose shoves my hand back down.

"Too slow!" She laughs.

"I'm paying for the ice cream then!" I say, putting the money back in my wallet.

"All right, it's only fair." I'm going to have to be quick whenever we get ice cream. I don't know how she got her money so fast, and mine is in my pocket!

We get our food and realize we did not think this through. There's nowhere to sit. We look around, and Rose points across the street. "Nation's has tables outside. Let's go sit there."

We cross the street and sit down at the tables. I look inside Nation's and get an idea. I turn to Rose. "Would you rather have ice cream or a milkshake?"

Her eyes light up immediately. "Milkshake!"

I walk inside Nation's and order two chocolate milkshakes and some fries. They smell too good to resist. Rose snaps some photos as I return to my seat. My phone goes off, and Rose has tagged me in an Instagram post.

"You posted me already?" I laugh, liking the photo.

"Yeah!" Rose's smile hasn't left for even a second. She's jumping in her seat. "I'm so happy. I've been waiting for this moment for so long!"

"H-huh?" My face is red again and Rose laughs.

"Why are you surprised?" she says between giggles. "I've had a huge crush on you since spring of seventh grade. I was too shy to tell you." Spring of seventh grade? Spring of *seventh* grade? "When did you start liking me?"

"First day of seventh grade," I whisper.

She smiles, then sighs. "I'm sorry if we can't do much for dates. Mom and Dad are like... Actually, this should explain it." Rose gives me her phone. It shows a map and an icon with her picture. The app itself looks very familiar.

"A tracking app? How come?" I zoom in on the map, closer and closer, until the picture clears up. It shows Rose's exact location, with the tip of the icon on the seats we're in. The break-in of my house makes sense now. If Diane managed to even screenshot where Olive was, she could find my house with no issues.

"They say it's to keep me safe. I get it, but I worry they don't trust me."

"You wouldn't do anything like that though."

"I know."

We dig into our food. Sparkles are in Rose's eyes as she drinks her milkshake. I look to my left. There's a small market next to Nation's with a dusty-orange truck parked on the side. Wait a minute. Is that... Sam's truck? I stare at it for a few more seconds. Yep, that's her truck.

I take another bite of my tacos and pull out my phone. I decide to text the group chat. Who knows, maybe all of them are stalking my date. I can't help but laugh when I send the text.

Me: Are you guys following me? I see your truck, Sam.

Yann: Lmao, I wish. I'm at home.

Sam: Damn! I knew I should've parked somewhere else. Owen can't decide on a bag of chips. We've been inside for ten minutes.

I chuckle and put my phone away. I continue eating and talking with Rose. Salsa falls from her face, and I grab a napkin to rub it off. She smiles, holding my hand to her face. So beautiful. I've been wanting to do this with her for so long. Dates, holding hands, just being with her. I can't believe this is even real.

We finish our food and throw it away. I don't want this date to end, but there's not much we can do. Even if I had the car, I don't think her parents would let us go far. In this part of Pittsburg, there aren't a lot of shops, but there is one place I have in mind.

"Want to go to the park? Buchanan's nearby, right?" I ask.

"Oh, yeah! I'll ask Mom just in case. I'd feel horrible if we got there and she got mad."

I feel bad that I can't give her much. I know we're only in high school, so in general, we can't have fancy dates. We can't afford it. But I still want to make her happy. She deserves it. She smiles brightly as we walk past her house. And when I ask if she's having fun, she answers yes immediately. I hold her hand a little tighter.

My phone buzzes. Then again, and again. There are a bunch of messages from the group chat, and they don't stop coming.

Sam: OH SHIT.

Sam: SHE'S HERE.

Yann: What? Who?

Sam: DIANE! She just walked out of the market!

Me: What?

Owen: We lied! A car followed you when you left your house. We've been following it since.

Me: Why didn't you say something?

Sam: We weren't sure if it was her! It looked like her, but we lost track of the car near Rose's house. We're on it now!

Oh crap. I look behind me. There's a car approaching. Crap. Crap. Where's Sam? I thought she was right behind her!

Sam: SHE SLASHED ONE OF MY TIRES!

Pachi: What?! Paco, where are you? I'll be there in two minutes. Time me.

I'm sweating as I send my location to the group chat. The car comes closer. It's a gray Honda Civic. Rose taps on my shoulder, asking what's wrong. "We're being followed." Rose's eyes go wide. She turns to look, but I squeeze her hand. "Don't. If it is her, I don't want her to see you."

"Who is it?" Rose questions.

Diane's car speeds up and stops a few feet in front of us. "Stay behind me," I tell Rose, keeping my body in front of hers. My hands are sweaty, and my heart wants to explode. The door opens, and Diane steps out of the car.

It's her. It's really her. She stands tall as she looks at me from her car. She looks horrible. I don't think she's slept in days. She's wearing old clothes with rips and stains. Her blonde hair is shaggy and falls in front of her face, and the roots are growing back. She has heavy bags under her brown eyes. Eyes that are staring into my soul.

"Can I help you?" I ask, trying to make my voice sound deep.

Diane slams the door shut and steps closer. She stops just in front of the passenger door. My eyes dart around me, trying to find some way to get Rose to safety. Rose puts something in my hand. It's a can of pepper spray. I hope I don't have to use it.

"Yes, actually." Diane pauses. "I was wondering if you've seen my daughter, Olive."

The blood drains from my face as Diane continues. "She's fourteen, about five-two. She has tan skin and medium-length, wavy brown hair."

I shake my head. "N-no, I haven't seen her." My eyes flicker to the car. Someone's head moves, and there's another person next to them. The kids are in the backseat. The kids are in the backseat!

Diane sighs and holds up her phone. "Are you sure? She has a tracking app, and your house was her last known location."

"H-how do you know that's my house?"

Diane steps closer. "This is funny. I know you're lying to me." Rose and I step away. I softly push Rose back as Diane creeps closer. *Run, Rose. Please, run!* Diane grabs my wrist. "I think we need to chat."

Rose snatches the pepper spray out of my hand and jumps in front of me. She sprays Diane right in her eyes. A car honking cuts through Diane's cries. Pachi comes flying down the street. Rose and I run to his car, get in, and Pachi drives off.

Pachi turns around once we've left the street. "Are you okay?"

"Y-yeah, we're okay," I say, taking a breath. "Where were you? You got here quick."

"On a pool date." Helen smiles. I didn't realize she was here. Her blonde hair is soaking wet. "We were getting ready to leave when Pachi got the texts. You sure you're okay?"

I nod. Maybe we would've run into them regardless. Buchanan Park also has a pool. Pachi's on the swimming team and goes swimming whenever he can. That's how he met Helen, actually.

"Rose, do you want us to take you home?" Pachi asks.

Rose shakes her head. "I'll figure out what to tell Mom."

When we get to my house, everyone is there waiting. Thankfully, Sam always keeps a spare tire with her. She changes tires fast. Olive sighs in relief when I walk through the door. For the lie, Rose texts her mother that during our date, my stomach started to hurt, and I got a friend to take us home. It's not exactly a lie.

"Are you two okay?" Olive asks.

"Yeah, we're okay." Rose fiddles with her hair, looking at me for a split second. "We saw Theodore and Christina in the car."

Olive's eyes widen. "Really? Are they okay?"

"I couldn't get a good look at them, but they were in there."

Olive looks down at the ground. She walks to the couch and sits. "Did she think I would be there?" Olive mumbles.

"That doesn't make sense," Sam says. "Why would she go after you guys? There's no reason for her to think Olive would be with you."

Helen steps forward. "Okay, so what's going on? Some psycho mother is after you?"

"It's my psycho mother," Olive says. "I ran away from home, and she wants me back."

"Oh." Helen's eyes flicker at the scar on Olive's arm. "Well, if you need to, you could stay with me," Helen says softly, and Rose nods in agreement. Olive stares at them, shocked and confused.

Rose looks down at her phone. She frowns. "My mom's outside." Rose gathers her things and turns to the door. Olive runs to her, pulling her into a hug. Rose is taken aback, but rubs her head, whispering words to calm Olive down. She always knows what to say.

Olive lets go, and I lead Rose to the door. Mrs. Serrano is approaching the porch steps when we close the door. "I would like to apologize," she says, catching me off guard. "It was very rude of me to question you like that. I'm sorry. I didn't mean for you to feel that way at all."

She means it. Guilt still clouds her eyes, and her low face makes me sad. I give her a smile. "Thank you. That means a lot."

Mrs. Serrano nods. "I'm sorry your date was cut short, but I hope you had fun." She reaches into her pocket and hands me a bottle. "Here, for your stomachache."

Rose and her mom walk away, but I call Rose back. I dig into my pocket and pull out the letter. "You can read it later, but I've been meaning to give it to you." Rose smiles, her hand going over the little heart I drew. She gives me a hug, and Rose heads to the car. After making sure no one is following them, I go back inside.

I shut the door, feeling the icy glares of my friends burning on my back. Yann clears his throat. "Okay, will someone catch me up on what happened?" Yann looks at me. "How does she know you're involved? The house robbery is one thing, but Olive wasn't there!"

"I made it worse." I tense up. "I called Theodore and tried to pretend I was Olive."

"You did what?" Pachi yells, and I flinch. Pachi puts his head in his hands and takes a deep breath. "Paco, I swear to God, sometimes you are the dumbest person I've ever met. Why would you do that without telling us?"

"I didn't think he would answer! It was ten at night!"

"Well, how did she know it was you? Theodore doesn't know what you look like," Sam says.

"Theodore knows his voice. If Mom forced him to tell her, she'll know." Olive sighs.

"You knew about this?" Sam asks.

Olive nods. "Owen too."

"Only because I was there!" Owen defends.

Olive sighs. "Theodore wanted me to come to the house to get what I needed, and he wants me to take Christina. I don't know if he convinced her, but he wants me to come tomorrow at noon."

Pachi's jaw drops. "After what happened today? Are you sure that's a good idea?"

"I need to check on them," Olive responds, her voice firm.

"What we should do is tell your dad. We need to get you somewhere else before we make any more moves. She might know where you are!" Yann says.

"No. I don't want to go anywhere else. And even if I did, what do we do if she finds out I'm there? Theodore said they'll be gone tomorrow. I'm going tomorrow, with or without you guys. I'm tired of being a sitting duck."

I sigh. "I'm sorry I didn't tell you guys. I didn't want to bother you." I ignore my friends' glances and turn to Olive. "But I'm going with Olive to the house."

Pachi walks up to us. "I'm going with you. You need a car, and Paco, I'm tired of you doing shit on your own." Pachi grips my shoulders. "You're like my brother, and I'm here to help. Just stop being a dumbass!"

"I'm coming too." Sam stands from the couch. "Maybe I can sock the shit out of her."

"Don't forget about me," Owen says. "I was going in the first place, and I still am. We won't let anything happen to you."

"Me too. I'm coming with you," Yann says.

I nod, somehow out of breath. "Okay. We'll meet here tomorrow."

Helen looks at Olive. "I'll help out any way I can, and my offer still stands." She looks at the rest of us. "Just let me know, and please stay safe."

That night I stare at the ceiling, trying to fall asleep. If we take one wrong step or do something wrong, everything will fall to pieces. We're this close to getting Olive and her family back together. We can't afford to screw up now. I can't do everything. I know that, and that's what everyone has been telling me all day. But if I don't do it, then who will? If I don't act now, will Diane act first? I don't want to bring the cops into this, but I'm starting to worry they'll be our outcome regardless.

I just hope Diane hasn't talked Theodore out of helping us.

10

— · —

PACHI PICKS US UP right before noon. We pile into the van and drive to Olive's house. She doesn't know the exact address, but she tells us how to get there. If she was able to run to my house in the middle of the night, it should be nearby. After a few minutes and one wrong turn later, we arrive.

It's an old house—easy to determine by its size—and it has one of the smallest garages I've ever seen. The house is a withered shade of blue with brown windows, and two are cracked. The grass is unkempt with weeds popping up everywhere. Not to mention that the grass is a burned brown, with only small patches of green scattered throughout the lawn.

There's no car in the driveway. Only a few cars at the neighbors, even one with a tarp. Olive digs into her pocket and pulls out her house key. Her hands tremble as she puts the key inside and turns it. Olive pushes the door open. We follow her inside, except for Pachi. He's staying outside with the car in case we have to bail.

The living room lights up when we turn on our flashlights. We can't have the neighbors know someone's here when they're not supposed to. We look suspicious enough. The inside isn't better than the outside. The door leads us to the small kitchen and the even smaller living room. The trash bag is overflowing, and dishes are piled in the sink. The dishwasher beeps, scaring the hell out of all of us.

"Christina?" Olive calls out. There's no answer. Olive disappears down the hall. Sam follows her. Yann, Owen, and I stay in the front area.

Owen's near the dining table. He picks a piece of paper up and reads it. "It's about Peter. He won a chess competition a few weeks ago."

"Why would she keep it?" Yann asks.

Owen shrugs. "No idea. It's printed in color too. Maybe she found it online."

I step over to him. "Is there anything else?" I grab another piece of paper. It's the rest of the article, but this page has a picture of Logan and Peter. Peter's holding a chess trophy and Logan has his arm around him. There's a yellow Post-It on the photo with scribbled writing.

So much for stopping homeschool. I need to leave ASAP.

"She knows Logan is here," I say. "That's why she's leaving."

"That explains it." Owen sighs.

Yann shines his phone down the hallway. There are five doors. He pokes his head through the first door on the left. Owen and I go after him. It's the bathroom. Blue-tiled floors, white walls, a bath, and a sink. The cabinets under the sink have a padlock on them. My stomach drops. I shake my head and go to the room next door.

No surprise, it's Diane's. A huge bed with covers thrown back and pillows on the floor. Her hamper is overflowing, and her closet is half gone. Owen finds something under her bed. An empty bottle of wine, a few of them, actually.

I reach Diane's nightstand and pull open a drawer. There's a gun with ammo next to it. Chills run down my spine and I step back. "She has a gun. There's a gun in the drawer."

"Are you serious? Is it loaded?" Owen says in one breath.

"I don't know. I don't want to touch it." I slam the drawer shut and walk toward Diane's desk. Yann follows me, putting a hand on my shoulder.

Her desk is a different story. Despite everything else in the room, her desk is spotless. Papers are neatly organized and stacked, with files in the drawers. She has a laptop on her desk. The lock screen is a photo of the kids when they were younger. Olive is in the middle, wearing a pink dress and pouting. Christina is also in a pink dress, but her curly hair is longer than Olive's and she's snuggled against her mother. Theodore's on Olive's right, and his hair is really curly too. His smile is wide, and he's missing one of his front teeth. Diane's bags are still there, but her smile looks real.

I press a button on the keyboard, and it asks for a password. Judging by Diane's secretive nature—and obvious favoritism—Olive probably doesn't know what it is.

Yann makes it out of the room first. He heads toward the room across the hall. Before following him, I stop at the closet door. I pull on the handle, but it doesn't budge. Not even after Owen tries. Why would Diane have a locked closet? Closets don't lock, do they? I sigh and go into the next room.

Theodore's bedroom is next, and it's rather small. A twin bed, a desk, and a closet with some clothes. He doesn't have a lot on his desk, other than the homework that he has from homeschooling. I pull open the desk drawers. There's a beginner's Spanish textbook and a photo of him and his sisters. It's more recent. Theodore's hair is big and just as curly. Olive sits next to him, and there's a bruise on her cheek. Christina's also next to Theodore, and she's holding his hand. Diane's in the photo too. She sits off to the side, and someone scribbled her out in red Sharpie. When I brush my thumb against the ink, my thumb turns red.

Yann walks down the hallway and nearly crashes into a vase. Olive follows behind, catching the vase before it breaks. She turns to face us. Her eyes look distant as they cast to the ground. The only thing she has is a small bag. We searched the whole house. Christina isn't here.

"Are you okay?" I ask, but Olive shrugs. I take a step toward her. "Hey, Olive. Do you know why your mom… has a gun in her drawer?

Olive blinks. "That's where she keeps it? Mom's always had a gun. She's scared that people will come after her, or that they'll take us away." Olive turns around. "Maybe she thought Dad would come after her, or something like that."

Yann frowns. "I don't understand. I thought Christina would be here."

Olive sighs. "Maybe she changed her mind." With that, Olive walks out the front door.

Sam pokes her head out of the last room. "Hey, can one of you help me get Olive's things?" she asks. I nod and walk inside.

Olive and Christina's room is bright pink. The walls are empty. No posters, or stickers, or anything like that. There's something eerie about it. Most of the room is covered with boxes, and the carpet is old and filthy. Which is why I shiver when Sam gets on her knees and reaches under a bed.

"What are you doing?" I ask.

"Grabbing stuff under the bed. What does it look like?" Sam gets up and brushes off her knees. She comes up with a stuffed animal. She puts it in a plastic bag with *Olive* written across it.

"Did you see the laptop?" I ask.

"No, but Olive doesn't know the password." Sam frowns and points to the desk. "Olive sorted some things out on that desk. She didn't put it away though. I'll grab the rest of her things if you clean that up."

I gaze at the desk on the left. Loose pieces of homework and drawings are scattered across it. I find an open book under the pile. I pick it up and read, using my phone to see. The handwriting on the page is fast, messy, and I can barely read some words.

I still can't believe Olive pulled it off. I don't know how she did it. I saw her in the house. As soon as Mom got to the stairs, some other lady came in and smacked her. She ran back to the car, grabbed my hand, and shoved me inside.

Oh shit. This is Christina's diary. There's a rip in the paper, and some parts of the paper feel thinner than the rest. I want to look away, but I can't stop reading.

Mom hasn't been the same since Olive left. I've never seen her so angry. She keeps yelling at me, blaming me for everything. She says it's my fault Olive's gone. She gave me all her chores too. I don't care, whatever distracts me from this nightmare. If all the chores in the world stop Mom from yelling at me, I'll do it a million times.

Theodore's been sleeping in Olive's bed. I can't sleep alone. He even stays with me until I fall asleep. He's the best brother ever. He's doing his best to calm Mom down, but it doesn't work all the time. The few times I wake up in the night, I hear him crying. He's lost his patience with Mom, and he yells *back. Mom hit him. She <u>never</u> hits Theodore, only me and Olive. I know we deserve it because we misbehave, but Theodore doesn't. He's not bad.*

My heart sinks as I turn the page. She still has more to say.

I've even thought about running away, and I never think that. I love Mom. I love her so much, but I can't take this anymore. I've always listened to her and did everything she wanted. I do all her bidding, as much as I hate it. I'm the best in our homeschool, and I'm Olive's tutor sometimes! Why does she think Olive leaving is my fault? My cheek still hurts. I hate this. I just want Olive home, and then we'll be happy again.

What... what the hell? My heart goes up to my throat and my stomach curls. Part of my mind tells me to take it. If shit goes down, this is evidence of abuse. But this is a fourteen-year-old's diary, something meant for her eyes only. But what else is in here? Are there more stories of Diane hurting them? I shut the diary and toss it on the desk.

"You're reading Christina's diary?" Sam asks.

"I didn't know that's what it was."

Sam sighs. "Yeah, same. Olive and I read a few pages. There wasn't much. Nightmares, Olive getting into trouble..." I look at Sam, and she looks away. "Olive stopped reading once we hit the more recent entries. Those are messed up."

"Is Olive okay?" I ask.

"I don't know. She's upset about Christina, but won't talk to me about it. She just grabbed her stuff and left."

The front door opens. I step in front of Sam. "We should start heading back." Pachi calls out, and I sigh in relief. "Diane could be home any minute."

There's a brief silence before Sam clears her throat. "I'll meet you in the car. Don't forget to pick everything up," she says as she walks out of the room.

I put the papers away and look at the closet. The few shirts hanging are pushed to the side, with cardboard boxes taking up space. There are only clothes and a stuffed animal. The stuffed animal falls, revealing a locked, small, silver box.

There has to be something else. This can't be it. There has to be some way I can help them. Chills crawl down my spine as I turn toward the diary. I've already invaded her privacy enough. I can't look through it again. What if I find something worse?

… What if I find something worse?

I grab the diary and skim through the pages. But page after page, entry after entry, nothing. There are weird time gaps too. One entry says March, then the next one says June.

Something silver falls to the ground as I turn a page. I dive for it. It's a small key. My head swivels around the room, landing on the silver box. I jam the key inside and turn it, revealing a small scrap of paper.

Mom's letting me use the computer! She said I can't share the password, so I'm writing it down to remember it. 0118456.

I run back to Diane's room and type the code into the laptop. It opens up, showing several tabs on the screen. I click through them. Prices of plane tickets, apartments, schools, and IDs that are all for the same state. Tennessee. They're moving to Tennessee, across the damn country. I check the plane ticket tab again. There are no tickets in the cart, but she's looking at the price of four.

"Paco! What's taking so long?" Owen yells from outside.

"J-just a minute!" I turn the laptop off. This isn't enough. This isn't enough. There has to be some other way I can help them. I pull open the desk drawers. Empty folders, spare paper, nothing good. I run to her nightstand, pulling open the drawers I didn't get to. The second drawer has a cell phone. The screen is cracked, but I'm able to open the phone. There's no password. I go to the contacts and only see three names.

Mom. Christina. Olive. This is Theodore's phone. My number's on the call log too. Putting my number in it would only tell Diane she was right, and now the lack of the password makes sense. But I need to tell Theodore I still want to help. He wasn't able to convince Christina, but he could try again. We can try again.

I grab a pen and paper from Diane's desk. I scribble what I need to, then put everything back the way I found it. I run to the girls' room. I read the paper over, making sure I wrote everything down.

Theodore, this is Paco. I still want to help. Your mom is catching onto me, but I'm not backing down. I've written my contact info down on this paper in case you need another way to reach me. Your phone is in your mom's nightstand drawer. Please let me know if you're okay.

I fold up the paper and tuck it under Olive's pillow. The bed is wrinkled and unmade, so he must still be sleeping there. At least now I've done something. I go to put the laptop password back. When I do, I notice something else. Papers, and lots of them, with sides ripped and torn. All of them have the same fast and messy handwriting.

Olive's curled up in bed crying. ~~*Mom hit her hard. I think she gave her a black eye.*~~ Underneath the crossed-out sentence is another. *Olive's overreacting. She'll be fine.*

The rest of the page is a normal entry, so I look at the next. The pages are the same. More crossed-out sentences, with more lies underneath. My knees hit the floor as I keep reading.

Mom brought Olive home ~~*kicking and screaming. She locked her in our room and didn't let her out till this morning. She just wanted to say hi.*~~ *Olive didn't listen to her warning, so she got punished. She won't listen.*

Every time Mom yells at us, my heart hurts. I hate it. ~~I hate it! I hate it~~ ~~so much!~~ But Mom does it because we don't listen to her. It makes her sad.

Olive and Mom have been fighting this whole week. ~~They've been throw-~~ *~~ing things at each other. Mom keeps telling her horrible things. She said she~~* *~~was a mistake. And she hit her so hard.~~ Olive still won't listen to her. I hope they stop soon.*

Mom says we'll be moving away. ~~I wish I could move away from her!~~ *~~I hate this!~~ I'll be sad leaving, but it'll be fun! I wonder where we'll go. ~~I~~* *~~wonder if I can escape.~~*

~~Mom messed up. She messed up really bad. Olive just wanted to help.~~ Olive should've known better! There's a reason Theodore does all the cook-ing.

Olive lied to me. She said she loved me. She said she loved Theodore. But she left us behind. Mom was right, she's just like Dad. I hate her! ~~What did~~ *~~I just write? Why would I say that?!~~ I hate her!*

~~Why is Mom so mean to me? Why does she hate me?~~ Mom loves me, it's for my own good. Everything is for our own good.

I CAN'T TAKE THIS ANYMORE! Christina's final entry is written in all caps, covering the entire page. My hand trembles as I flip it over, praying there's writing on the other end.

Mom is a monster.

My head jumps from the papers as something creaks. My body freezes. *Don't move. Don't move at all.* No noises follow, so I get up from the floor, pocketing the papers. I need to get out of here and putting the papers back will only waste time. Christina won't care if these disappeared, would she? She doesn't want anyone to see them.

I leave the room and head toward the door. I move slowly, trying not to make a sound. The house creaks again, and it sounds like the closet door I couldn't open. It creaks slowly, getting louder and louder.

I don't look back. Maybe it's the door giving out. This is an old house anyway, it's just that. Maybe if I move so slowly, I'll have more time to run. I'll get closer to the door and then move so fast that she'll never get me. Maybe she'll think I haven't noticed her.

Creak.

Keep moving. Don't stop.

Creak.

I'm so close. So close.

Creak.

Almost, almost!

SMASH!

I turn around as soon as the vase hits the floor, my phone's flashlight shining on the debris. I move it to the left and slowly go up. Past the ripped jeans and shoes, past the tattered jacket and brown shirt. I land on the short blonde hair and brown eyes with nothing but anger inside.

Oh.

Fuck.

I sprint to the door. The moment I touch the handle, Diane grabs my shirt and slams me against the wall. The throbbing in my head only gets worse as I look at her. The grin on her face is evil. "I knew it. I knew it was you! I knew you had something to do with this!" she yells at me.

I shove her off with all my strength, but she blocks the door. I run into the kitchen. She follows me, but I cut her off by opening the fridge door. Either way, she'll have to go around the kitchen island to get to me. But I'm faster. God, I hope I'm faster.

Diane slams the fridge door shut, and I run out of the kitchen to the front door. My hand reaches for the handle before Diane yanks it backward, nearly taking me to the floor.

"Get off of me!" I yell, tugging my arm back and forth.

Her grip only gets tighter. "You're so lucky I don't have my gun, or I'd blow your brains out just for being here!" Diane pulls me back harder. No. No. NO!

I scream louder. "Get off! Get off!" I yank my arm out of her grip, and before she can grab me again, I turn around and slam my fist into the side of her face. She cries out in pain, and I rip the door open and run outside.

"Start the car!" I yell to Pachi, nearly falling over. "Start the car!"

Pachi's eyes grow wide, but he quickly gets inside. Owen pulls the door open so I can hop in. The moment that door shuts, Pachi drives off. I push past my friends to the backseat so I can look out the window.

"Paco! What happened?" Owen asks for the fifth time. But he never hears my answer. No one needs to. We all see the gray Honda Civic creeping up behind us. That blue tarp from earlier is now on the side of the road.

"Shit! Shit!" Owen screams at the top of his lungs.

"It's Diane! Diane's after us!" Sam yells.

"Where did she come from? I didn't see her car anywhere!" Pachi asks.

"Was she here the whole time?" Yann questions. "How did she know?"

I finally catch my breath. "She knew we were coming," I turn to Owen, whose face is paler than normal. "She made Theodore tell her everything."

"Goddammit!" Owen turns to the front of the car. "We need to lose her!"

"Working on it!" Pachi turns to the right, and Diane follows. Pachi groans. "Fuck! Hold on! This is going to be a bumpy ride!"

I think I'm going to throw up.

11

I DON'T KNOW WHERE the hell we end up after leaving the house. Pachi turns left and right whenever he can, but Diane follows every time. The car swings back and forth with every turn. One hand is on my stomach, the other on my mouth. I don't get carsick often, but I have the tendency to throw up when I'm scared. Add the two together and...

"Hold it in, Paco!" Owen moves through the aisle and grabs onto my shoulder. "Not in the car, man. Not in the car."

"Get me a bag or something," I tell him, my hand covering my mouth. Owen looks around, grabs a plastic grocery bag under a seat, and gives it to me. I open it up and keep it in front of me. Every movement of the car makes me want to hurl my guts out.

Sam moves to the back row and sits next to me and Olive. She pulls Olive into her arms, trying to comfort her. After a few seconds of rubbing her back, she puts a hand on mine. Sam and I discovered years ago that rubbing my back somehow helps me overcome nausea. I shake my head. Olive needs it more than I do.

I turn around and look out the window. Diane has a death grip on her steering wheel, and her movements are jerky. She turns the wheel hard and her car shakes with it. Her face is red, and she clenches her teeth. Her gaze is burning a hole in my head. I twist around and hold my head over the bag.

"A U-turn? No! That's too risky!" Pachi waves his hand around. "You see how packed this street is? I'll hit another car!"

"We need to lose her!" Yann shouts.

"I know! I know!" Pachi's head swivels in all directions. He groans. "Fine! Hang on!"

Pachi reels around and speeds back the way we came. We barely miss the other cars and fly past Diane's. Her car comes to a screeching stop, then she turns around and catches up to us.

"*Ojos del diablo*," Pachi mutters under his breath. Eyes of the devil. I keep thinking the same thing. There's something sinister in them.

Olive lifts her head up from Sam and gets out of her grip. "Is she gone?" she asks.

I turn around. "No, she's catching up." I look away from the window with my head over the bag. With her hands free, Sam puts a hand on my back and starts rubbing circles. It doesn't help much. She looks at Pachi and then back at me. I nod, telling her it's okay.

Sam lets go of my back and sits behind Pachi. "We have to go somewhere. Any ideas?"

"I can get to Railroad from here," Pachi answers, looking at the street signs.

"It's lunch hour! Hell no! Railroad will be packed, and if we get stuck, she'll probably storm up to the car!" Sam argues.

"Fine! But what do you want me to do? I'm going to run out of gas!"

"Why didn't you fill it beforehand?"

"Oh, because I forgot to." Pachi looks at her. "Because I didn't think we'd be in a high-speed chase!"

Diane is still close behind. Her grip only gets tighter, and she leans over the steering wheel, trying to get closer. Her hands are turning white, and the moments when her car almost catches up to us, I see veins bulging out of her neck. I lean my head against the window. Deep breaths, take deep breaths. Deep breaths...

SLAM!

The entire car shakes, followed by everyone's scream. Pachi struggles to get the car straightened out. I slam my hand against my mouth and push it hard. I hunch over. If there's one more sudden movement, I won't be able to hold it back.

Olive leans over quickly and starts rubbing my back. I turn to her, confused. Her eyes are glossy, but she shakes her head. "If you throw up, I'm going to throw up, and it will be messy." Her pats help a little, but my body is still trembling.

"This bitch hit my car! She really hit my car!" Pachi yells once he gets everything under control. He looks in the mirror. "You guys okay back there?"

"Haven't thrown up yet," I answer in a strained voice. Olive lets go of my back as I look in the back window. Diane's frown turns into a smirk, an evil smirk. Her car goes faster, and I turn to Pachi. "Speed up! Speed up!" I yell.

Pachi looks in the rearview mirror and floors it. Diane's car slows down to her earlier speed. We have a little head start, but it's not enough. We need to get to somewhere we can easily lose her. Neighborhoods aren't enough, we need to get somewhere faster. Somewhere with a bunch of cars.

"The freeway," I say. "Pachi, hit the freeway." It's perfect. With lunch-hour traffic, we can lose her in all the cars.

"The fuck do you mean the freeway?" Pachi glances at me before returning his gaze to the road. "We'd have to go down Railroad! That's the only entrance!"

I frown. "I know, but I don't think we have a choice."

Pachi grits his teeth and adjusts his rearview mirror. He changes into the right lane and turns. Now we're on West Leland, and the next turn takes us to Railroad. Cars follow behind, but none of them go in front of Diane. All of us, except Pachi, turn around and watch her speed up.

The light turns green, and Pachi makes the sharpest left turn I've ever seen. Our bodies slam against the windows as Pachi straightens out in the lane.

Railroad Avenue is infamously known for being one of the busiest streets in Pittsburg. If you get a message from someone saying they're stuck on Railroad, you better expect them to be ten to twenty minutes late. My abuela always jokes about it. "Such a small town, yet so much traffic," she says. Cars come from all over the place, and mostly from other towns, so they can get on the freeway. Not only that, Railroad has a bunch of fast-food restaurants and a Starbucks. It's always packed. It sucks when you're in a rush.

Like we are right now.

It's a miracle that most of the traffic is behind us. When we approach the light, it turns yellow. Pachi floors it, and as soon as we pass the light, it turns red. I smile, but Diane is coming behind us. Cars honk as she catches up. She ran the red light!

"East or west entrance?" Pachi asks, his words coming out quickly.

"What?"

"East or west!" Pachi asked again.

I look around to see two freeway exits. The one on the right is closer to us, but it leads us out of town. If Pachi's running out of gas, that's not a good idea. "East!" I say in a panic. Pachi puts on his blinker and looks over his right shoulder. Dammit! Wrong one! "No! West! Go west!"

Pachi drives into the left lane and turns onto the freeway. He does it so fast that I can barely process it. Sam leans out of her seat and looks out the window. Her smile falls. "She's still there!" Sam announces, and the rest of us groan.

"Why won't she quit? Give it a rest already!" Owen yells at Diane. He puts his head in his hands.

Olive turns to the window for the first time. I look too. Diane stares at Olive. Her frown turns into a smile, her face goes soft, and she gives Olive a small wave.

Until Olive flips her off and mouths *fuck you.*

I can't help but laugh, but Diane snaps. She switches moods real quick, and I swear she drives even faster. I turn away after that, but Olive doesn't. Her smile fades and her eyes fill with fear. She dashes from the back row into Sam's arms, who pulls her in close. Owen hops into the seat next to me and starts rubbing circles on my back.

"What now? I don't have much gas left?" Pachi says.

"How far can it get us?" Owen asks.

"I'm not sure." Pachi tries a few lane changes, but Diane follows every single time. A few cars honk at her. We're going to cause a crash if this keeps up. Imagine the headline. *Six teens and one mother cause a pileup crash trying to get away.* Yeah, no, it'd be a disaster.

I'm so angry at her. So damn angry. She'll stop at nothing to get Olive back. She doesn't care what she has to do, doesn't care who she has to hurt. What the hell did she do that got Olive scared so quickly?

Her flipping off Diane is the first time I've seen Olive not afraid of her, and it changed so fast. Olive's still in Sam's arms, and her eyes are red.

I finally sit up and push the bag to the side. My nausea is still shit, but I can handle it now. I look around. Taking the freeway was a mistake. Whatever exit we take, she'll follow. Even with all the surrounding cars, she's never far behind.

Pachi's hands are gripping the steering wheel tightly. Despite all the conditions, he's driving safely. He's already risking his license for this, and it took him a while to not fear driving on the freeway. I have to pay him back for this, if I ever can.

"I need to get off. I can't drive for much longer," Pachi says.

Owen pulls out his phone and looks at the map. "The exit up ahead has a gas station," he says.

Pachi looks in his mirror. "She's right on our tail. How do I lose her?"

A light bulb goes off in my head. "We juked her with that U-turn, and we can do it here." Pachi stares at me confused, so I continue, "We'll act like we're not going to the exit, then switch at the last minute. She won't be able to react in time."

"How do we do that? I need to be close enough to the exit."

"Move one lane over. We're in the one leading to the exit."

Pachi moves to the left, and Diane follows. It's working. The exit sign comes closer. We look back. I make eye contact with her, and Diane steps on the gas.

"Step on it, Pachi!" I shout, and the rest of us start to scream.

SCREEEEEEEEEEECH!

Pachi zooms into the exit lane and drives down the ramp. As we make it to the stoplight, we turn around. Diane is gone.

Halle-fucking-lujah.

We all sigh in relief. Pachi turns right and pulls into the gas station across the street. Yann and Owen step outside. Sam, Olive, and I wait inside the car. Finally, I sit up without my head spinning.

"I thought you were asleep," Sam says. "Are you feeling better?"

"Yeah, thankfully," I say. Olive's sitting in the seat in front of me. She's leaning against the window. "Are you okay?" I ask.

"I'm okay," she answers in a quiet voice. Olive turns to face me. She fumbles for words. "Did you find anything? You were in the house for a while."

I completely forgot I took the papers. I take them out of my pocket, doing my best to flatten them. Olive's eyes grow big, and her hands are already out. I give them to her, and she reads in silence. Olive brings them close to her chest, tears rolling down her face. Guilt eats my chest. I didn't mean to make Olive cry.

The door slides open before I can apologize. Pachi leans against the doorway with his arms crossed. He glares at me. "Paco, come here. We need to talk."

Oh no. I gulp and get out of the van. Sam shuts the door for me. Pachi takes the nozzle out of his car and puts it away. He closes the cap and shoves the receipt into his pocket. I'm sweating as he leans against the gas pump, turning to face me. His eyes are narrow, and he crosses his arms again. I look around. There are no other cars waiting for us to move. *Oh, I'm so dead.*

Pachi's mouth moves, but I speak first. "How's the back of the van? Did she damage it bad?"

Pachi blinks a few times before answering. "No, no. Just a small scratch, surprisingly. It'll be fine."

"Oh, that's a relief." I'll have to check later. That didn't feel like just a scratch.

I stare at the birds nearby. Two are squabbling over a bag of chips. A third bird flies down and swipes a chip. The first two don't even notice.

"Paco, what happened inside the house?" Pachi asks.

I freeze. "What do you mean?" I keep my eyes on the birds. One puffs up his feathers and flies away with the chip bag. The other squawks and pecks at the crumbs.

"You know what I mean. I've never seen you that scared before." Pachi sighs. "This past week, you've been... overly adventurous."

"I thought that was a good thing." I look at him and feel like disappearing. The look of disapproval on his face is something I can't describe.

"Not when you're taking all these dumb risks." Pachi steps closer to me. "You called Theodore, knowing it was risky, and Diane obviously found out. You were willing to go to their house without telling the rest of us, and I'm pretty sure the only reason Owen knew was because he was there."

Red creeps into my face and I look down. "I didn't want to bother you guys," I mumble.

"Stop hiding shit." Pachi sighs. "How did you even get Theodore's number?"

"Diane was the one who broke into my house. Theodore left a note saying to call him. I tried to pretend I was Olive, but he figured it out. Theodore... well..." I trail off, hoping he drops it.

"Spit it out," he says sternly. It's the same voice he scolds his siblings in. God, it does not feel good.

"Diane's lost it. She's been taking it out on them, especially Christina. She gets the worst of it. I found her diary, and it was bad."

"You remember how we said Theodore wanted us to get Christina?" Owen comes from around the corner. I forgot he was out here. "He was trying to convince her to stay behind so we could take her." Owen sighs. "I don't know what happened. He said they were ready."

"Do you think it might've been Diane who texted? I found Theodore's phone in her nightstand drawer. If he hasn't had it at all, then she might've done this." I put my hands in my pockets. "Theodore's been wanting to run too, but he can't leave Christina. If he wasn't caught, I'm sure Christina would be in the car right now."

"*Ay dios mio.*" Pachi groans. His face is cold when he looks at me. "You still haven't answered my question. What happened there? And don't bullshit me with 'oh, it's nothing.' Your nausea never gets this bad."

"Yeah, what happened?" Owen repeats. Yann walks up to us at the same time, so of course he hears the question. The three of them stand there, waiting for my answer.

"Diane caught me, that's all." It grows very quiet. Their faces turn pale with worry, so I continue, "No, don't worry. She didn't do anything. I punched the shit out of her because she wouldn't let me go." I refuse to tell them she threatened to kill me. If they're that worried that she caught me, hell will break loose if I tell them what she said. My hand burns, and I shake it. "Damn, it still hurts."

"We need to tell Logan, or have her stay with Rose or Helen. I don't know what else we can do. If she could, we'd have a bounty on our heads," Owen says, and we all nod. He looks at me. "She knows you're involved. It's too dangerous for her to stay with Sam now."

"You guys are right." The van door slides open. Olive is sitting in the seat, and Sam is behind her. Olive clings to the diary papers. "You've all put yourselves in danger to help me, and I've only made things worse. I thought you guys were lying about wanting to help me, but even Rose and Helen offered, and they don't even know me." Olive tightens her grip on the papers. "I know what to do now. I need to go home."

My mouth falls open. "You mean?"

"Yeah, I'm ready to meet Dad."

Yann goes back inside the store to find something for my hand. The bandage is cheap, but Yann's done it so many times for himself that he makes it work.

"Is that better?" Yann asks when he finishes.

I flex my hand a few times. "Yeah, it feels great. Thanks." I grab a water bottle from the shopping bag and open it.

The car is silent, uncomfortably silent. Owen's in the front seat and Sam and Olive are in the back. All three of them have fallen asleep. I don't get how, it's still the afternoon. But other than that, the tension is thick. Guilt slowly builds in my stomach.

I turn away from Yann and lean back in the seat. His gaze doesn't leave me. He knows something is up. I close my eyes, but I can still see that look in Diane's eyes. I can still hear the tone in her voice. Hell, if she knocked me down, would she have killed me right there? Her words ring in my ears, and I sit up quickly, my hand over my stomach.

Yann groans and gives the bag back to me. I shake my head, but he doesn't stop until I take it. "I'm fine, really," I tell him.

"You don't look fine. You look like you've seen some shit."

"What did you guys find in the house?" Pachi asks. "I know about the diary, but anything else?"

My eyes widen. "Oh shit. Yeah. There was a laptop in Diane's room. I found the password and where they're moving to. Tennessee."

"Tennessee? Why there?" Pachi wonders.

"I don't know. She was looking at apartments, schools, plane tickets, and other stuff."

"Did she book them?" Yann asks.

"No, they were pretty expensive. Plus, there are a bunch of boxes in the house. They can't take all of that on a plane."

Yann sighs. "I saw the backyard when I left. The side gate was open. Nothing was there, just a broken-down swing set. Other than that, it looks forgotten."

I put a hand on my head. I have a piercing headache, and I can't stop thinking about Diane. It feels like she's still near me. I clench the bag in my head. I'm not sick enough to need it, but my stomach's doing twists and turns.

"It's Diane, isn't it?" Pachi asks bluntly.

I groan. "I don't know. She barely touched me, but I can't stop thinking about it. The way she looked at me, and the way she was acting at that moment. She looked unhinged." I shudder. "I can still feel her grabbing the back of my shirt."

"I get what you mean. The few seconds I made eye contact with her..." Pachi shivers.

A few minutes of silence pass before Yann speaks, "What did her diary say?" I look at him, confused. Yann fiddles with his hands. "Sam said the bitch put Olive through a lot. She hasn't told me what, but is it as bad as she said?"

"Yeah, bad." I struggle to find my words. "I don't even want to say it. I don't get how a mother could do this to her own kids!"

"Did she hit them?" Yann questions.

I slowly nod. "Diane's been after Christina the most, but she snapped at Theodore too. Christina wrote that she never hits him, only her and Olive."

"I knew that story she gave about the burns was bullshit, but I was hoping it wasn't." Yann pauses. "At least she has her dad. She'll be safe there."

"You think she'll be okay?" I ask. Olive is curled up next to Sam. The two of them are still fast asleep.

"I know she will." Yann looks at Olive. "Last night, she called me with Sam's phone and asked for stories about Logan. Dad's been sharing stories about him since you and Pachi came over, so I told them to her. She seemed excited."

I smile, but it doesn't last long. I let out a heavy sigh. "I don't know we should do about Christina and Theodore. I found his phone in a drawer, but I don't know when he'll get it back." I pause, wondering if I should say what I did. My friends stay quiet, waiting for me to continue. Screw it. "I hid my contact info under his pillow."

"You what?" Pachi asks.

"I had to." Yann and Pachi glare at me, and I cross my arms. "I didn't want to leave him with nothing. I doubt Diane will check under his pillow. If he finds it, he can let us know he's okay. And maybe we can get them out of there."

The car comes to a stop a few seconds later. Pachi shakes Owen awake, and I wake up Sam and Olive. Sam takes the house key from my pocket and runs to open the door. I go around to the back of the car to look at the damage. Pachi wasn't lying, only a few scratches. I'm surprised.

The car goes off as Pachi locks it. He's waiting for me at the door. He puts a hand on shoulder. "Just be careful," is all he tells me, and we walk inside.

12

— · —

IF I TOLD HIM any earlier, Leo would've broken down my door in excitement. He calls after I text him the news, and his screams of excitement make me drop my phone. He runs to tell his siblings, and they also scream.

It turns out Rose is there tutoring Leo. She texts a few moments later, asking if I'm okay and what happened. I tell her everything, just not the threat to kill me. It doesn't matter though. My nerves disappear as I talk to her. Her voice pushes every worrying thought out of my head. She assures me it'll be okay. Olive's going home now, and that's a reason to celebrate.

I can't deny that. My friends stay at my house until it's late. We watch TV, play games, I even cook dinner for everyone. Good thing my parents are going out tonight. Otherwise, they would see Olive.

My friends leave after dinner, but Owen and Olive are coming back tomorrow so we can meet Logan. Sam wanted to join too, but her sister is coming home from college today. Her flight lands early this morning. Owen calls when he and Olive get here. In a few minutes, we're in the car and driving to Logan's house.

"How are you feeling, Olive?" I ask.

"Excited? Nervous? I don't know." Olive looks down, clutching the bag Sam gave her. "I'm going to miss Sam. Her family's been so good to me."

"You can always visit." Owen turns around with a smile.

"I'd like that."

We arrive at Logan's house a few minutes later. It's a small blue house, with a freshly mowed lawn and flowers along the side. There's a big tree in the front yard with a wind chime hanging from the branches.

I knock on the front door, and Leo answers it within seconds. His smile is wide. "Hey! Dad's upstairs, come in!" Before he shuts the door, he turns to Olive. "Are you ready? I was about to call him down."

Olive nods. "Could you stand with me?"

Leo's eyes are teary. "Of course I will," he answers, taking her hand and guiding her inside the house. Lucy walks to the stairs and calls for Logan.

"I'm coming! I'm coming!" Logan says, somewhat laughing. "What's going on?" He can barely finish the sentence as he reaches the bottom. He leans onto the railing the moment his eyes land on Olive.

Olive takes a step forward, and Logan does too. Another step forward, then another. They inch closer and closer until they stand in front of each other. Logan gets onto his knees, and he's still as tall as Olive. Olive's hands are tightly at her side, Logan's are loose. He's fighting the urge to wrap her in his arms and never let go.

"Hi, Dad," Olive stammers.

Logan bursts into tears and pulls her into a hug. Olive freezes, but quickly, her arms wrap around him. Leo can't wait any longer and starts a group hug. Owen and I smile, then walk outside to give them some time together.

We lean against the house in silence. Owen holds up his arm, leaning his fist toward me. I follow suit. Owen sighs. "We did a good thing today, man."

I chuckle. "Yeah, we did."

Owen clears his throat. "Pachi caught me up with what you found. You got any ideas?"

I shake my head. "No, not really. I think the only thing we can do is wait for Theodore to respond. Anything else is too risky."

Owen pats my shoulder. "Don't stress, we'll figure it out."

The front door opens. Leo's eyes are red, but he has a smile that radiates pure bliss. "Ha, sorry. Come in. Dad wants to talk to you."

The tuplets are sitting on the couch. Logan walks over and shakes both of our hands. "Please, have a seat," he says. We join him on the couch. Logan takes a deep breath. "I can't thank you enough."

"Of course," I answer with a smile.

"Leo, grab them something, will you?" Logan asks, and Leo runs to the fridge.

"We have water, Gatorade, Capri Sun..." Leo announces, and he shoves a Capri Sun into his pocket.

"I'll take water." I look at Owen, then back at Leo. "Two, please."

"How did you find Olive?" Logan asks as Leo comes back with our drinks. Logan glances at Olive before speaking. "I just don't get how. We searched and searched everywhere. The police ruled them deceased after a year."

"Olive found me. She broke into my house." I smirk. Olive nearly chokes on her water. "And she took a bite out of my friend's sandwich."

"In my defense, the door was unlocked." Olive takes another sip of water. "And the sandwich was good."

Owen continues, "Our friend remembered the triplets from Lumpy's and realized they look similar. We invited them over, thinking they were cousins or something. They told us the story."

Logan sighs. "I'm glad, but something still doesn't add up. How did the police never find them? We searched everywhere, and I pressed them constantly for updates."

I turn to Olive. This thought has been running through my head for a while. It's worth a shot. "Do you remember moving here?" I ask.

Olive nods. "We moved here a few years ago, and more before that. I don't remember where, though."

"She fled town. That makes sense. I can't believe I didn't think of that." Logan groans.

"She goes by a different name too, all of them do. She's going by Susan Rodgers," I say.

Logan tilts his head. "All of them? What do you mean?"

"We're all alive," Olive says.

Logan's mouth falls open. He looks away, and tears run down his face. Olive freezes. She looks at her siblings with panic in her eyes. Logan sniffles and wipes his eyes. His voice is shaky when he asks, "H-how are they?"

Olive looks away. "As good as they can be."

Logan frowns. "So, your mother hasn't changed?"

"W-what do you mean?"

"Believe it or not, she wasn't always like this. There were times we dreamed of a large, happy family." Logan walks to the bookshelf at the end of the room. He pulls one out. It's a high school yearbook.

"I met Diane my freshman year of high school, and it was love at first sight. She was kind, beautiful, funny, everything. I asked her out to junior prom, and we had been together since then." Logan flips through the pages, landing on the hall of fame. There they are. Cutest Couple: Logan Page and Diane Hall.

She looks completely different in the photo. She's smiling. She looks happy and healthy, with color in her cheeks and light in her eyes. Nothing like today.

"What happened?" I ask.

"She changed over time. She wasn't as kind as she used to be, and she was quick to anger. But everything spiraled after we became parents. We started fighting over everything. The kids, money... us. I know things change after becoming a parent, but this was different. She stopped caring."

Logan shuts the yearbook. "One night, I came home from work. The kids were crying, and Diane wasn't home. I found her at a bar out of town, and when we got home, we had the biggest fight in our entire relationship. I yelled at her, asking why she would leave them home alone, not even bothering to call her parents or mine. Diane snapped, calling me an unfit father, regretting ever being with me, and calling our children a mistake. That night, she packed up her stuff and left. I filed for divorce the next day."

Olive blinks. "I think I remember that night." Logan's eyes go wide. "I saw you through the doorway. All I remember is yelling, and someone getting hit."

"You saw that?"

"Yeah. I mentioned it to Mom a few years ago, and she said you slapped her." Logan's mouth falls open. Olive rubs her hands over her arms. "She said a lot of things about you."

Logan shakes his head. "I would never. No matter how many times we fought, I would never *think* about hitting her!" Olive looks away, and Logan slowly puts a hand on her shoulder. "If you ever want to talk about it, I'm here, okay? This is your home now."

Lucy peers around the corner of the stairs. Once she realizes they're done talking, she clears her throat and steps forward. "Olive, do you want to try on some of my clothes?" Lucy holds up a purple dress that shines in the light, and it's covered in sparkles. "I don't know what you're into, but we can find out!"

Olive gets up to the couch and runs up to her. Lucy puts the dress in Olive's hands, and Olive runs them over the fabric. "It's so shiny," Olive says with a twinkle in her eye.

Lucy grabs her hand. "I have a bunch more you can try on. Come on!"

The girls run upstairs. Leo and Peter go up after, saying they're going to their room. The three of us sit in silence for a minute. Logan turns to us once the doors close.

"Since they're upstairs now, is there anything I need to know?" he asks.

Owen and I look at each other. There are a lot of things, but we don't know how to start, or what to say. "Christina and Theodore are with Diane," I finally say, but I want to slap myself. That part is obvious. He already knows that.

"We're waiting for Theodore to text us and let us know he's okay," Owen says.

"Then we'll figure out what to do next," I finish the sentence.

"Okay, no. You let me handle this." Logan leans forward. "You've done enough. This woman is dangerous. I'm sure you already know that. Let me handle it, okay? I don't want you getting hurt."

"We can't call the cops," I say, and Logan tenses. "If Diane finds out, she's leaving the state, and she'll take the kids with her."

Logan freezes. "O-okay, well... Christ, that complicates things." Logan's resolve shatters with each breath he takes. "There has to be something I can do. T-there has to be. I can't..." Logan puts his head in his hands. A sob escapes his throat.

I don't speak for a moment. "We'll bring them home, Mr. Page. Whatever it takes," I tell him.

"Please, call me Logan," he says, sitting up. Logan puts a hand on his left cheek. "God, if only I wasn't so stupid. Had I changed the locks earlier, this never would've happened."

"What do you mean?" Owen asks.

"She was able to get inside because she still had her key. I knew I had to change them at some point, but she hadn't seen the kids in months. It was in the back of my mind. She wasn't even interested in custody at first. The night she kidnapped them was the day we were set to go to court. Her car alarm went off, and I saw her drive away. I put the kids in my car and chased after her, but I lost track." Logan lowers his voice. "I feel like it's all my fault."

"But you had no idea," Owen says quickly.

"I know. I know I didn't, but I can't stop thinking about it." Logan looks away. "We moved out of Pittsburg a few years after graduating and got married at twenty-one. Next to nothing to our name, but we had each other. Stockton had too many memories, so I moved back home." Logan takes a breath, but his voice is still shaking. "I've been in this town for two years and haven't seen her once. I can't believe it."

Logan wipes his eyes. The words wheeze out of him. "Please, let me know when Theodore messages you. I need to know my kids are okay. I *need* to get them back."

"We will," I tell him.

Logan slowly rises from the couch, muttering something about making lunch. Owen and I look at the clock. It might be best to leave everyone be. We walk up the stairs to say our goodbyes. Olive and Lucy have the door closed, so we head toward the boys' room.

The walls are painted blue, with twin beds on each side of the room. Above the red bed is a framed soccer jersey, and more sports posters on the wall. Peter's side of the room is covered in video-game posters.

Leo walks around with a ruler, measuring every inch of the room. Peter is sitting at his desk, drawing on some paper. He crinkles it up and tosses it on the other side of the desk. They probably share it due to the size. It takes up half of the room.

"What are you guys doing?" I ask.

"Trying to figure out the layout for our room." Peter turns around to look at his brother. "Maybe we can loft one of the beds? There's no way the three of us could share a desk."

"Do you think it'll fit? The room's small enough as it is." Leo points around the room. "Why does the closet have to be over there? It's ruining the plan! Maybe if we move the dresser..."

Leo walks to the dresser between the two twin beds. The dresser is covered in clothes and gold trophies. One is Peter's. It's the chess trophy he held in the newspaper. The rest are soccer trophies. Leo grabs the dresser and squats. The dresser scrapes on the carpet. Clothes fall off it and I run to catch anything else.

"What are you two doing?" Logan asks as he comes up the stairs. Owen steps away from the door and lets him inside the room. Leo explains, and Logan chuckles. "You let me figure that out. Leo, do not pick up the dresser. You're going to hurt your back, and you do not want back problems."

"Maybe we should wait for Theodore. He might not want the loft, maybe he'll want to bunk with one of us." Peter suggests.

"Well, whatever one he wants, I'm not on the bottom bunk! I am not going through that night again!" Leo crosses his arms and looks away. He has a devious smirk on his face.

Peter puts his hand on his forehead. "We were nine! I had a bad dream!" he defends.

"You drank a whole bottle of Dr. Pepper!"

"It was a small bottle!"

Logan watches his two sons bicker with a soft smile filled with joy. Lucy walks past her dad and into the room. Olive follows behind. The dress she has on is sky blue, with white lace sewn throughout the skirt to resemble clouds. It's a pretty dress. She has barrettes scattered in her neatly brushed hair.

"I think it suits you a lot better than me. Blue was never my color," Lucy says.

How does that work if they're identical? You know what, never mind. "It looks nice!" I smile. "You like blue, huh?"

"Yeah, but a light blue. Not dark." Olive spins around, watching the skirt rise and fall so smoothly. The twinkle in her eyes hasn't left since she got here.

"Did you bring anything?" Logan asks, and Olive nods. "You can keep it in Lucy's room. You'll be sharing a room with her and Christina when she comes."

"Really? Christina too?" When Logan nods, Olive dashes into Lucy's room. The walls are light pink with posters of boy bands and movies scattered all over. Olive stands on the right side of the room in the empty corner. "I claim this corner."

Logan chuckles. "It'll be a bunk bed. Do you want to wait for Christina to—?"

"Bottom bunk. I hate heights." Olive looks at me. "I-I mean, Sam's is fine. Hers isn't that high. But I like the bottom bunk more." Her speech stammers as she tries to explain herself.

"Bottom it is." Logan smiles. "I'll go finish lunch. Let me know if you need anything!" he says as he disappears down the stairs.

"Do you want to try on another dress, Olive?" Lucy asks.

Olive gazes at Lucy's closet. It's extensive. Beautiful dresses, bright colored shirts and sweatshirts, everything. There are more clothes on Lucy's bed. Olive turns to her sister. "No, I think I'm okay."

"Okay! I'm going to help Dad with lunch. You can go through my clothes and take what you like." Lucy opens a bin on the floor, revealing some more clothes. "These are all clean. I was getting rid of clothes I don't wear anymore, so take what you like." Lucy turns to leave, but she runs back to Olive. She gives her a tight squeeze before going downstairs.

Olive steps toward the closet. Owen and I follow her. "Hey, Ol." The nickname comes out of my mouth faster than I realize, but Olive doesn't make a face. "We were about to head out. You feeling okay?"

Olive half-smiles. "Yeah. But… could you guys help me tidy up? I made a mess going through the clothes." It's nothing more than a small pile on Lucy's bed. But if she wants help, I won't say no. Owen and I nod and pick up the clothes.

Olive puts the clothes on the hangers and into the closet, not saying a word. There's a pink dress she pulls out of the closet. It's covered in sparkles, and Olive smiles. "Christina would love this," she says before putting it back.

Olive sets a few shirts aside for her and Christina. She puts them on Lucy's vanity. As she puts down another shirt, she knocks over some makeup. Lipstick rolls off the vanity and brushes fall onto the floor. Olive dives toward the makeup and puts it back quickly. Her eyes look distant and swollen. She notices me staring and turns away.

"Are you okay?" I ask.

"I'm fine," Olive mutters. As she puts the lipstick back in its place, she looks in the mirror. Olive runs her hands over her hair and takes a barrette out. It's in the shape of a flower. Her fingers caress it. "I don't think I deserve this."

I frown. "What makes you say that?"

Olive grabs her bag and dumps it on the bed. Her sketchbooks and some clothes fall out. She grabs a pair of jeans and unfolds it. There's a bright-colored star patch on the left knee, a small heart patch right under, and stitches that run up the side of the pant leg.

"The diary entry, the one where Christie said she hated me... We got into a fight the night before I left. I called her so many names. Said she was a horrible big sister, and that she's nothing but a pet. Now that I'm here, I see it. Mom used all of us for her own benefit. Hell, I saw it then too. Christie never listened to me. She loves Mom more than anything, after all, more than me." Olive holds the pants in her hands. Her hands gloss over the stitches and patches. "Even though I'm gone, she still fixed my clothes."

Olive wipes her eyes. "She doesn't deserve to be there. Theodore doesn't either. If anyone deserves it, it's me. I'm so horrible. I'm horrible to them, and to all of you."

"But you deserve to be here too," Owen says. "All of you deserve to be here."

Olive looks at Owen. "I'm sorry for being so rude to you."

Owen's eyebrows raise. "When were you rude to me?"

"At Paco's house. You were telling me the truth about my mom, and I wasn't listening. I kept snapping at you. You were just trying to help."

"It's okay, don't apologize. I know it's hard to hear. I'm always here if you want to talk."

"You mean it?"

"Yeah, you're not alone."

Olive walks to him and hugs him tightly. Owen freezes. He doesn't hug much. He puts his arms around Olive and tries to comfort her, even though it's just a small pat on her back. When she lets go of him, she runs to me and pulls me into a tight hug.

"Thank you," she whispers.

"Of course," I say as her tears fall onto my shoulder.

13

THE NEXT DAY I spend working at the bakery, with today as well. I've taken the past few days off because of Olive. Now that she's with Logan, I don't have to worry as much.

Business is slow today, and we've been open for four hours now. Today's Saturday, and that's one of our busiest days. Well, it's not so bad. Any business is better than none.

I can't stop checking my phone. I still haven't gotten a response from Theodore. The fireworks show is in two weeks. It's been confirmed that it's Diane's last shift. Paula messaged me today that she overheard one of Diane's conversations with their boss. Diane's waiting until then to get more money for the move. I really don't want to wait that long, but I don't know what else to do.

I don't know what to tell Logan either. We've been texting back and forth, but there isn't much to say. He's got his hands full, and every day that passes without an update makes me want to explode. I'm absolutely terrified.

Antonio, Tío Harvey, and I are the only ones here. Antonio's in the kitchen frosting some cakes, and Tío's in the back with paperwork. I'm packing an order for pickup when the door opens. The ringing of the bell makes me rush to the counter. I smile at who it is.

"Owen, Katie, how's it going?"

"We're good, man," Owen answers, wrapping an arm around Katie.

"I've been craving your family's cakes literally all week." Katie laughs. Her brown hair is pulled out of her face, showing her freckles. She's wearing a short-sleeved dress that shows the rest of them. I smile. They must be on a date. Maybe I'll take Rose here. A remake of what could've been my confession.

"Do you still have those monster cupcakes?" Owen asks.

I snap back to the conversation. "Yeah, which one do you want?" I ask as I step closer to the glass display. "We have chocolate, vanilla, red velvet, strawberry…"

"Strawberry, please!" Katie beams.

The monster cupcakes are the size of three normal cupcakes smashed into one. It was my tío's idea, and the strawberry one is his favorite. It has pink frosting with a strawberry on top, and the cake comes out a light red. It's not the most popular flavor, but enough people like it, so we still serve it.

Owen gives me the money as Katie digs for some in her purse. She stops once she hears the cash register. "Babe! I was going to pay!" Katie says.

After I ring them up and give them the cupcake, Katie pulls Owen to a nearby table. Normally I don't pay attention, but Katie runs to the seat that faces the exit. It's odd.

"Do we have to come here?" I hear a voice under the bell that makes my blood turn cold.

"Girl, yes! This place has the best pastries!"

It's Renise and one of her friends. My eyes fly to Owen. He flinches once he hears her voice. He pulls out his phone and quickly reaches for Katie's hand. Katie sticks the plastic fork into the cupcake and gives Owen a bite to distract him.

"Ah, jeez. I need to call my mom real quick. Can you order? I'll pay you back," Renise's friend asks as she steps away. Renise comes up to the counter and crosses her arms.

"What do you want?" I ask, not even hiding the tone in my voice.

"Look, I don't want to be here either, so don't even start." I don't answer, and Renise rolls her eyes. She looks at the glass display. "Can I have two monster cupcakes, one vanilla, and one chocolate?"

I place the cupcakes into their containers and put them in the bag. Renise flips the card reader around and sticks her card in. It's an uncomfortable silence as she puts her pin in. I glance at Owen. His eyes are on his phone. Katie gives him another bite.

"Ugh, sorry about that." Renise's friend comes back from her phone call. "You are coming to the fair, right? It's in two weeks."

"The one at the marina?" she asks as she puts her card away. "I don't know. I have to see if I'm free."

"Come on! The whole town will be there!" Her friend grabs the plastic forks from the counter. She waves her hands around. "There's going to be food, games, and even fireworks! At least see if you're free."

"I'll check. I might have a date that night," Renise says, her eyes on Owen. He doesn't budge, and she frowns. She swipes the bag off the counter, takes one last look at Owen, then leaves the bakery with her friend following behind.

I hop over the counter and run to Owen. I put a hand on his shoulder. "Don't worry, I'm okay," he says. "She doesn't stress me out that much anymore."

"What were they even talking about? I haven't heard anything about fireworks at the marina," Katie asks, and Owen shrugs. Crap! I never told him what Paula said about the fireworks!

"I think I know, but I'll tell you later. You two enjoy your date," I say before going back behind the counter.

A few minutes pass before the door opens again. A boy wearing a hood walks up to the counter. His hands tremble when he approaches.

"Hi, how can I help you?" I ask softly. Maybe he's nervous about ordering.

His mouth moves, but nothing comes out. He pulls at his fingers, still not saying anything. "Are you okay?" I ask.

"Not really," he mutters. His hood moves. He has big curly hair, a bruise on his cheek, and a bandage on his chin. We make eye contact, and I'm staring into a pair of eyes I've seen before. His dark brown eyes are red, with tears rolling down from them.

"Theodore?" I whisper. His eyes widen.

"H-hi."

I don't know what to do. He's standing right in front of me. How did he get here? How does he know I work here? There are so many questions I have, but dammit, we don't have the time.

"W-what happened? Are you okay?" I ask.

"I-I'll be fine," he stammers. "I still don't have my phone, and I didn't want you to worry anymore."

"How did you find me then?"

"I stole Mom's phone to see if I text your Instagram account. I found the bakery's account and saw you in a video." Theodore looks behind him, staring at the window. "Can I have a chocolate cake, please?"

"A... a what?"

"Chocolate cake. Please, it's the only way I convinced Mom to come here."

I grab the cake out of the display and place it in a box. Theodore sticks his mom's card in the reader. He puts the pin in and looks back, his hands moving faster.

"Do you have to go? Is there any way you can get away now?" My voice cracks when I ask.

"I can't leave Christie." Theodore looks back again. "I-I have a plan. Meet me at my house, around 3:20. I know it's late, but Mom's asleep by then."

"I'll be there." I give him the cake, and he takes the card out. The receipt prints. I hand it to him. "Be careful, please."

Theodore nods. "I will." He grabs the box and walks out the door.

After a few seconds, Antonio comes up behind me and puts a hand on my shoulder. "*¿Que pasó? Parece que has visto un fantasma.*"

I catch a glimpse of myself in the glass display. With how white my face is, I really do look like I've seen a ghost. "*N-nada. No te preocupes,*" I answer.

Owen and Katie leave a few minutes later. I wave goodbye as they walk out the door. I get a text after. I pull the notification down, reading the message preview.

Owen: Hey, who was that kid in the hood? You looked pale.

For some reason, my hands don't move, my brain can't think. I just... can't.

I swipe the notification away, not even responding.

The bakery closed early for maintenance. It's a bit of a relief. I could barely focus for the rest of my shift. It's been three hours since I got home, and I still haven't gotten a message from Theodore.

One hour I spent alone with my thoughts, but the past two hours I've been playing games with Yann. When he's not boxing, he's a fierce gamer. By that, I mean he carries the entire team. He's M.V.P. in almost every match. We're on a FaceTime call, and Yann leans back in his chair, shooting the player that killed me.

"How was work?" Yann asks.

"It was good. What have you been up to?"

"Not much." The game announces that Yann's on a kill streak. He looks at the camera for a second. "How are things with you and Rose?"

"We're good." I smile. "I want to take her out on another date to make up for how the first one ended, but I don't know where to go." Despite how it ended, it was nice. My face reddens as I think of her in her dress, and how excited she was that day. She's so beautiful.

"You'll figure it out, don't worry too much. You won't be able to enjoy it." It's funny to hear romantic advice coming from Yann. He doesn't have the best luck.

"Now that I think about it, why were you telling me to confess to her so much? It was random," I ask.

Yann smiles. "Oh, do you remember how I had third period with her?" I nod. "We were talking, and she admitted to liking you."

"W-what?" My jaw drops, and Yann bursts into laughter. "When? How? Why?" My brain stutters with all my questions, and Yann laughs harder. My face is red from embarrassment, and his is red from laughter. "H-how long have you known?"

"This happened... uh..." He's pausing for dramatic effect. The smirk on his face widens. "Last month."

"You've known for a whole month?"

"Since her birthday. She told me as she was gushing over the present you got her. She was so embarrassed." My head is in my hands, and Yann's laughter subsides. "Don't be mad! I told you she likes you! And I was right!"

The round ends. Yann, once again, is M.V.P. He leans back in his chair and stretches. "Do you want to keep playing? We could do a different mode, or a different game," Yann says, but I don't answer. An Instagram notification pops up on my phone.

"Hold on," I say as I snatch my phone off my desk. Yann chuckles, saying how funny I look from this angle.

Theodore: Paco? Is this you?

Me: Yeah, it is. Are you okay?

Theodore: Yeah. Mom just gave my phone back. Are you still coming?

Me: I'll be there, don't worry.

Theodore: Thank you.

"You okay, Paco?" Yann asks. I realize he can only see my forehead.

"Theodore texted me," I say as I return to the camera.

"Oh, cool." It takes him a few seconds to realize. "Wait, he did?"

"He wants me to go to his house so we can talk about what to do next. He doesn't want to risk his mom finding out again."

"What time? Now?"

"3:20." I sigh. I haven't been able to sleep anyway, no big deal.

"Goddamn! Sorry, there's no way my parents would let me go out that late. And I can't sneak out even if my life depended on it."

"It's all good. I'll figure something out."

"Whatever you do, don't go alone. You got that?"

"I won't, don't worry." I hear another voice on the phone. "You gotta go?"

"Yeah, Mom needs help downstairs. And I need to take Lobo on a walk. I wasn't able to earlier." As if on cue, the camera flips, and Lobo sits in front of Yann, wagging his tail.

"All right then, goodnight," I say. Yann waves goodbye, then hangs up the call.

I don't want to go alone. Just thinking of Diane waking up and finding out what we're doing gives me a headache. I look at my messages. Owen's text sits there unread. My thumb hovers over it. No, I don't want to bother him. I don't want to bother anyone. I can do this on my own. It won't be so bad, right?

Chills run down my spine as I think of her eyes. I shake my head. I'll be fine. Theodore and Christina are going through hell right now. I'm not chickening out because of their devil of a mother.

My thumb taps Sam's contact. I type out the message and wonder if I should hit send. It's ten o'clock. Maybe this won't wake her. At least I could say I tried.

Me: Sam, you awake?

She calls me five seconds later.

"Is everything okay?" Sam asks in a hushed voice. A door creaks in the background.

"Is this a bad time?" It's around the time Ruby finally falls asleep. She fights it like no tomorrow. I hope I didn't wake her. One time I did, and it was a nightmare.

"No, Ruby's asleep," Sam says, and I sigh in relief. "I'm in my room now. What happened?"

"Theodore showed up while I was working."

I hear Sam fumble around her room. Does she already know where this is going? "What? Really? How is he? Is he okay?"

"He says he's fine, but he doesn't look like it. He had a bruise on his face, and his eyes were red. He wants me to meet him at his house."

"What time did he say?"

"3:20, tonight."

"Damn!" Sam responds. I wait for her to continue. Maybe I shouldn't have sent the text. Sam loves her sleep. "Well, we're biking then. I won't be able to get the car. I'll bring my pepper spray too."

"You sure you don't mind?" I can't help but ask.

"I'll be at your house ten to three. That should give us enough time. I'll see you soon," Sam says, then she hangs up the call.

Sam: Hurry up! It's cold!

I place the note on the kitchen counter and slowly go out the front door. Our security cameras still aren't here; I got lucky. As long as my parents don't wake up and question why I'm going on a "walk" at three in the morning, we'll be fine.

Sam moves her bike into the street, and I grab mine from the side yard. I type the street name into my phone and we're off. Despite all the time we spent at the house, none of us looked at the address. I barely caught the street name as we sped out of there.

We don't get that far before I start to slow down. I take a deep breath. "Hey, thanks for coming with me."

"Of course," Sam answers.

"I would've been stressed if I had to go by myself." A nervous chuckle escapes my mouth. Sam doesn't respond. "I still would've gone, but I feel a lot better with you here."

Sam slams on her brakes. Her bike comes to a screeching halt in front of me. "Stop doing shit on your own, for fuck's sake, Paco!" Her tone catches me so off guard that I nearly fall out of my seat. She sighs and hops off her bike.

She takes a deep breath. "Who do you think you are? Telling us to be careful, then doing the riskiest shit without telling us. Pachi said it, I damn well know Rose said it, even Olive said so!" Sam grabs my shoulders and shakes me hard. "Get it through that thick skull of yours!"

"That's why I texted you!" I defend. "Even I didn't want to go alone at this." Sam stops shaking me and lets go of my shoulders. I get off my bike with a sigh. "Look, I know I'm being a dumbass. I'm sorry. But this whole thing's been keeping me up the past few nights. And after reading Christina's diary... I'll never forgive myself if I can't get them out of there."

Sam sighs. "You've always been like this, others before you. I don't get it."

I look at the ground. "Having no one to trust when it feels like the world is after you messes you up. If being there for them helps them feel better just a bit, then I'm going to do all I can." Sometimes, I wonder if helping is all I'm good for.

Ka-thunk.

There's only one person that can be making that sound this late at night. *Ka-thunk. Ka-thunk.* We bike over to the house. Sam and I climb the fence and look into the backyard.

It's Owen, bow in hand, shooting a target in the backyard. He learned for fun, but he uses it as a way to de-stress. He says it helps him focus on the moment right now, instead of the past or future. The arrow flies out of his hands and lands on the target. Bullseye.

"Damn, I think you've got him," I say from the fence. Owen whips around, pulls out another arrow, reloads, and aims at me. It's all in one motion. I fall off the fence. "Ah! Don't point that at me!" Sam stays on the fence and grins.

"Don't sneak up on an archer, man." He puts his arrows away as I get back on the fence. "Why are you guys up? Wait, why are you here?"

"Wanted to say hello since you're up." Sam smiles, then frowns. "But seriously, we're going to see Theodore."

"What? Why? What happened?"

"He showed up during Paco's shift. Wanted to meet at 3:20."

Owen slowly turns toward me. He blinks a couple of times before yelling, "Why didn't you tell me?" He picks up his arrows with a groan, jabbing a finger at me. "I'll be back. Do not leave without me."

A few minutes later, we're back on the road. Pittsburg feels different at night. Instead of busy streets, there's no one out. The town is quiet. It's funny seeing the streets this empty, knowing they'll be packed a few hours later. We avoid the wrong turn and arrive on time.

We park our bikes behind a neighbor's car and walk to the house. I find the side gate Yann told me about. I drag the door open. Yann wasn't kidding. Other than the swing-set, the yard is empty. The grass is yellow and patchy, there's trash littered everywhere. Do they even come out here? I look to the right. There's a broken chair near the house with a small child sleeping on it. Wait a minute.

"Is that him?" Owen asks.

I step toward Theodore. "Yeah, it is. I hope he wasn't out here for long." I put my hand on his shoulder and slowly shake him. His eyes pop open, and I back up in shock.

"Hi," his voice comes out so quietly. He looks over. "Who are they?"

"This is Sam and Owen. They're my friends, and Olive's friends too."

His smile is wide as he jumps up. His small arms try to wrap around all three of us. Christ, he's so small. I hug him back. I fear if I squeeze too tightly, I'll break him. He feels fragile. Owen puts a hand on Theodore's back, and Sam wipes her eyes.

"Thank you, just thank you." Theodore sniffles. "I don't know what I'd do without you guys helping me."

"Are you okay?" Sam cuts to the chase. That's our biggest concern.

Theodore cups his hands together. "Yeah. Yeah, I'm fine. How's Olive?" Why does he keep avoiding the question? "Is she okay? She's safe, right?"

"She's safe," I assure him, and the relief on his face hurts.

"Does she talk about us at all?" he questions.

Sam nods. "Yeah. She talks about you guys a lot. She tells me stories and memories. She misses you."

Theodore's smile quickly drops. "Well, tell her not to." Theodore looks at the ground. "I'm sure she's not coming back, but she's stubborn as hell. I need her to know that she can't come back. That she can't go looking for me or Christie."

"Look for you? Theodore, did something happen?" I ask.

"It doesn't matter," Theodore says in a hurry. "I need your guys' help, because I need to get Christina out of here, and fast."

14

Desperation makes people do crazy things, and Theodore's no exception. His words come out faster than I can comprehend. I keep telling him to slow down and explain it again. He's going off on a whim. His plan isn't fully thought out. The only thing that's clear is we have to distract his mom long enough for them to escape.

"How are we supposed to distract her?" I question. "If she sees us, we're screwed."

"Then I'll distract her, and you guys take Christina," Theodore says with no hesitation.

"What about you? We can't leave you behind."

"I'll be fine. I'll figure it out."

"Does Christina even know about this?" Owen asks. "Have you talked to her at all?"

"Well, no, but—!"

"You need to talk to Christina about this," Owen interrupts. "She might have an idea."

"You don't get it! Mom said something to her, and she won't listen to me anymore!" Tears run down Theodore's face. "No matter what I tell her, no matter what Mom does, she keeps defending her!" Theodore grips his hair. "I don't know what to do, and I'm running out of time."

My eyes widen. "What do you mean?"

"We're leaving in two weeks, with or without Olive. Mom's finalizing the apartment. She's lost hope that Olive's coming back, but she won't stop trying."

"Does she know where Olive is?"

"Not anymore. She wasn't at your house, and she didn't find her in the other house. But she's been going out and looking for her." Sam and I freeze. I rethink all the noises that have been waking me up the past few weeks. "She said something weird though. She was in one of those moods. Slurry, dizzy, giggling at whatever." Drunk, but I guess he doesn't know the word. "She thinks Dad has her. But that doesn't make sense! Dad's dead. He's been dead for years."

The tension thickens as I look at my friends. Theodore tilts his head, staring at us with a confused look. "When did she say he died?" Owen questions.

Theodore holds his chin and looks away. "She said he died when we were three, a year after she saved us from him. But I don't get why she didn't save the rest of us. We're sextuplets, did you know?" Theodore looks down at the ground. "But Mom was only able to save us. She couldn't get the others in time because Dad woke up."

I look at Sam and Owen as Theodore continues. "I don't think she had a plan. She only had seats for three of us, but she tried to save us all." I can't speak. How do we tell him that he's grown up on a lie? A sick, twisted lie? When we stay silent, the light fades from his eyes.

"How much of it was a lie?" His voice is quiet.

"... Everything."

Theodore's face hardens. His eyes grow dark, and his body shakes. "I wanted to believe her. I wanted to be a good son. I was her only son left. That's what she told me. Why would she lie? What else is a lie?"

"Theodore," I call.

He looks down at his shaky arms. He rotates them, looking over all the old wounds and bruises. "All these years, she said she was protecting us. That we had a chance now that we were away from him. Was that a lie too? Was everything she told us a lie?" I call his name again. No response and he continues to talk. His words are coming out at high-speed and his tears fall faster. "What would she get out of it? What was the point? She was still being an—!"

"Theodore!"

Theodore stops immediately and mutters an apology. "I just don't get why."

"They're alive," I finally say. I step toward him and put a hand on his shoulder. "Your dad and your siblings. They want you home."

Theodore's eyes go wide. "You mean they want me to go with them?"

"You and Christina. They want all of you home." I glance at Sam, and she nods. "Olive's there too. She's safe."

The light returns to his eyes, and his frown curls into a smile. "You mean it?"

"I wouldn't lie about this."

Theodore leans forward, cupping his hands together. His body tenses up as I let go of him. I can't imagine what thoughts are going through his head. He looks back at the house, then looks away.

"Okay. Okay," he says, taking deep breaths. "I have a plan. A new one. A better one." When he opens his mouth again, his watch goes off. His eyes widen in horror. He looks at the house and then back at his watch. "No! No!"

"What's wrong?" I ask.

Theodore's face pales. "You guys need to go."

"What? Why?" Sam questions.

"It's Mom. The past few nights, she's been waking up at the same time and checking on us. I have five minutes before she gets up. I thought it would be fine if we went through with the plan!"

We follow Theodore out the side gate and to the front door. He opens it slowly, stopping at any small creaks. Before he enters, Sam lunges forward, grabbing his hand. "Come with us."

Theodore's eyes grow big. "What?"

"Grab Christina and come with us," Sam pleads. "We can get you guys out of here."

Theodore looks back and forth between us and the house. "I can't. She won't believe me, then we'll both get in trouble."

Sam swears under her breath before speaking again. "Then promise me you'll talk to her as soon as she wakes up."

"I will," he answers, and Sam lets him go. He stands in front of the door and turns around. "Promise you'll come back for us?"

"We will," I answer, and my friends nod.

"Okay, see you soon," Theodore says as he closes the door.

"Theodore!"

My body freezes. Theodore squeaks out a yes as the door shuts. We run to the side of the house and lean against it. I tilt my head forward despite the alarms going off in my mind.

"M-Mom, I just wanted to help pack! I swear that's the only reason I'm up!" His voice trembles, and he takes a shuddering breath, trying to fight back tears.

"Pack what? The front door?" The tone in her voice sends chills down my spine. The door creaks open. We back up, and Sam steps on a twig. The air thickens. My face pales as her threat creeps into my mind.

You're lucky I don't have my gun, or I'd blow your brains out just for being here.

She's armed. She's armed! When she takes a few steps, I shove my friends into the backyard. I should've gone alone. I can't let her get them. I'll never forgive myself if something happens to them.

Sam leans against the wall near the gate. She pushes me and Owen away. Her hand gestures around the yard. Owen and I run around, trying to find some sort of exit. The other side of the yard doesn't have a gate. But when I try to haul myself over the tall fence, I get a splinter in my hand. I take it out as Owen steps on the fence. A piece snaps and falls. It won't last long enough for us to get over it.

Sam runs to us. Footsteps approach the gate, and I can't hear Theodore's voice. Sam tries to jump over, but the fence creaks, and she hops off. We're cornered. This is it. We're done for.

The window on our left flies open. Theodore's on the other side and reaches his hand out. We push Owen up first, then Sam and I. Thank God it's a one-story house. I shut the window as Diane rounds the corner. Theodore runs out of the room, and we drop to the floor. Owen crawls under Theodore's bed, and Sam and I move to the closet. We duck under the hangers and go to the far back. I shove my hands on my mouth. *Please don't throw up. Please, not now.*

The front door slams shut a few seconds later. "I told you to get in bed." Diane hisses. "Why are you still up?"

"I remembered I left my window open, so I went to close it," Theodore answers, his voice in a higher pitch. "I was going to bed now."

"Why were you in your room when you've been sleeping in Christina's?"

"Christina snores, and it got too hot. She hates being cold." Theodore has an excuse for every question Diane asks him. He answers her with no hesitation. Diane grows quiet.

Diane lets out a loud groan. "Fine. Just go back to bed. I'm too tired for this shit." Diane stomps down the hallway. "Don't do anything like this again. You stay in bed. You got that?"

"Yes, Mom," Theodore responds. Diane opens her door and slams it shut. Theodore walks into his room and closes the door. I walk out of the closet, careful not to knock anything over.

Theodore wipes his eyes and steps toward the window. He opens it slowly. Owen comes out from under the bed and Sam exits the closet. "Go out the side gate," Theodore whispers.

We leave in the same order we came. When my feet hit the ground, I turn around. "If anything happens, you tell me. I'll come get you."

"You mean it?"

"I promise."

Theodore nods and gives a sad smile. "See you soon." With that, his window closes. For a few seconds, I stare at his window. I want to get them out of there now. I want to get them far away from her.

It hurts to leave them there, but I don't know what we could have done. And now we really have a time limit. I thought they wouldn't leave Olive behind. Not only that, Theodore's bruises look horrible. How did it get worse than this morning? Can we afford to play the waiting game, especially when she has a gun? I'm so stuck in my thoughts that I don't realize we're almost home.

Sam's bike slows to a stop. "You don't know what Olive went through, do you?"

"Did she tell you?" I ask, my bike slowing down as well.

"Yeah. During the days she stayed with me, she opened up, and she finally told me what happened. Let's just say Christina's diary wasn't that far off."

"What do you mean?" Owen asks. His face has a frown.

"Diane's a damn monster. The way she treats her kids, I can't believe it." Sam steps off her bike. Her arms wrap around herself. "She's so mean to them. And she expects them to do everything. On top of the homework, chores have to be done every day, no exceptions. Theodore cooks every meal, even when he's sick. Christina cleans the house from top to bottom and teaches their lessons when Diane doesn't. Olive does the heavy lifting. Trash, groceries, shit kids shouldn't do."

Sam takes a deep breath. "And when they don't do something right, Diane gets so pissed. Yelling, throwing things, and even hitting them. When she's drunk, it's even worse. Like full-on punches." Sam takes shaky breaths, and she clenches her fists. "She hurt them so much. Olive has nightmares about it. The week she left, they were fighting every day. Olive wanted to cook dinner to make up for it, and burned the whole pot, so Diane..." Sam can't finish the sentence before she bursts into tears.

My bike falls to the floor as I run to her. I pull her into a hug, and she cries on my shoulder. "I don't get it. How could someone who's supposed to love you hurt you so much?" I hold her tighter, and Sam's breathing finally calms down. She picks her head up, and my hands fall to my side. "We need to get them out of there," Sam says.

"I know, and we will."

"Theodore's smart," Owen says as he walks over. He puts a hand on Sam's shoulder. "He'll convince Christina, I'm sure of it."

"But they're leaving in two weeks. What if he doesn't?"

"I have a plan," I say, and they look at me. "But I'll tell you when we get to my house. I'll make breakfast if you guys are hungry."

Sam and Owen crash on the couch as soon as we get home. I can't fall asleep. I keep pacing around the kitchen, trying to figure out a way to help Christina and Theodore. Every idea has too many risks; too many consequences if we get caught. Part of me wants to go back. Get Theodore and Christina in my car, then drive them to Logan's. Theodore would be fine with it—it's Christina I'm worried about. God, I wish I could help them. I feel so useless.

Sam and Owen finally wake up after eight. When Sam's head pokes up from the couch, I grab eggs from the fridge and get to work. Owen and Sam watch some TV as I cook. They text their parents that they're at my house. None of us got caught sneaking out.

Today's breakfast is spam, eggs, and potatoes. I cook everything the way my friends like it. Over-easy eggs and thick slices for Sam, sunny-side and thin slices for Owen. I make scrambled eggs and whatever spam is left for myself. I don't care.

They grab drinks from the fridge and sit at the table when I call them. We eat for a bit before I decide to tell them about the fireworks. My friends stare at me, confused.

"Fireworks?" Sam asks. "What do you mean? Does Pittsburg even do—?"

"Well, are the rumors true, Jim?" The TV interrupts.

"They sure are! Pittsburg has had fireworks shows in the past, but this year, the city is going all out! Fourth of July weekend, the city will fill this parking lot with stalls of food, games, anything and every-thing! Clubs from Pittsburg High School will be here raising money and setting up some games as well, so come with empty stomachs!"

The camera changes, showcasing the yacht club. Jim continues to speak, "The show will be at the marina, and if you're interested in partying, the yacht club is opening its doors to everyone! No membership or boat required! Drinks will be served throughout the night."

"It's in about two weeks, right, Jim?"

"Ah! Yes, it is! Forgive me, Harry. I haven't had my coffee today!" Jim laughs.

Sam and Owen glare at me. I take another bite of my food. "Why didn't you say anything?" they both yell.

"A whole fair? Here? That's so cool!" Owen says in awe.

"How long have you known?" Sam points her fork at me. "Were you going to tell us?"

"I was going to! I just... kept forgetting."

"Don't tell me you were planning to do something on your own." I can't deny that, so I take a bite of my potatoes. Sam rolls her eyes and reaches over the table. "*¡Pendejo!*" she shouts, lightly slapping the side of my head.

"I was going to tell you, honestly," I say.

Sam puts her fork down. "Then tell us now. What do you have planned?"

"Diane works at the yacht club, and her last shift is the fireworks. She's probably too paranoid to leave the kids at home, meaning they'll be there with her." I pause. "If we can't get them before..."

"We can get them there," Owen finishes my sentence.

I nod. "At least if Theodore can't convince her in time, we have a backup plan."

"How do we find her though? And when we do, how do we keep track of her?" Sam says.

Owen perks up. "Wait. The reporter said clubs from school will be there raising money. Who do we know that's in a club?"

We sit in silence for a moment, racking our brains trying to think of people we know. Sam's eyes widen. "Helen. Helen's in Key club, and Key club will definitely be there. She can keep an eye on the fair and let us know if she sees anything."

"That's perfect. Paula works at the yacht club too. That's how I found out. She can keep an eye out there." I put my fist out, and my friends do the same. "We're getting them home, one way or another."

As we finish our breakfast, I text the group chat and let them know what we've learned. Pachi says he'll tell Helen. A few seconds later, Helen texts yes. We're all in.

The other thing the news mentions is a severe heatwave. For the next few days, temperatures are in the high nineties, and some days in the hundreds. What's worse, the county is rotating blackouts. It's now day two without power at Pachi's house. He's at mine, sitting in front of a fan with a wet towel draped around his neck. Paula's power went out too, but it came back on last night.

"*¿Tus abuelos estan bien?*" Pachi asks.

"*Si, estan bien.*" I finish washing the dishes and walk over to Pachi. "Are yours okay?"

"Yeah, my family's there right now. Dad fixed their AC, so they're living life over there. Thanks for letting me come over."

"Of course, don't worry about it. Do you know when it's coming back on?"

"No clue, but if it doesn't come on soon, we'll have to spend the night at my abuelos' house. It's too hot in that damn thing."

"Same with Paula. Dad's going to her house after work to see if he can fix her AC. Her power came back, but her AC's busted."

"Doesn't she have a pool?"

Pachi and I look at each other. And when the lights in my house go out with a *whoosh*, we run upstairs to my room. I grab some swim trunks and we hurry to Pachi's car.

We drive down the road and I text Paula that we're on our way. Quickly, she responds. I read the message. "Aw, damn. Pachi, we have to turn back. Her power went out again."

Pachi stares at me for a few seconds. "So? We can still use the pool." Oh no, the heat's getting to his brain.

"The pool won't be clean. When the power goes out, it messes up the filtering or something like that." I show him the text Paula sent. She attached a file stating what to do for pools when the power went out. The first step is to get people out of the pool.

Pachi pulls over so he can read it. When he finishes reading, Pachi groans and leans back in his seat. "It's too hot for this shit!"

We sit in the car for a bit, trying to figure out what to do. Honestly, we don't want to get out because Pachi's AC is blasting on us. I don't care where we go as long as we're out of the heat. I watch the heat waves sizzle in the street. The temperature on my phone says ninety-nine, and it's not even noon.

Pachi pulls out his phone. He turns to me. "Mom needs me to pick up something from Target. Want to come?"

"Yeah, we can get ice cream."

Pachi pulls out from the curb and gets back on the road. The heat is keeping people inside. There are barely any cars out. We arrive at Target quickly, and it's just as hot. Pachi and I run inside the store.

Even the store is emptier than normal. Only two cashiers and no customers in sight. I grab a hand basket and we walk to the food aisle. Pachi wants to get the order when we're done, but I think it's so he can look around the store. After dragging Pachi away from the dollar section, we make it to the ice cream aisle.

"I'm telling you, the cheesecake ice cream is hella good," Pachi says, pulling out a small tub of ice cream.

"You said that about the last one." I laugh. I reach in and pull out another tub. "I'll try it if we get this one." It's a double fudge ice cream. Pachi stares at me, and I grin. He rolls his eyes.

"Who says you're paying?"

"I owe you, so I'm getting it." I throw both containers into the basket and run off. Pachi follows me, still asking what I owe him for.

We run down the aisles. My eyes widen. Flour! I need to get flour. I throw some into the hand basket and continue down the aisles, grabbing more ingredients. I've been craving cupcakes as much as I've been craving to bake. Pachi watches from afar. His eyebrow arches.

"I'm buying this, don't worry." I chuckle.

Pachi goes to the back of the store. It's the seasonal section, and it's filled with lots of pool toys and accessories. He stares at the selection before grabbing some green goggles.

"How many green goggles do you have?" I ask with a smirk.

Pachi rolls his eyes. "Hey, I gave Helen mine." He tosses it into the basket. "You ready to go?"

"Paco! Pachi!" We turn around. Olive runs up to us, carrying a bunch of clothes. Logan and her siblings are behind her.

"Hey Olive!" Pachi smiles. "How have you been?"

"I've been good." Olive holds up her clothes. "We're clothes shopping, and I've never been here before. This place is cool!"

"Olive! Come look at this!" Peter calls from one of the toy aisles.

Olive tosses the clothes into the shopping cart and runs after her brother. Lucy and Leo poke around the video game aisle. Logan pushes the cart and stops next to us. Pachi quickly introduces himself. He hasn't seen Logan since the day we met Olive.

"How's Olive doing?" I ask. She said she was doing good, but I want to make sure.

"She's doing great." Logan smiles, but it drops. I ask why. "It's just... there's so much she's missed out on. I make big breakfasts on the weekends, and Olive got confused. Not to mention, the first morning she went downstairs to make breakfast. Lucy stopped her before she burned down the kitchen."

I wince. "I think they had to make their own food. Theodore does most of it, but Olive helped once or twice."

"I know. That's what she was telling me." Logan sighs. "How's Theodore and Christina? Anything new?" I already told Logan and Olive what happened on Sunday. They're grateful the kids are okay, but still worried. I don't blame them, I am too. We're just waiting that this point. As painful as it is, we don't know what else to do.

"No, he hasn't convinced Christina. I'm just happy I can talk to him." Now that Theodore has his phone, we can text each other. He's been responding faster than I thought he would. I turn to Logan. "He's excited to meet you."

Logan smiles widely. "I never thought this would happen. Never in a million years. I wake up in the morning wondering if this is a dream." Logan looks at his kids. "You know, I've been thinking that since it happened. Hoping it's all a nightmare, and that I'd wake up with her next to me and all our kids home." Logan pauses. "But for the first time, I don't want to wake up. I want it to be real."

Logan turns to us. "I can't thank you and your friends enough. My dream's finally coming true."

Olive runs through the video game aisle with her siblings. She stops to look at the giant TVs, then looks back at us and smiles. It's not fake, not forced, it's a genuine smile.

She's finally home.

15

— · —

I'm back at their house. I look through every closet and open every door. No one is there. Theodore and Christina are gone. Another failed attempt. I close the door to Christina's room and start walking toward the exit.

Creak. Creak. Creak.

Not again, dammit, not again.

SMASH!

She doesn't wait for me to look, and I don't wait for her to move. I run to the door and swing it open. She pulls my arm back, but I punch her again and run down the steps.

"Start the car!" I yell, nearly falling. "Start the——!"

But the car isn't there. Nothing is there. No one is there.

"Pachi? Pachi!" I cry out. I call all of their names, but no one answers.

Diane grabs me. Her hand is covering my mouth, and she pulls me back into the house. I reach out to the light, but the door slams, leaving me in the darkness.

I wake up in a cold sweat and grab the trash can near my bed. I hunch over it and wait for something to happen. Once the room stops spinning, I throw the trash can off to the side. It's the third time this week I've had that dream, and every single time I wake up soaked and want to throw up.

I've always had vivid nightmares, even when I was a kid. It got worse after my dad's assault. It tends to be the same dream over and over, only now someone else haunts my dreams. I shudder. This is so stupid. I'm fine. I'll be fine. I can handle it.

Soft knocks ring throughout the house. I step out of my room and move toward the stairs. I listen closely. The knocks continue, and this time more clearly. I creep down the stairs and walk to the door.

I open the door as slowly as I can. The hot air hits my face. There's a boy at my door. A boy with thick curly hair, tattered clothes, and a giant bruise on his cheek. Not just the bruise. Cuts and scratches all over his face and arms. Tears pour from his eyes. My heart falls, and Theodore starts to shake.

"What happened to you?" I question. My hands reach for him, but he flinches. He lets out a cry and steps back. My arms are frozen. Oh god. What if I hurt him? What if I make it worse?

"I-I'm sorry! I didn't know where to go!" Theodore cries. I shush him. My mom is home, and the door being open isn't —

"*¡Mijo!* What's going on down there?"

Crap! "Nothing, Ma! J-just a salesperson!" I gently grab Theodore's hand and bring him inside. I shut the door behind me and guide him upstairs.

"I might be home late, sweetie! I have a lot of appointments and a lot of hair to cut!" Mom says from behind the door. Her footsteps run up and down the room. Theodore and I tiptoe around my parents' bedroom and make it to mine. As I shut the door, Mom comes flying out. She runs to kiss my forehead. "*Te amo mucho.*"

"*Te amo, Mama.* Have a good day at work!" I tell her as she runs down the stairs and out of the house. I dash to my room when the front door closes. Theodore is sitting on my bed, crying in silence.

"Theodore, what happened?" I reach for his arms more slowly. They're covered in small scratches and cuts, with dried blood around the edges. "Are you okay?"

He shakes his head. "M-Mom kicked me out. I tried to go back inside, but she said she'd kill me." My blood runs cold as he continues. "She's said things like that before, but I think she meant it this time. And I can't reach Christina. She's not answering my messages at all."

She threatened to kill him? And why would she kick him out? Unless... I gulp. "You didn't try your plan, did you?"

"N-no! I didn't!" Theodore cries. "I was talking to her about it like you said, and Mom heard me!" His words come out fast, and he's hyperventilating. His nails dig into his arms. "She found our messages and threw me out! She said to go with Dad and die from God knows what! And that... and that she never wanted me! S-she didn't even want to save me!"

Theodore falls into my chest and bawls. I wrap my arms around him, but he can't stop crying. I rock him back and forth, pat his head, and soothe him in any way I can, but nothing helps. He cries and cries. Tears fall down my face when he finally speaks again. "She yelled at Christina to stay out of it. But she tried defending me, and Mom got angry at her, and I got angry, and... and I yelled at her!" He chokes for air. "I-I tried! I tried, but I couldn't get her out! I'm a failure!"

"You are not a failure," I tell him. I move his head so I can look at him. His eyes are bloodshot. His hand brushes against his nose, trying to clean it. "We're going to save Christina, I promise."

"I've failed both of them. What kind of brother am I?"

"You're an amazing brother," I say, but Theodore shakes his head and falls back onto my chest. Snot dribbles onto my shirt. I hold him tightly, listening as his bawls turn into sniffles, and finally, they stop.

I look at his arms again. Nail marks run up and down, but some scratches are too straight to be from his nails. A couple of them spill blood. I tap his shoulder, and he gets up. "Hey, let's get you patched up and cut your nails." I look down again. His eyes follow. My thumb brushes by a straight mark. "You can't be doing this."

Theodore looks at his arms, his face full of guilt. "I don't mean to. It just happens," Theodore mutters. "I don't even realize I'm doing it."

Theodore follows me to the bathroom. I clean the cuts, and he winces as I wipe them down and put Band-Aids on them. As he clips his nails, I grab my phone and call Sam.

"*¿Qué?*" Sam's voice is groggy. Looks like I woke her up. "What time is it?"

"Can you come over? It's an emergency."

"What happened?" Sam sounds a little more awake. "Are you okay?"

Theodore leans into the phone. "Hi," he says.

"I'll be there in five," Sam says before hanging up.

Sam nearly knocks Theodore over when she gets there. She pulls him into a hug. We're not at my house for long. We get into Sam's truck and drive to Logan's house. Theodore's eyes go wide as we pull up. He looks around the house as we walk to the front door. Sam knocks, and Peter opens it a few seconds later. He steps away to let us in. Theodore hides behind me, not sure what to expect.

Olive walks out from the kitchen. She has orange juice in one hand and a bagel in the other. Her smile widens when she sees us. She puts her food down and runs to Sam, giving her a hug. Sam smiles sadly, and Olive's face falls. "What's wrong?" She looks over Sam's shoulder, and that's when she sees him.

Theodore's arms are stiff at his side. His eyes are watery, but nothing can wipe the smile off his face. They run to each other, embracing immediately. Theodore picks Olive up and swings her. He's crying all over again. The triplets are confused for a few seconds, then it finally hits them.

"Theodore?" Leo asks.

Theodore lets go of Olive and looks at his siblings. He cries harder, and to my surprise, he starts the group hug. He nearly takes Leo to the ground as he pulls him into a tight hug. "You're here! You're really here!" he cheers.

"I don't understand," Olive says, wiping her eyes. "What are you doing here? How did you?" The silence falls quickly. "Where's Christina?"

Theodore frowns. "Mom kicked me out, and I can't call Christina."

Olive's face pales. Worry fills her eyes and she mutters under her breath. But before she can say anything, Peter steps forward. "Did she do that to you?" Peter points to Theodore's cheek. He grabs his arms, eyes going over all the Band-aids and scratches.

"Those are old," Theodore says.

"Is your dad home?" I ask Lucy.

She nods. "He's upstairs in his room. He has to work in a few hours." Leo's already walking up the stairs. A few minutes later, Logan comes downstairs.

Theodore doesn't give Logan time to process. He runs straight into his arms. Logan's doing everything he can to not cry. It's a quicker reunion than the one with Olive. With tears in his eyes, he tells his dad what happened. Logan's face turns red with anger, but he's trying to hide it.

"This isn't your fault." He looks his son in the eyes. "It will never be your fault."

Theodore wipes his face with his hand. "But I couldn't save her," he whispers. "I-I'm a horrible brother."

"You're not." Logan crouches down to his level and pulls him in close. "You protected them in any way you could. You did so much for them. So never, ever think that." Logan hugs Theodore for a while longer, before letting him go to call his work.

Despite his attempts, Logan can't get the day off. Too many people called in sick. Sam and I stay at the house with the kids. Leo and Peter are upstairs, getting Theodore's bed ready. Logan already bought the bunk beds. The boys don't want any help, saying it's a surprise.

Lucy is downstairs with us, listening to Theodore's story. He talks about what happened since we visited him that night. He's been telling Christina about his plan every day. From what it sounds like, she was getting more interested in it.

His stomach interrupts him. It growls loudly, and Olive glares at him. "When's the last time you ate?" she questions in a tone I've never heard before.

Theodore turns pale, and he visibly shrinks. "Last night," he responds, but there's a level of uncertainty in his voice. Olive groans, grabs his hand, and drags him to the kitchen. She pushes him into a chair and opens the fridge, taking out eggs.

"Olive, I'm not hungry," he protests.

"Your stomach shouted otherwise," Olive responds. Theodore protests again, saying he doesn't want to eat. Olive sighs. "You're going to get sick again. You can't keep doing this."

"Olive, please. I don't want you to get hurt." Olive freezes. She says nothing as she pours oil into the pan.

"I can make it, Olive," I say, poking my head into the kitchen. She doesn't move. "Or I can show you tips." She nods.

I show Olive how to flip the eggs over. Theodore asks for over-easy. As Olive keeps an eye on the eggs, I look in the fridge. What else can I make for him? Theodore is *skinny*, about as skinny as Olive was when I first met her, if not more. I'm guessing by Olive's reaction, this happens a lot.

I find the bagels the kids were eating earlier and give one to Theodore. He puts jam on it. When we put the eggs in front of him, he licks his lips. At first, he eats it so fast, but then he stops. Olive sits next to him, giving him the other half of the bagel.

Olive stares at him. "I'm not leaving until you finish it all. You need to eat."

"I'm full already." He's only eaten one egg and a few bites of the bagel. His stomach growls again. Olive grabs his fork, stabs his food, and holds it up to his mouth. Theodore quickly takes it out of her hand and eats some more.

"These are the best eggs I've ever had," Theodore admits. "Thank you."

Olive smiles, but it doesn't last. Her eyes go over her brother's wounds, and then her hands. Her fingers brush over the wounds and she sighs. "What happened? Why haven't you been eating?"

Theodore shakes his head. "Nothing. Just with everything... I haven't had time to eat. I didn't want to." Theodore says, and I think he's about to cry again. "Mom doesn't care anymore."

"Is Christie okay?" Olive asks.

"I don't know. Mom's not yelling at her as much anymore, but she's still angry. I yelled at her, Olive. I actually yelled at Mom. And even more, Christina yelled at her."

Olive's eyes grow big. "She did? How come?"

Theodore chuckles. "I couldn't believe it either. But she was defending me. I think I got something through to her. Maybe she's finally realizing."

I take a seat at the dining table when they finish talking. "Theodore, why didn't you call me?" I ask. "I could've come and got you. How long were you outside my house?"

"Not long. Mom kicked me out at four. It took longer getting there."

"Still, you should've called. Hell, Sam and I both drive! We could've picked you up!"

"I didn't want to bother you," Theodore says.

I hold out my hand, and Theodore gives me his phone. His screen looks worse than before, but it's usable. I put my phone number in, and Sam puts hers in. I give him Owen's, Pachi's, and Yann's. Just in case.

"Theodore! Your surprise is ready!" Leo yells from upstairs.

Peter comes down and takes us to their room. He pushes the door open. The bunk bed is the first thing I see. Leo lies on the top bunk and points to the right. It's the loft bed they were talking about, with green blankets and stuffed animals. A small desk is under the bed, along with a dresser.

Theodore gasps and walks closer to the bed. Stars sparkle in his eyes. "This is mine?" Theodore climbs up the ladder. "This is so cool!" He looks at a plush on the bed. It's a lion. "I love lions," he says.

Theodore gets off his bed and pulls his brothers into a hug. Leo's smile falls when Theodore starts to cry, but he smiles. "They're happy tears, Leo. Happy tears."

He seems to be taking everything well, but I'm still worried. I step toward him. "Theodore, can I talk to you?" He nods. I look at the tuplets and Sam. They take the hint and leave the room. Olive looks at me with worry in her eyes, but she shuts the door.

"How are you feeling?" I ask.

Theodore tilts his head. "What do you mean?"

"About everything. You've been through a lot, and I want to know if you're okay."

Theodore looks at his lion, running his fingers through the mane. "I'm fine," he says, giving me a wide smile.

His voice gets higher when he lies. The night we stormed Diane's house, his voice was high whenever he gave her excuses. It was high when he told Olive he ate last night, and it's high now.

I frown. "You don't have to lie."

Theodore's face falls. His eyes are droopy, with heavy bags under them. They cast off to the side, and a tear rolls down his cheek. "I'm worried about Christie. I don't know what to do now."

"Has she answered your texts?"

He looks at his phone again. "No, but she's read them." He exhales. Theodore types another message, asking Christina if she's okay. She reads the message instantly but doesn't reply.

"I can still text her." Theodore's voice is brittle. "If she's reading my messages…" His head perks up, and he smiles. "I can convince her to come here!"

My eyes widen. Theodore looks at his phone and takes a deep breath. "I can tell Christina everything. How nice Dad is, and how fun our siblings are!" Theodore's smile drops. He looks down at his phone. "And how they actually love us."

I put an arm around him, and he leans into me. "She'll be able to run. She's quiet and quick. Confidence is what she needs. She doesn't like breaking rules, disobeying Mom, or anything like that. If she knows she'll be okay, then she'll do it." Theodore sighs. "I just have to convince her. I just have to wait. Wait for her to come. Wait for her to realize she's in a hellhole." Theodore chokes on a sob. "I hate waiting!"

I hold him in my arms and listen to him cry. Minutes later, Olive comes in to check on us. When I look at him, Theodore's fast asleep. She gasps, and tears fill her eyes.

"He's never been able to sleep like that," Olive says. "He wouldn't let us hug him whenever he had a nightmare. He couldn't sleep with someone holding him."

I pat the bed and Olive sits next to me. She stares at her brother. A curl falls in his face. Olive pushes it behind his ear. "He looks so happy." Olive hiccups. "He's the best brother I could ask for. And I stressed him out, so much."

"You're both here now. That's all that matters."

"Not all of us."

There's a pit in my stomach when she says that. "We won't rest until she's here," I assure her. All I can do is assure her. Olive looks at me. "I swear on my life."

"I know." Olive sighs. "I know."

I keep losing track of the days. It's been almost a week since Theodore was kicked out, and the fireworks show is in four days. I've been texting him back and forth, and he's a lot happier now. Olive says he's eating more, but other than that, there's nothing new. He had one message from his mother, saying he'll regret not coming home.

Christina hasn't responded to any of his texts, but she's been reading them. Theodore texts her small things, like what he's been up to and what food he's been eating. He tells her that Logan already loves her and sends a picture of her new room. Even Olive's sent a couple of messages. She tells Christina about us, Rose, and that she misses her. Christina hasn't responded to Olive either. Theodore calls every day, but she never answers. I can't shake the feeling that something bad is going to happen.

It makes my blood boil. Diane's doing this on purpose, I know it. The moment I see her, she's going down. But I can't fight. Sure, give me a bat and I can swing hard, but with my fists? I'm screwed. I'm surprised I didn't get put in the hospital after the fight with Renise.

I knock on the white door and wait for it to open. Mrs. Torre is behind it. She smiles and lets me know Yann is upstairs. I catch him just in time. He looks like he's about to go work out.

"Are those boxing lessons still on the table?" I ask him. He offered them sometime after we stormed Diane's house.

Yann blinks, trying to process what I said. Once he does, he nods and smiles. "Yeah, of course."

I follow Yann down the stairs and into the gym, grabbing two water bottles before we leave. Lobo watches curiously, but stays in the kitchen, waiting for crumbs to fall. Mrs. Torre is making lumpia. If I was Lobo, I would wait there too. Yann turns on the lights in the gym and grabs two sets of gloves. He throws the black ones at me and puts his red gloves on.

"Okay, we're going to start off with a peek-a-boo stance," Yann says, turning toward me.

"Peek-a-boo?" I wonder, putting on the gloves.

"Yeah, that's what it's called. Basically…" Yann put his hands up, blocking his face. "You hold your hands in front of you like this. That way, you can block punches coming at your face. This is more of a defensive stance. Like this, you can wait for an opening."

"I never see you do that." I've been to a few of his matches, and most of the time, he throws the first punch. "You just start swinging."

Yann chuckles. "Oh, believe me. When I first started boxing, I only did that stance. I don't use it that often because of how long I've been boxing. I'm more of a swarmer boxer, but I'll get to that later." Yann smacks his hands together. "Put them up."

"Like this?" I put my hands up and try to copy how he's standing. I feel like an idiot.

"Yeah, but fix your feet." His foot kicks my shoe a bit. "You look like a tree. And don't forget to bend your knees." Yann moves around me, adjusting my form before we move on.

"I know the whole point is to wait, but what if there isn't an opening?" I ask. "What if I get hit over and over?"

"Oh, believe me, there will be. If you keep it up, they're going to get tired. Then mad, and then their punches will be sloppy. They'll be slower to react. I know it's tedious, but it works. That's how I've won a few matches, and how I've lost some."

I nod. Yann throws a few light punches. I think he's more concerned if I can block them or not. They're quick, but not full force. His speed increases as we practice more. When I block ten in a row, that's when we move on.

The next few minutes we spend working on punches. Follow through, using your hips, even fixing my fists. Yann has a lot of patience with me. Something is wrong with my punch every time, but he corrects me with no complaints. Once Yann decides it's enough, he turns back to the punching bag.

"Okay, pretend the bag is someone you hate." *Diane,* I think to myself. Yann touches the bag lightly, enough for it to start swinging. "Let's pretend the fight started, and they've thrown the first punch." The bag comes toward him, and Yann hops out of the way. The bag comes again, and Yann once again dodges it.

"You have to be prepared to move. Don't stand still," he says, jumping out of the way. The tension builds. It's like a cat-and-mouse game. I know the bag can't hurt him, but watching it come close makes shivers go up and down my spine.

Yann waits till the bag slows down, then *WHAM!* He hits the bag square in the middle. The bag flies backward, falling toward him crookedly, not like it was earlier. Yann doesn't have to move for the bag to miss him. Yann throws another punch at it. The same thing. The bag jolts in different directions. Then Yann goes all out. He throws punch after punch, to the point where I feel bad for the punching bag.

The bag's chain is the only thing keeping it from hitting the wall. He punches it one last time. The thud sends the room into shakes. I stare in fear. I know Yann is stronger than the average fifteen-year-old, but holy shit! He sent it flying!

Yann laughs at my expression and stops the bag. He presses a button on his phone, and music blares out of the speakers. "Okay, now your turn."

The one thing I hate about sports is the one-on-one training. It's embarrassing when the coaches pull me to the side to work with them. Yann shouts comments here and there. Fix my form, react quicker, hips, full force. When I finally hit hard, Yann cheers so loud that I almost get hit by the punching bag on its way down.

Yann smiles and turns down the music. "Yeah! I think you're ready now." I turn to face him. He smacks his fists together. "Let's do this."

"Huh? What do you mean?" I stare at him, then my eyes widen. "Wait, I have to fight you? I don't want to do that! What if I—!"

I barely block Yann's fist as it comes flying toward me. I hold it, staring at him in shock. Yann smirks as he brings his arm back. "You need to be prepared for anything. You ready for real?" I nod, and the fight begins.

I block a few more of Yann's punches and land one on his side. I grin and go for another. Yann blocks it, but I'm ready for whatever he's got planned.

"Your mom's a bitch!"

"What?" Yann's fist hits the left side of my face. My hand flies to my cheek and I back away. "What the hell was that for?"

"I don't mean it! But look, once I said that, your guard dropped," Yann says. Jeez, he's right. "You need to ignore what I'm saying. If you let your emotions get the best of you, you're going to lose."

I put my hands up again. Yann throws a right hook, and I move out of the way. I jump back when he throws another one. My hands guard my face as I wait for an opening.

There it is. I throw a right hook at him, and it lands on his left temple. Yann puts a hand on his face. "Not bad." He hops, his arms hanging loosely at his sides. "But can you block this?" He throws a jab at my left. I can't block it, but I move just in time. It doesn't land.

"You're an asshole!" Yann yells. I flinch and barely avoid his punch. "You... smell weird!" I block that one easily and push him back. "Your pink hair's stupid!" His punch lands right in my chest, knocking the wind out of me.

Yann frowns as I wheeze. "You okay? We can stop if you want."

"No." I cough. "Keep going."

No matter what I throw at him, he never breaks eye contact. His swarmer style makes a lot more sense now. I feel bad for whoever he fought. There's no space between us, and he moves fast. All I can do is block. If I try to fight back, he will nail me. What's worse, he's still throwing insults and taunts to distract me. I keep having to remind myself he doesn't mean it.

"You're stupid!" He throws a jab, and I move back. "You suck at video games!" That one is easy to block, and I punch his chest. Dodge after dodge, taunt after taunt, I block them all. Yann's getting tired. He's drenched in sweat, and his punches are slowing down.

"You're a shitty friend!" Yann yells. I block Yann's punch. His eyes go wide, and there's a clear opening. My uppercut lands clean. He backs off, groaning in pain. "Shit! Damn, that was good!" Yann holds one hand forward, keeping the other one on his jaw. "You did really good."

I fist-bump him. He smiles and takes off his gloves, and I take off mine. I know he was trying to get to me, but is that what he really thinks? I turn to him. "Do you really think I'm a shitty friend?"

Yann's eyes go wide. "No, of course not! I've never thought that." Yann throws his gloves to the side. We stand in brief silence before he takes a deep breath. "In fact, have I ever told you why I got into boxing?"

I shake my head. Yann and I sit on the weight bench. He sighs. "I wasn't well-liked at school, and my parents wanted to put me in a sport. I got picked on a bit, so I chose boxing. Fought a classmate in the ring and lost what friends I had. You and everyone else are my first real friends." He pauses. "When you guys invited yourselves to my match, I didn't expect you to show up. But all of you were in the stands cheering me on, and I started crying."

Yann smiles. "So, no, you're not a shitty friend. Never have been." Now I want to cry. Yann gets up from the bench. "And before you ask, your pink hair isn't stupid."

I smile back. "Thanks for this."

"Don't mention it. You did good." He hands me a water bottle. "I'm always up for a rematch. No insulting this time."

"No, it's okay, I'll throw some out myself." I chuckle. "I'm kidding."

Yann rolls his eyes, and we run back inside his house to escape the heat.

16

TWO MORE DAYS. THAT'S all we have, and I think we have the upper hand. Theodore just called to let me know that Christina finally responded to his messages. She sent him a text saying hi. Theodore doesn't know why, but he's happy she finally answered. She still hasn't answered his calls, which isn't sitting right with any of us. But now is our chance. Theodore's going to text her all day to convince her to run.

Rose is at my house. Her parents are at work, and her power went out. I picked her up and brought her here. To my surprise, her parents were okay with it. We're upstairs, lying on my bed, staring at the ceiling fan. Despite it being on the highest setting, I'm sweating like crazy. I look at Rose. Her cheeks are pink, and she's also sweating. My face gets hotter as she looks at me. She gives me a soft smile. No matter what, she's so beautiful.

"Do you want to eat something?" I ask. I'm not sure what time it is, but I haven't eaten, and my stomach is growling.

"Yeah, food sounds good," she says.

We go down to the kitchen and look inside the fridge. Rose isn't that hungry, so I decide to make a charcuterie board. I pull out some cheese, salami, and grapes. Rose and I stare inside the fridge for a while, letting the cool air hit our faces. Rose grabs crackers from the cabinet, and I pull out a board to use. A minute later, it's ready to eat.

Rose and I take our food to the couch. I place the board on the coffee table, and Rose grabs the book next to it. I turn on the TV and flip through a few channels before landing on the news. The heatwave isn't going to stop anytime soon, and the hottest day of the week is Saturday, with a high of 104. I turn off the TV after that. There isn't anything good on.

The book Rose grabbed turns out to be the family album. Mom was going through it last night. Rose flips through the pages and smiles. "Oh my gosh! Is that you?"

I look quickly. She points to an old photo of me and Sam. I cringe. I hate looking at old photos of myself, hate seeing what I looked like. I only like this photo because Sam is in it, and back then she was the only one who didn't care what I looked like. The photo was of us on the first day of sixth grade. My hair was still brown, and Sam still had braces. The jacket I had on was visibly tight on me.

"You look adorable." Rose rubs my cheek. "Still do!" I try to smile and she frowns, asking me what's wrong.

"Nothing, just glad I got rid of that jacket."

Rose slams the book shut and sits up straight. "If you keep talking like that, I will throw you on the couch and compliment you for an entire hour."

I laugh. "You can't pick me up."

"Bet." Rose and I stand. She wraps her arms around my waist and tries to lift me. I don't budge. "My point still stands." Rose pouts, sitting on the couch in defeat.

Rose hands me my phone as I sit. It buzzes with a text message from Lucy. However, it's a heavily edited photo of her, and it's a meme. She sends a message after.

Lucy: OMG! Theodore made that!

Rose and I laugh. She lets out a sigh as she leans on my shoulder. "Has Christina responded? Other than the first text?"

I look at my texts with Theodore. He's sent screenshots of his conversation with Christina. It's mostly him talking, but Christina has answered a few times. "Yes, but they're quick replies," I tell Rose, and my phone goes off again. It's a text from Lucy.

Lucy: Dad's getting pizza tonight for Olive and Theodore. You and your friends are invited. We want to thank you for everything. It'll be at six.

I turn to Rose. "Do you want to come too?"

"I'd love to!" She pulls out her phone and goes to her mom's contact. "Mom's been more lenient too, so I should be able to stay late!"

"Did you end up making a PowerPoint presentation?" I joke.

Rose shakes her head. "We talked it out. She apologized for the argument. They still have my location, but I have theirs too. It's not that bad. I can see when they're coming home with dinner." I love that about her. She finds the good in everything.

"You want to help me make cupcakes for the party?" I've been wanting some for the past few days. Now I finally have time, and an excuse to make them.

Rose and I start baking. I show her the measurements of flour and sugar, and she pours it in. I made the recipe myself, and I haven't used box mix since. I add the rest in and whisk it. Later, I pull the first batch out of the oven. Rose and I frost the cupcakes and eat some, while the second batch bakes. She frosts the second and I grab more flour and eggs, getting ready to make a new batch. I crack the eggs into the batter. We stay silent as I whisk. Rose clears her throat.

"You know, Owen told me that you bake a lot when you're stressed."

The whisking slows. "Oh, he did?" I ask, trying to play dumb.

"Yeah." She puts the tub of pink frosting down and takes a few steps toward me. "He said your house smelled like dough for over a week because of marching band auditions."

The whisking stops. Dammit, Owen! He's not wrong. I was so worried I wouldn't make it in. If I wasn't practicing, I was in the kitchen. Bread, cupcakes, cookies, and I made dinner the whole week. I was stressed for nothing; I did amazing on the audition. I don't get why he told her though.

"Sam mentioned it too, and Pachi, and Yann. They're kind of worried about you." So that's why Pachi looked at me funny when I grabbed everything at Target. I put the bowl down on the counter and turn to her. She's fiddling with her hands. There's flour and frosting all over her adorable face.

"I'm okay, Rose. Really." I give her a smile, but she doesn't smile back. She doesn't believe me.

"You can tell me anything," she says, taking my hand in hers. "What's wrong?"

"It's nothing, *mi amor*. I don't want you to worry."

Rose pulls me close. My face turns red, and I look away. She holds my face and turns me toward hers. There's so much concern and love in her eyes. I melt under her touch and lean into her hand. She rubs my cheek with her thumb. "Please, talk to me," she whispers.

I hold her hand against my face. I don't want her to ever let go. "Do you remember when my friends and I stormed her house?" Rose nods. "I've been having nightmares about it. Each time, I get out, but when I yell at Pachi to start the car, he's gone. All my friends are gone. So, Diane catches me, drags me back inside, and... she kills me."

Rose turns pale. Worry fills her eyes and I stare at the ground. "You said she scared you, but I didn't know it was that bad. What did she do?" Rose asks.

My mouth opens and shuts, but she holds my hand tighter, urging me on. "She said if she had her gun, she would've killed me." I feel her body tense. "I didn't want to believe it, but Theodore said she threatened to kill him too."

"Why do you hide things? You don't have to keep it to yourself. You can talk to me about it, or any of your friends. We're all here for you."

"But I'd be saying the same things over and over again. She scared me, and I'm stressing over it. That's it." I look away again. "That's it, really."

"That doesn't mean you keep your feelings to yourself!" Rose's frown makes me want to cry. This is why I didn't want to tell her. I don't want to worry her. I don't want anyone to worry about me. Rose squeezes my hand, holding back tears. "It won't bother me. I *want* you to tell me what's going on. I'm here for you, no matter what. You believe that, right?"

I sigh. "I'm scared. I'm just really scared."

"If I were you, I would be too. You're doing a lot for these kids, but you can't do everything. And with Christina, we just have to wait." I frown, and Rose sighs. "I know. I'm worried too. It'll be okay."

Her soft smile makes my heart race. My cheeks get hotter. I let go of her hand and put mine on her cheek, holding it gently. There aren't a lot of things I'm afraid of, but losing everything is one of them. Everything has grown over the years. My family, my friends, and now Rose and the tuplets.

My thumb brushes against her cheek. I mutter her name, and she looks at me. Blush creeps on her face as we step closer. Closer, closer, so close. My lips land on hers. Her lips taste like the cupcakes we made. So sweet and full of love. I hold her close to me as the kiss deepens. This life I'm living, and the friends I have, I'll always fight for it. I'll always fight for them. So, I'm going to keep my promise to Olive. I'm going to get the tuplets home no matter what.

And I swear on my life I'll keep everyone safe.

I park in front of Logan's house. Rose gets out of the car and helps me bring the cupcakes inside. Logan waves as we put the cupcakes on the kitchen counter. He's on the phone ordering pizza. I take Rose up the stairs to find the tuplets.

The bedrooms are almost complete. Both rooms now have bunk beds inside. I poke my head into the girls' room. The tuplets are playing a board game. Owen and Yann are there too. Olive gets up to greet us.

"I brought cupcakes," I say, and the tuplets' eyes light up. "After dinner!"

The front door opens, and Sam's voice follows. Olive runs past me and dashes down the stairs to greet her. She crashes into Pachi on the way down. No one else comes. Logan's saving the big party for when Christina comes home. He comes upstairs to let us know he's leaving to get the pizza. We play some games to pass the time.

"No insane dares," Peter pleads, and Olive smirks.

"I dare you to run around the room and sing that song you showed me earlier. Very loudly." Olive laughs. No mercy for Peter.

"Okay! Let's play a different game," I say. Olive pouts, while Peter sighs in relief.

"What about that random question generator?" Sam suggests. "We did that during band. Maybe they have better questions now."

Owen pulls out his phone and looks up the generator. Once he finds it, we form a circle, and he places his phone in the middle. Lucy yells "nose goes" to pick who goes first, and I'm the last one to react.

"Have you and Rose kissed yet?" Olive asks with a smirk.

"W-what?" I turn bright red, and Rose excuses herself to get another drink. "A different question!" I stammer.

Pachi asks the same question in Spanish. "*¡Cállate!*" I yell, smacking him on his arm. My blush deepens as I remember this morning. "Yes," I whisper.

It's like someone's on fire. Cheers erupt and Yann cheers the loudest. He's jumping and pointing to Sam. "Twenty bucks! You owe me twenty bucks!"

Sam holds her head in her hands. Twenty bucks? If Pachi and I are bad at bets, then those two are even worse! "How could you do this to me, Paquito?" Sam cries.

"You bet twenty bucks on a kiss!" I defend. I look between them. "What exactly was the bet, anyway?"

"Nothing!" Sam and Yann answer. Yann sits back down, and Sam reaches for her wallet. She hands Yann a twenty, wiping a fake tear from her eye.

"Am I coming to the wedding?" Olive questions.

"Ooh! Can I be the ring bear?" Theodore asks excitedly.

"Considering you're dating *my* tutor, can I be a groomsman?" Leo smirks. "Which, by the way, I give you my blessing." I hear Rose chuckle as she comes up the stairs.

My face is hot and I roll my eyes. "One question only! And we're using the generator!"

"This seems way more fun though." Pachi grins. Rose returns and sits next to me, her face as red as her hair.

"I'll try it," Theodore says, and he presses the button. "What's the best thing you got from your parents?" His face falls, and his mouth hangs open. His lips form words, but nothing comes out.

"Let me try." Olive presses the button, but her question isn't good either. "Biggest regret?"

Owen takes his phone out of the center. "Well, that was a bust. Olive, I can ask a different question if you want."

"No, it's okay." Olive sighs. "It's obvious, stupidly obvious, but trusting my mom. Now that I'm here, I can see it. She never loved me." She looks at Theodore. "Never loved us. All these years, I've been begging, praying for her to love me. She said she did, but it wasn't the truth."

The door opens after Olive stops talking. It's the pizza. We don't move, even after Logan calls for us. We stare at Olive, who looks at us, confused. "Why are you just sitting here? Go eat! I'll clean up." She shoos us away.

Rose takes the triplets downstairs. Olive makes Theodore go with them. He protests, but in the end, he goes down. Now, it's just the six of us in this quiet room.

"Are you okay, Olive?" I ask.

Olive shakes her head and stomps to her bed. "No. No. Dammit, no."

My friends and I look at each other with worry. I sit next to Olive, asking her what's wrong. Olive shakes her head, but tears fall from her face.

"I was a tool. A punching bag. A scapegoat. And yet... I miss her." Her own words hit her like a truck, and she sobs. "I don't know what's wrong with me. She was horrible to me, she hated me, and she said I should've died. And I miss her. I don't know why I miss her!"

My heart breaks into pieces. I don't know what to do. I can offer comfort, hugs, and even food, but words of advice? I can't give anything. Although... maybe I can tell her something.

"I kind of get it," I mutter. Olive looks at me. "When I was younger, I didn't have a lot of friends. Good ones, I mean. Sam was my only true friend throughout elementary school. The few I did make ended up turning on me. I wasn't smart enough, wasn't popular, my looks weren't great, anything, really."

I sigh. "For a long time, I let the bullying happen. I thought they were good people. They were in the memories I had. I thought they would change, and I didn't want to lose them. In the end, I did, and if it wasn't for Sam and everyone else, I don't know what would've happened."

Owen steps forward, catching our attention. He sighs. "I know how you feel. For a while, I missed Renise. Despite everything she put me through, there were still some good moments, and I loved her. I missed who she used to be."

I place my hand on Olive's shoulder. "It's okay to miss her. I think it's a bit hard not to. But you need to know she should've never treated you like that. No one should ever treat you that way, especially people who claim to love you. Someone who loves you wouldn't do this." I look at the scar on her arm. I sigh. "I know it's hard, but you can talk to me, your siblings, your dad, hell, any of us. We're all here for you."

Olive can't hold back anymore. She puts her head in her hands and cries. We sit with her, showing our support in any way we can. The stairs creak, and I turn to look. Logan is standing in the doorway, holding a plate of pizza. The tuplets and Rose are behind him. Logan gives the pizza to Lucy and walks to Olive. Olive looks at him, tears in her eyes, and hugs him tightly.

Everyone eats dinner in the girls' room. We sit on the floor, the beds, it doesn't matter where. Olive's ready to go downstairs when everyone finishes eating. Part of me thinks it's because of the cupcakes, but in the end, as long as she's happy.

The night goes on. We play games and share stories, but time flies by. Rose leaves around nine. Her parents come to pick her up. They greet Logan and they take a few cupcakes home. I kiss Rose's head and wave her off. The party winds down. Pachi leaves after he falls asleep on the couch, then Sam and Owen. I offer Yann a ride home, and he agrees. The tuplets head to bed. I say bye to Logan and toss Yann the keys. He's about to fall asleep and I need to use the bathroom.

I reach the top of the stairs and see Theodore coming out of his room. He's not in his pajamas. The floor creaks, and his hands jump to his chest and his body shakes. Once he realizes it's me, he puts them down.

"Are you okay?" I ask.

"Can I talk to you? About Olive?" Theodore asks softly.

I nod and step closer. "Is everything okay?"

Theodore stutters, "Could you keep an eye on Olive? I know we're here and everything, but could you still?" He trails off. "I'm just worried, and I know you're a good person. She talks about you and your friends a lot."

"She does?" I ask, feeling a bit flattered.

"Yeah. She trusts you guys a lot. We all do." Theodore's smile is sad. "You've saved us. You really did. I never thought this would be my life, our lives." Tears fill his eyes, and his voice cracks. "You're truly one of the best people I've ever met."

I wrap him in a hug and pat his head, hoping to make him feel a little better. It's not a long hug, but he looks happier. After that, Theodore goes back to his room, and Yann and I head home.

Will I ever be able to sleep in again? At least I didn't have that nightmare. My phone rings loudly. I don't look at who's calling. When I say hello, I tense up. The voice on the other end is frantic and breathing heavily.

"He's gone! He's gone!"

My body turns cold as the voice continues to cry. "What? Who? Wait, who is this?"

"Theodore! Theodore's gone!" The hysterical voice is Leo's, and everything clicks into place. Theodore is gone. Theodore is... what?!

"What do you mean he's gone?" I throw off the covers and grab some shorts off the floor, putting them on as fast as I can. I run around my room, trying to find a clean shirt.

"He's not here!" Leo cries. "The front door was unlocked, but his stuff is still here! We can't find him anywhere! We searched the whole house!" Leo is five seconds away from a breakdown. His breathing worsens, and he can't stop sobbing.

I snatch my keys off the counter and fly out the door. I start my mom's car and take off. "I'm on my way. Leo, please try to calm down. We're going to find him."

"Why is this happening? Why is this happening?" Leo wails. "Dad's not even home! He's at work! I don't know what to do!"

"You have to tell him," I say. I slam on the brakes, realizing there's a stop sign. "Look, I'll be there soon. We'll figure it out together."

We tear the house upside down. The closets, the backyard, the garage, we look absolutely everywhere. I take Lucy down the block, and we yell out his name. No response. He's gone. It's like he disappeared into thin air.

Is that why we had that conversation last night? Was that a goodbye? Was he trying to leave then? Why didn't I notice? I should've stayed longer. I should've talked to him more. I should've done something to help him. I should've done something to help Christina.

Lucy and I return to the house. The tuplets' faces fall when we walk inside without him. Leo paces up and down the hallway. His phone is in his hand, practicing the words to tell his dad. Peter is with him, but he can't stop crying either. Lucy sits on the couch. She presses herself against the cushions, her arms tightly around her body. Olive is in her brothers' room, and I find her in Theodore's bed under the covers.

I climb up the ladder to check on her. She sits up and looks at me. I don't know what to do, so like always, I offer her a hug. She cries into my shoulder, snot dripping onto my shirt. After a few minutes of that, she returns to the covers. I leave her alone.

I enter the girls' room to start cleaning the mess we made. It's the least I can do. After I make Lucy's bed, I go to Olive's. As I pick up the pillow, a piece of paper comes with it, stuck to the fabric. It's like déjà vu.

Olive, I'm so sorry, but Christina's in danger. I don't want to leave you, but I have to protect her. I failed you both once, and I won't fail again. Leo, Lucy, Peter, I love you guys. This isn't your fault, it's hers. Tell Dad I love him. Thank you for everything.

I can't help but cry. But as I read the letter over and over, my blood starts to boil. I take the letter back to Olive. She comes down from the bed and reads it. Her eyes go wide, and her fists clench the paper. She curses under her breath, damning her mother and all the hell she puts them through.

Olive throws the letter to the floor and runs to her room. I chase after her. She grabs her phone and taps quickly. The phone rings. My face turns pale. Is she… is she calling her mom?

"Theodore." I sigh in relief. "I'm not mad. I promise I'm not." Olive's voice shakes. "But please let me know if you're okay."

Olive hangs up the call and stares at her phone. I look over her shoulder. It's her messages with Theodore. She's sent a bunch since this morning, but he's finally responded. They're screenshots of a conversation. Olive taps on it.

Christina: Mom keeps spending money. She just bought a firework and a bunch of wine bottles. I don't know what she's doing, but it's scaring me.

The timestamps of the messages are during the party. Right when Logan came home with pizza.

Christina: She drank a whole bottle. She keeps going off about you and Olive.

Christina: Can you come home?! She's yelling at me again! She's trying to break down the door!

Christina: She's waving the gun around again! I don't know what to do! She won't listen to me! She won't put it away!

Christina: Theodore!

The second screenshot shows three missed calls from Christina. One right after the other. Olive taps on the third screenshot, showing the last messages.

Christina: PLEASE COME HOME I'M SCARED!

Theodore: I'll be home by morning. I need to sneak out. I'm so sorry.

My heart shatters, and Olive starts to cry again. For a while, we sit on the bed. Holding on to each other as the tears roll down our faces.

What do we do now? What can we do? If Diane has them both and is willing to threaten them, anything can happen.

No. I can't think like this. I can't give up yet. There's still time to save them. We have a whole day to figure out our plan. I was hoping it didn't come to this, but we don't have a choice now.

My phone goes off. I take it out of my pocket, tears falling on my screen as I read the message.

Theodore: This is my last message. I'm so sorry. Please take care of Olive for me, and thank you for everything.

The floorboards creak, and we turn to the left. Leo's standing in the doorway. He steps into the room, holding his phone in his hand. "Ol, Dad wants to talk to you," Leo stammers.

Olive slowly rises from the bed. She walks to her brother and takes the phone out of his hands. She mutters hello and leaves the room. I stumble out into the hallway and go inside the bathroom. My body trembles as I grip the sink counter. *Breathe.* Tears fall down my face. *Breathe.* They turn into sobs as I sink against the wall. *Breathe. Breathe. Breathe.*

I need to stay strong for the tuplets. If they see me like this, they might think it's over. It's not. There's still a chance. We still have time. God... I'm praying we still have time.

I pull my phone out of my pocket. My fingers linger over the keys. Each click from the keyboard makes my heart hurt more. I send the message to the group chat, still hoping this is a nightmare.

Me: Theodore's gone.

17

"T-THERE HAS TO BE something we can do!" Sam says through tears. The FaceTime call started not even ten seconds after I sent the text. "Is he answering calls? Texts?"

"No, not really." My voice cracks. "He sent Olive the screenshots after she called and sent me one last text. It's been radio silence since."

"What do we do?" Owen cries.

"We'll have to go with the backup plan. That's our only option now."

"We've barely talked about it!" Sam groans.

"It's better than nothing," Yann admits. "At this point, it's all we got."

I sigh. "I'll talk to Paula later today. Pachi, will you talk to Helen?"

Pachi nods. "I will."

My phone buzzes. The ringtone is the default one, but the contact is saved. My eyes widen. "Theodore's calling me."

"Answer it!" Owen yells.

I leave the group call and answer Theodore's. "H-hello? Theodore? Are you okay?" My questions come out fast. There's heavy breathing on the other side. I call his name out again. "Are you okay?"

"I knew you would answer for him."

I sit straight up as fear runs through my body. Why the hell does she have his phone? "Where's Theodore?" I question.

"I'm only going to say this once..."

"Where are the kids?" I yell.

"They're home. And if you interfere with justice tomorrow, you will be sorry."

"Bring it on, bitch." I hiss. "If you try anything, if you hurt them in any way, I will break every bone in your goddamn body." Part of me doesn't want to believe the words that just came out of my mouth, but dammit, I'll do anything to stop her from hurting them.

I sit on the bathroom floor for a few minutes after Diane hangs up. My friends blow up my phone. The buzzing becomes static in my ears. I look up at the ceiling. How the hell did this happen? Theodore said Christina was open to it, and now... this.

I splash water on my face and step outside. I meet the tuplets downstairs, where they're helping their dad through the door. Sobs leave him as he sits on the couch. "My boy," he mumbles through his cries, "my little boy."

Olive watches as I take my keys out of my pocket. I wave to the triplets, although none of them are looking at me. Olive follows me out the door. She stares at me with bloodshot eyes.

"We're going to get them back." I pull Olive into a hug. "It's going to be okay."

"I hope you're right." Olive sniffles.

The hours leading up to the fireworks show are uncomfortable and stressful. My friends gather at my house around four. The fair doesn't open until six. Helen will be our eyes down there. Paula's shift ends at eight, and Diane is supposed to start after. We sit on the couch in silence. Dread runs up and down my veins. I send a few more texts to Theodore, but he hasn't responded.

Someone knocks on the door. I run to open it. To my surprise, it's Logan. The tuplets are behind him, so I let them inside. Olive gives me a hug. She's wearing the blue tank top and star-patterned shorts I saw her get at Target. Her hair is pulled up into a bun.

"Dad did it." She smiles, showing it off. She sits next to Sam, and her siblings sit on the couch with their dad.

Logan looks at me with bags under his eyes. The usual sparkle behind them has faded. He looks horrible. "Leo says you have a plan?" His voice is hoarse.

I nod. "Diane's working at the yacht club tonight, and they're leaving the state right after. Theodore and Christina are going to be with her. My sister works the shift before hers, and we have someone keeping an eye on the fair. The moment we find them, we grab the kids and run." It's not the best plan, but it'll do.

Logan sits in silence. I can't imagine what the past twenty-four hours have been like for him. His son was ripped away from him for the second time in his life.

"Do you want anything?" I ask, unsure what else to do. Logan shakes his head. I know what he really wants. Everyone does.

Logan turns to his children. "I want all of you to stay together during the fair. You are either with each other or Paco and everyone. Don't let each other out of your sight." His kids nod. Logan turns to us. "When you find Diane or my kids, call me immediately."

"We will," I say.

Logan steps outside, saying he needs some air. I follow him a few minutes later, closing the door behind me. He's leaning on the porch fence, staring at the heatwaves dancing in the street.

He doesn't realize I'm out here. Looking at him like this, I see the tuplets in him. They all have his eyes, Olive especially. Certain faces he makes look exactly like Olive. Theodore has his curls, but I don't know about Christina.

"Logan?" I finally speak. His head turns slightly to acknowledge me, but he says nothing. "Do you want to talk about it?" I ask, because all I can do is listen.

"It's not right to dump it on you," he answers. "You're a kid. You shouldn't even be involved in this." Logan turns to me. "You can't go after her like this. I know you're trying to help, but it's too dangerous for you."

"I'm already involved."

"Stubborn like your mother." Logan sighs. "All right. Well, for the past few days, I've been having dreams that we were all together. That the kids were never taken. I would have them on my birthday, but now they keep coming." Logan looks out into the road. "For twelve years, I've been wishing for a dream that will never come true."

I turn to him. "You still love her, don't you?"

"I think I always will. At least who she used to be." Logan wipes his eyes. "I wish I could've helped her more. Sometimes I wonder if there was something I could've done to prevent this."

We stay silent for a bit before Logan speaks. "Thank you for everything. And..." Logan pauses. "No matter what happens, thank you for wanting to help."

It's a nightmare getting to the marina. Roads are closed and there's no parking anywhere. The response to the fair was so great, they extended it to the patch of grass nearby. It has more space for stalls, but holy shit, I've never seen this many people at once. Between the two fair locations are The Waterfront Grill and Cafe, and Dalé Vino. I feel so bad for whoever's working there tonight.

Two spots near the curb open up, and Pachi zooms into it fast. Logan follows behind. "All right, we are walking the entire time," Pachi says as we get out of the car. "This parking is insane."

Logan and the tuplets hop out of the car. It's weird not seeing Logan's cheerful attitude. His eyes are narrow and dark. His friendly stance is hunched, emitting determination and anger. Olive walks up to me, and her family waits nearby.

I take out my phone as she approaches and swallow the dread in my body. "I know what this looks like, but hear me out."

Olive glares at my screen and crosses her arms. "A tracking app?" Her eyebrow arches.

"Only for tonight. In case anything happens, you have my location and I have yours. I'll delete it as soon as we find Christina and Theodore."

Olive stares at me without saying a word. Her frown drops and she chuckles. "I'm messing with you." She takes out her phone. "It's a good idea, and I trust you."

Leo steps forward. "Put mine on there too. Just in case." After we set everything up, the kids follow their father to the fair.

Sam double-checks that she brought her pepper spray and tightens her ponytail. Owen pulls a flashlight out of his pocket. I stare at him, and Owen shrugs. "Because of the blackouts. You never know."

The whole town is here. Children run up and down the stalls, laughing all the way. Music blasts from the speakers. Metal rings clink against glass bottles. A splash erupts down the row. A head comes up from the water, and the kid cheers. There are more games down the rows. Ring toss, darts, and so much more. We pass the smells of fresh pizza and tacos, and the stalls of cotton candy, hot dogs, snow cones, anything and everything you can think of.

Someone taps me on the shoulder. I turn around, sighing in relief at the sight of Rose. Katie pokes her head around Rose, and Owen runs to her. Rose puts some tokens in my hand. We need them for the games and food. We follow Pachi to the ice cream stall. Helen looks up from her scooper and smiles.

"Hi, honey," she greets Pachi. Her cheeks flush when we appear behind him. She clears her throat. "No sign of her yet. If she hasn't started work at the yacht club, she might be down here. I'll keep an eye out for the kids too."

"Do you know anything else?" I ask.

"The yacht club is packed. To be honest, she'll have to park somewhere else and walk there. I'll see her when she passes by."

"Okay. Let's have Logan cover the top part of the fair. Helen has this part, and Paula has the yacht club." Owen says, and we nod.

A line forms behind us, so we get some ice cream. Katie and Rose brought enough tokens. Owen gets the biggest ice cream scoop ever. Chocolate syrup drips from the top, with gummy bears and sprinkles covering it all. Some of the gummy bears float in the melted ice cream.

"You better pray you never become lactose," Sam says. She takes a spoonful of Yann's ice cream right under his nose.

Owen laughs and takes another bite. He hands the spoon to Katie. "It's not going to change anything."

My phone vibrates. It's a message from Paula, letting me know her shift ends in ten minutes. It'll take that long to get there with this crowd. I call Olive to let her know. The tuplets and Logan meet us at the ice cream stall. Olive begs to come with us, and it takes a bit of convincing for us to say yes.

Logan gives Olive a tight hug. "Please be safe. I love you," he whispers.

"I love you too, Dad." My heart jumps at it. She knows he's never stopped loving her.

We start the march to the yacht club. Our stone faces stand out from the surrounding laughter. The crowd disappears as we approach the yacht club. Cop cars are nearby. I keep my eyes ahead, and Rose squeezes my hand tighter.

We arrive at the yacht club at 7:59. Paula's shift ends in one minute. Paula sends me another text.

Paula: No sign of her yet. Where are you?

Me: I'm outside.

Paula: You're what? Okay, get in here. We need to talk.

I tell my friends to wait outside and dash up the stairs. Rose follows behind. We push the door open. It's packed. People squeeze past one another just to go to the bathroom. I step into the dining area. It's covered in red, white, and blue. The tables are blue with star cutouts scattered across. Near the DJ booth is a cutout of Uncle Sam. I follow the smell of cocktails and margaritas and end up in the barroom.

Paula is still behind the bar. I push through the crowd to reach her. She slides a drink to a man sitting down. Her eyes narrow when I reach her.

"What are you doing here?" Paula questions.

"What do you mean?"

"You know what I mean." Paula leans in. "You shouldn't be here. It's too dangerous."

"I'll be fine," I say. Paula glares at me. Her eyes are burning a hole in my face. "Have you seen her anywhere?" I ask.

"No, but she's here. She clocked in early." Paula looks around. She drops her voice to a whisper. "The schedule changed. She was supposed to be bartending, but she's doing something else. I'm getting overtime unless someone takes over."

"Crap. I'll look around then."

"No, Paco," Paula says firmly, "go back to the fair."

My eyes go wide. "What? What do you mean? I need to—!"

"You need to go back to the fair! This is too dangerous!"

"But Paula!"

"Paco Alejandro!" Paula's tone makes me flinch. "I want you back at that fair right now!"

I sigh. "Fine, I'll go. But if shit happens, I'm coming back."

"If shit happens, *I'll* take care of it. She won't be able to sneak out. The managers are pissed at her." Paula cleans a spilled drink. "I'll keep you updated, okay? Just stay away from her."

I nod, looking down at the ground. "Paquito," Paula calls softly. She sighs. "*Te amo mucho.*"

I look at her. "*Te amo mas.*" With that, I leave the barroom and follow Rose outside.

My friends are waiting near the steps. I scratch my neck. "Well, I'm banned from the yacht club. Paula doesn't want me to go inside at all, and I know she'll throw me out," I say with a sigh.

"Has she seen Diane?" Yann asks.

"She hasn't seen her, but she's there. She was supposed to take over the bar, but she got moved or something."

"How do we find her then?" Pachi questions.

"Hold on, do you think she'll throw *me* out? I have to use the bathroom and I refuse to step foot in those porta-potties." Olive makes a face.

I nod. "Yeah, I'm sure that's fine."

"I'll go with you. I hate those things," Owen says. The two of them go up the stairs and inside.

Yann looks at his phone. "What time are the fireworks?"

"I think at nine," Katie answers.

"We have a whole hour to kill. What do we do?" Yann questions.

"Maybe back to the fair," Sam suggests. "If the kids are here, where can they be? They either have to be in the yacht club or at the fair."

"What if they're in her car?" Rose asks.

Pachi shakes his head. "It's too hot for that, and someone would've called the police."

We share a few more possibilities before I get a text from Logan.

Logan: Haven't seen her yet. Anything on your end?

Me: No, not yet.

An idea pops into my head. I'm sure the triplets want to run around, and Logan might need some help keeping an eye on them and looking out for Diane. "Hey, Rose. Maybe you and Katie should go with Logan. I think he could use a hand."

"That's not that bad of an idea," Katie says.

Rose tilts her head. "I know what you're doing." Rose grabs my hand and takes me a few feet away. "I'm not leaving you alone."

"I won't be alone, Rose. It'll be safer for you to go with Logan."

"You're not being safe either." Rose looks me in my eyes. "Babe, you said it yourself. She threatened you."

"Exactly. I don't want you getting hurt."

"So, it's okay for you to run into the danger?" I look down and Rose sighs. "I don't want anything to happen to you. I don't know what I'll do if she hurts you. You can't go after her alone."

"I won't be alone. I'll be with my friends the whole time. I'll be safe, I promise." I brush her hair off her shoulders, running my hands through it. I kiss her soft lips. "Please, *mi amor*, go with Logan." Rose holds up her pinky, so I do the same. After our pinkies lock together, we walk back to the group.

The yacht club doors open and close once more. Olive hurries down the stairs and comes up to us. "What's up?" Olive asks.

"Do you have an idea where Theodore and Christina could be?" I ask. Olive shakes her head. I look behind her. "Hey, where's Owen?"

Olive frowns. "He said his stomach was hurting. He might be in there for a bit." With that giant ice cream he had, it makes sense. I pull out my phone and text Owen to call when he's out.

Rose turns to Olive. "You keep an eye on him, okay?" she says, pointing to me.

Olive chuckles. "What do you mean?"

Rose gives Olive a hug. "Stay safe, okay? I'll see you later."

We watch Katie and Rose walk away. Olive blinks. "You know, I'm still not used to hugs."

The walk back to the fair is long. I look at my phone. It's now 8:15. Walking between both spots takes a while. If something happens at the yacht club, we won't get there in time.

"What's on your mind, Paquito?" Sam asks.

I don't answer at first. "Maybe we should split up. In case something happens and we're not close enough."

Pachi shakes his head. "No one's going alone. I've seen one too many horror movies to know how that goes."

"Yeah, no way. We'll split into groups. I'll head back to the fair with Olive." I turn to her. "Going to the bathroom is one thing, but I'm pretty sure she'll kick both of us out."

"I'll stay with you guys," Yann says.

"All right. So Pachi and I will head back to the yacht club," Sam announces.

"If anything happens, call us," Yann orders. Sam and Pachi nod and take off running.

The sun starts to set as we approach the fair. Sparkles shine in Olive's eyes. The fair lights up. Strings of lights hang off the stalls and tents. People are selling glow sticks. Yann and I get some. I hand Olive one, and she smiles widely. The fair's more crowded now. The passing conversations are all about the fireworks.

Olive stops at the ring toss game. Her eyes linger on the stuffed animals. The clerk notices. "Step right up! A game is three tokens."

I pull out two tokens, and Yann pulls out one. We give them to Olive. She slides the tokens to the clerk, and they give her the rings. Olive throws one ring. It clinks one of the bottles and falls to the side. She throws another one. It ricochets and falls to the floor.

"Let me try," I say, holding my hand out. Olive hands me the rings. I throw some, and they land on the bottles. Yann takes a ring and throws it. It lands on the high tier of bottles.

"Congrats, you have won! What prize would you like? You can pick one from this row right here." The clerk points outside of their tent. A row of small plushies ranging from dogs to dragons. Olive picks a pink cat. The clerk hands it to her and we walk away.

Olive is jumping with joy. She skips down the road, her eyes glancing at all the stalls. Music is still blasting and people are still cooking. I take out my phone and text Owen. He's been in the bathroom for a long time now. I'm getting worried. In fact, Sam and Pachi haven't sent an update. I send all of them a text, but Owen responds first.

Owen: My stomach's messed up. I'll be out soon.

Me: Do you need anything?

Owen reads the message but doesn't respond. Jeez, has he become lactose intolerant in the span of an hour?

Olive steps toward the fence. She looks out at the water, taking in the sights. Yann and I stand next to her. Her eyes flicker over all the boats.

"The town's so beautiful at night." Olive exhales. "I've never seen it like this."

"It's cool, huh?" Yann asks. Olive nods quickly. He turns to her. "Now that you're home, what do you want to do?"

Olive tilts her head. "What do you mean?"

"You missed out on a bunch of stuff. What are you looking forward to?"

Olive puts a hand on her chin. "Well, maybe going to the movies. Mom never liked going. And going to an actual school would be nice.

Homeschooling's all right, but it would be cool to see other kids. And then going to college or nursing school."

"Nursing school? You want to be a nurse?" I ask.

"I've always wanted to." Olive stares at the water. "Mom loves these doctor shows, and I would watch with her. Some of the shows were real, like with real people. The others were fake. But I've always loved the idea of helping people."

"That's sweet, Ol." I smile.

"Thank you." She looks down with a smile. "And thanks for helping me win the cat."

"Of course. What are friends for?"

Her eyes twinkle as she looks at me. "Friends?"

"Yeah, friends."

BOOM!

The fireworks burn in the sky. Another follows. They explode in many colors. Red, blue, purple, and green. Three more fireworks shoot up into the sky.

"It's nine already?" Yann asks. "How long have we been here?"

I turn to my phone. No new messages from my friends, but one from Paula.

Paula: Hey, someone took over my shift. I still haven't seen her.

"Paula's off," I say. I look at my phone again. 9:00. I call Owen's phone. He doesn't answer. Okay, not texting is one thing, but not answering calls? Something's wrong. I turn to Yann. "We need to check on Owen. He's been in there for way too long."

"Good idea," Yann replies.

We run back to the yacht club. Some people are leaving, eagerly heading to the fireworks. I catch the door from closing. The yacht club is hot and cramped. We push through the crowd and reach the bathroom door.

"Owen?" I call. All the stall doors are open. There's an occasional drop of water from the sink. Chills go through my body. If he's not here, then where is he? Maybe all of us should've set up the tracking app.

"He's not in here," I say to Yann.

Confusion is written on Yann's face. "Is he outside? He couldn't have gone far."

I call him again. The phone rings and rings. Pick up, dammit, why won't he pick up? What the hell is going on?

The room comes to a standstill as it falls into darkness. What once was a room filled with laughter is now a room filled with screams of horror. I barely see the outline of my feet. People come crashing through the doorway and run to the front doors.

"Yann! Yann, where are you?" I yell.

"Come on, Paco!" Yann shouts over the screams. He grabs my hand. "Let's get out of here!"

I grab Olive's hand and let Yann guide us out the door. We get away from the crowd and stand off to the side. The crowd keeps running out, desperate to escape the heat and darkness inside.

I pull out my phone and call Owen. His phone rings out, leaving me with a voicemail. I try Sam's phone, then Pachi's, and the same thing. Voicemails from both of them. My heart sinks to the pit of my stomach. Why is no one answering?

My phone buzzes, and so does Yann's. We look at our phones, buzzing with new messages in the group chat. I stop breathing.

Owen: HELP.

Owen: DIANE.

I shove my phone into my pocket and run up the front steps. I grab the door handle and pull, but it doesn't budge. I pull harder. There's no way it's locked. In the panic, no one stopped to lock it.

"Yann! Olive! Help me get this open!" I yell. The door moves, but it slams shut, making my body crash against it. "Open the door!"

Yann dashes up the stairs and grabs the door handle. We both pull, but it doesn't move. We listen to the commotion inside. Chairs knocking over, and footsteps running. What's going on in there?

Yann tugs on the door a bit more. It pulls back. Then it swings open, nearly hitting him. I run past the bathrooms and straight into the dining area. "Owen! Sam! Pachi!" I yell at the top of my lungs.

"Ah! Fuck!" My blood turns cold when Yann yells. My head turns slowly, just in time to see him hit the floor.

"Yann!" I fall to my knees and shake him. "Yann, come on. Get up! Please get up!" His eyes look at mine, but they're closing.

My head whips around. I find Olive standing a few feet away with her phone flashlight on. Her other hand is over her mouth, trembling with the rest of her body. "Olive, help me!" I yell, and she stands there. "H-help me!"

"I'm sorry!" She croaks. "I'm so sorry!" She drops her phone and starts sobbing. "I didn't want this!"

"Run," Yann's voice comes out in a whisper. A pain-filled whisper. "Run!"

I turn around, still on my knees. My head moves up, following the dark figure standing in front of me. I scream when they come toward me. I scramble out of the way and get on my feet. I push aside tables and chairs and run to Olive.

"Olive, come on, we have to run." She doesn't budge. She's trembling and sobbing uncontrollably. No other option. I stand in front of her, shielding her from Diane. I don't need a flashlight to determine it's her.

What does surprise me is Olive pushing me into Diane's hands. Hands that I can't get out of fast enough, hands that pull my arms tight toward her. In a last attempt, I reach out to Olive. Begging her to run, to get help, anything. But she just stands there.

Not even looking at me.

18

— · —

"*¡Ayudame!*" I scream at the top of my lungs for no one to hear. "*¡Ayudame! ¡Ayudame!*" But whenever Diane's hand slips off of my mouth, I yell out. Maybe Mom is nearby, or Dad, or Paula, or Rose. Somebody, anybody!

There's nothing I can do. Diane's grip is too tight. The few times I get my hands free, it isn't for long. Diane pushes me down into a chair. Another pair of hands pull mine back and tie them behind the chair.

"I'm so sorry." It's Theodore. He whispers apologies as he finishes tying my hands.

I'm gasping for air as tears stream down my face. There's so much pressure in my chest, like I'm being squished by a ton of bricks. Diane stands away from me. I can't see her face, but she stretches, cracks her knuckles, and adjusts her jacket.

"W-where are my friends?" My voice cracks when I yell. "What did you do?"

She steps closer to me, coming into view. Her lips curl into a smirk. "What do you mean?"

"You heard me!" I yell. I yank my arms back and forth, my restraints tugging at my skin. "What did you do to them? I'm going to…" I gasp for air. "I'm going to kill you! I'm going to fucking kill you!"

Diane leans her head forward and breaks out into vicious laughter. She smacks her leg. "Oh, please!" she says, wiping a tear from her eye. "You wouldn't hurt a *fly*. I told you, didn't I? You would regret this. And you sounded so confident yesterday when you threatened me."

I hang my head in shame. She's right. I was confident. I thought we could get Theodore and Christina home so easily. I let my guard down, and now my friends are paying for it. I don't even know where they are. I hold in my sobs. "J-just let them go. Please. They didn't do anything wrong." My voice shakes. "Whatever you have, it's between you and me! Let them go!"

Diane walks into the darkness. Something clicks and the room lights up. It's a lantern. With its light, I see Olive sitting in a chair. Her arms hold on to herself, squeezing the cat plush close to her. She looks at the ground and sniffles. I don't get it. She shoved me into her mother's hands, and she's going with her willingly.

"Olive." She doesn't move. "Olive, did you plan this? Was this your plan all along?" She doesn't meet my eyes, and my heart breaks. "I just want to know why."

Diane chuckles. "Oh, right. You're the only one that doesn't know." She turns to Olive. "You can let your hair out of that stupid bun, Christie. The cat's out of the bag."

Christie? Christie?! My jaw drops as "Olive" reaches for the bun in her hair. Long brown hair falls past her shoulders, and curls stand up and point in different directions. There's no way Olive's hair grew out that fast. Not only that, she wipes the scar away like it's makeup. It's Christina, it's been her this whole time. I can't believe I fell for it!

"Where's Olive then?" I question. "What did you do to her?"

"Nothing wrong," Diane responds. "She's perfectly fine."

"Not fine! Not fine at all!" This time it's really her. A chair scraps on the carpet, and Olive comes into view. She's wearing a pink shirt and black pants, and her hair is at her shoulders. Diane tied her hands behind the chair, but she continues to throw herself back and forth.

"Olive, are you okay?" I ask.

"No! This bitch grabbed me when we went to the bathroom! And she took Owen too! She took everyone!" Olive finds her mother in the darkness and yells, "I hate you! I hate you! I hate you!"

"You don't mean that, Olive," Diane says with a whimper. She walks toward Olive and places a hand on her cheek. Olive leans back as far as she can, but Diane doesn't stop trying. "I'm doing what's best for you. This is what's best for you, Theodore, and Christina. I love you, Olive. Why can't you see I'm trying to help you? I want to bring you home. I love you so much." Olive looks her mother in her eyes, and the fear in hers fades. She leans into Diane's touch.

"Get away from her!" I yell. Olive's head jolts out of Diane's hand. She tries to scoot away, but the chair nearly tips. Diane turns to me, her face twitching, and I'm scared for my life.

"Or what? What are you going to do about it?" The pounding of Diane's boots matches my heartbeat. Pounding harder and harder the closer she comes to me. "I'll answer that for you. You can't do anything. I've already won. My children will be home with me, safe and sound from people like you."

"How do you think Olive got to me in the first place? How come Theodore ended up with me? I know why. Trying to get away from a monster like you!"

I've struck a nerve. Diane scowls and her eyes are full of fire, but she turns away from me and looks at her children. Christina's arms are wrapped around herself. She turns her body away from Olive and their mother. Theodore stands next to her. His posture is tight, and he's trying to stand tall. His body is trembling despite his best efforts.

I scan the room. My eyes land on Yann, who is still on the floor. His chest rises and falls, and I sigh in relief. My head turns to the left, and my face pales.

Owen is sitting on the floor a few feet away from me. His hands are bound with duct tape. There are scratches on his face. We make eye contact, but I look away when his mouth starts to move. I can't. I can't look at him, not after I got him into this mess. But I see Sam and Pachi in the same condition. Duct tape, scratches, sitting on the floor and leaning against the chairs. There's a clamp on my chest, squeezing my heart until it breaks.

This is all my fault. This is all my fucking fault. I shouldn't have split us up. I should've paid more attention. I shouldn't have dragged them into this. If I had been more careful, they would be fine. They would be outside, having the time of their lives. I would be the only one here. I would be the only one in danger.

Diane chuckles. My head snaps back at her. "Who's the real monster here?" Her eyes gaze at my friends. "And besides, they only think I'm a monster because of you. If it wasn't for you, we wouldn't be in this mess. You manipulated my children into staying with you." Diane stomps to me, grips my shoulders, and shakes me. "What did you tell them?"

"Get off of me!" I yell. "I only told them the truth!"

Diane shoves me. The chair scrapes against the carpet as she steps back. "I knew I should've killed you when I had the chance." My body flinches, and my friends' jaws drop. Diane's hands clench and unclench into fists. Her whole body shakes as she glares at me. "And what truth? What *lies* did you tell my children to get them to stay with you?"

The lantern gives enough light to see the front door. It opens slowly. I can't tell who it is, but someone is here. I need to stall her.

"You're a piece of shit. You're wondering why your children hate you, and you can't see that you're the reason why. At least they know Logan loves them."

"You think they'd be better off with that man?" Her hand gestures to the door, but she keeps her eyes on me. Eyes that are wide and unstable. "He's even worse than me! Do you think they'd be loved? Well-fed? He has problems with money. Did he ever tell you that? We damn near went bankrupt!"

"That's because you weren't helping!" I snap. "Logan told me the whole story!"

"Logan did *nothing* for me or my children." Diane's fists clench tight. "He is a deadbeat. He is uncaring, and he is abusive."

"They're not terrified of him like they are of you." Whoever is inside is getting closer, just a few more seconds. "And if Logan was abusive, why did you leave half of your kids with him? If you *are* a good mother, why didn't you save them all?"

Diane doesn't answer my question. She spins her arm around, smacking the person coming up behind her. She fists their shirt and slams them to the ground, tying their hands behind their back.

Only when she turns them over do I see who it is. It's Leonardo. He winces in pain. I look at Olive and Theodore, who are both distraught. Christina, however, is confused. She tilts her head and looks back and forth between her two brothers.

Diane huffs as she gets up from the ground, a pair of scissors in her hand. "Really?" She turns them over. "You thought *this* would help?"

She drops the scissors and kicks them away. "How did you even find us?"

"Olive never came out, and I was worried. Isn't that obvious?" Leo snaps. I'm relieved that he doesn't mention he has her location. Leo rolls to his side, and something vibrates. His face pales.

"Who's that?" Diane asks.

"Dad," Leo whispers.

"Oh, give me that. I'd love to hear his voice again. It's been so long." Diane reaches down to Leo. He tries to squirm away, but she grabs his phone out of his pocket and answers it.

"Leo! Oh, thank God, where are you?" Logan asks.

"Hello, Logan," Diane says in a sweet voice with a sadistic smile. I can hear Logan's breathing halt from here. Hell, I can feel it. Diane puts the phone on speaker as she continues. "It's been a long time now."

"D-Diane?" The way she smirks at the fear in his voice infuriates me. "Where's Leonardo? What have you done to him?" he yells.

"Oh please. He's fine." Diane rolls her eyes. "You'll get him back soon."

"Where's Olive? And Theodore and Christina!" Christina's head perks up at the mention of her name. "I know you have them! If you've hurt them, I swear I'll—!"

"They're fine. I'm taking them home." Diane grins. "I'll take great care of them."

"Logan!" I cry. "We're in the—!" Diane races to me and shoves her hand over my mouth.

"Is that Paco? What have you done to him? And his friends!"

"You'll find out soon enough." That chuckle will haunt me for the rest of my life. "Have a good night, sweetie." She makes a kissing sound before hanging up. She chucks the phone on the ground, land-ing near Leo.

"You're sick! You're fucking sick! Haven't you traumatized him enough already? What the hell is wrong with you?" I yell at her.

Diane doesn't look at me. She returns to her children. "Christina, grab Olive. We're leaving," she orders.

Christina stands in front of her sister. Her hands move toward Olive, but they fall to her sides. She turns around. "No."

Diane stands still. "No?" she questions. "What do you mean, no?"

"I. Said. No!" Christina's voice shakes. "We're not going with you!"

"Don't tell me that the stories of Logan got into your head." Diane scoffs. "He's an abusive, neglectful deadbeat."

"You're the deadbeat!" Christina squeaks out. Theodore steps closer to her. She's shaking, and I mean shaking. Trembling in fear with the words she's trying to say. "Y-you went through five jobs in the span of two months! It's a miracle you're still at this one! I don't even remember the last time we went clothes shopping! And Theodore begged you to take him to buy us food! Food!" I look at Olive, and her jaw is on the floor.

The anger in Diane's eyes is visible. Her face is red, and her body violently shakes. "I work day and night to put a roof over you three! And this is how you repay me? By running away, acting out, and dis-obeying me? Now all three of you want to go back to your father, the man who put us here in the first place?" The louder Diane yells, the more Christina shrinks. She flees to the back of her brother. Theodore stands as tall as he can, protecting her.

Diane hunches over. "I am your mother. No one will take care of you like I do. No one will *love* you like I do."

"Liar! You fucking liar!" Olive screams. "Dad cares a lot more than you ever have!"

Diane steps back, and I can't help but chuckle, even if it's mostly from nerves. Her head twists toward me. "What's so funny?" Diane questions.

"I told you, didn't I? I told you they know the truth. And you know they will never forgive you for this."

Her hands clench into fists. "Shut up."

"Logan loves these kids. They're his whole life. They know that he loves them. That's more than I can ever say for you."

She turns again, her whole body facing me. "I said shut up!" She stomps toward me as she yells. "Just shut up!"

"And you know what, Diane? You know why I know they'll be better off with Logan?" I get as close to her as I can, and I can't help but smile as I say this, "Because he won't hit them for burning dinner."

Diane's hand flies across my face and my head jerks back. "They are my children. Mine. I carried them for twenty-eight weeks. I gave birth to them. I nursed them. I raised them. You have no right to tell me how to raise them, and you have absolutely no right to take them from me." Diane grabs my shoulders. "They're mine! No one will take them away from me! Not you, not Logan, not anyone!"

"They'll run away again. This will keep happening. You want this to be over, don't you? Let them go home."

She doesn't move, but she reels in her anger by digging her fingers into my shoulders. I wince. She sucks in a sharp breath. "Logan is not their home. *I* am their home."

"Home isn't something to run away from."

Diane lets go of me and kicks a chair. It falls to the ground with a thud, and she kicks it again, sending it across the room. The tuplets stare at her in horror. Diane marches to Olive and frees her of her restraints. Olive whines as the duct tape rips off her. Diane snatches her hand. "Come now, we're going home."

"No!" Olive hisses, and when her mother argues, she shouts again, "No! I'm not going with you!"

Diane growls. "I have had it! I am sick of you disobeying me! I am your mother. I am in charge of you. I know what's best for you! And I say we are going, *now!*" She yanks Olive out of the chair and drags her away. Olive pulls her mom's arm back hard.

Diane's free hand slaps Olive's face. The slap is hard enough for Olive to lose her balance. She grips onto a chair, stopping her fall.

"Olive!" I yell.

This is all my fault. This is all my fault. I made too many mistakes and look at what's happened. I can't even do anything to help.

Olive holds her cheek. She backs away from Diane and stands near Theodore. "I'll run away again. I don't care how many times I have to. I'll run away. I will never go with you."

"Olive, I'm giving you one last chance. You will come with me, you will get in the car, and we will go to our new home."

Olive shakes her head, yelling, "No! No!"

Diane sighs. "Then you leave me no choice." She reaches into her jacket pocket. "I want you to know." She pulls out a gun. "This is all because of you."

All the confidence in Olive has faded away, and I freeze. She has her gun! Diane has her gun! Olive's eyes go wide. "Mom. Mom, put that away." Olive's hands are in front of her as she steps away from her mom. "Please put it away."

"No. You need to learn that there are consequences to your actions." Diane moves her arm, and the gun lands on me. "Consequences if you don't listen."

My heart falls to the pit of my stomach and my blood turns cold. No. No. *No!* I want to scream at the top of my lungs, but I can't move a single muscle. Diane stomps toward me. My eyes stare at the gun pointing at my head. Diane holds it still. If she pulls that trigger, she's not going to miss.

"Mom! Mom! Don't do this!" Olive cries. She tries to get in front of her mother, but Diane's free hand pushes her away.

"If you don't want this boy's blood on your hands, come with me, now!" Olive shakes her head, and Diane cries out, "I'll change! I'll be better! Just come home!"

My throat tightens, and my eyes fly around the room quickly. My friends' voices clash with Olive's and Theodore's as they plead for Diane to put the gun down. I look at my friends. Their faces filled with fear. Did she threaten them? Did she hurt them? This is all my fault.

Diane looks away from her crying children and glares at me. I squirm in my seat, and she smirks. She fucking smirks. I'm freaking the hell out and she's over here enjoying it. My fear turns to rage.

"Don't do it! Olive, don't do it!" I look at Olive quickly. Her eyes are wide, and her jaw is on the floor. "She's not going to change! No matter how many times she tells you! You know it!"

"Are you crazy?" Olive yells with tears pouring down her face. She runs up to her mom and tugs her arm. "Please! Don't do this!"

Diane looks back at her kids. Theodore's pleading for Diane to put the gun down, but Christina only stares. Her mouth hangs open and her body trembles. "Why?" Christina cries. "Why?"

"See, Christina?" Diane calls out. "This is why I have my gun, because of people like this. People who want to take you away from me!"

"But he was kind to me! They've been kind to me!" Christina wails.

Olive sobs. "Why are you doing this? Why?"

"I'm doing this because I love you. I'm trying to protect you. Why can't you see that?"

My anger grows. "This isn't love! This isn't how someone should treat you!" Diane's grip on the gun gets tighter. Veins are popping out of her neck as she pushes the gun onto my forehead. My head tilts back with it. If looks could kill, I'd be dead a long time ago. I look away and find Olive. "Don't believe anything she says! You know this isn't right! Someone who loves you wouldn't do this!"

Olive is tugging at her hair. "Why are you doing this? Let him go! Let everyone go!" she screams.

Diane turns to Olive. "Then come with me!"

"No! I don't want to go with you! I don't want to!"

Diane cocks the gun. "This is your final warning. Come home!"

"Listen to your kids for once!" I yell. "You want to know why they won't go with you? I'll tell you why. It's because you're a shitty mother!"

Diane moves the gun to my left and fires. Glass shatters behind me, and I wince. My ears are ringing. My eyes fly around the room. What happened? Where did the shot land? I heard glass break, so everyone's okay, right? I find Diane, gun still in hand, waving it around the room.

"I am the only one who can raise them!" Diane yells. "No one else can! No one can do as good as a job as I can!"

"You're crazy! You're fucking crazy!" Owen screams. "No mother would do this to her kids!"

Diane whips around and points the gun at Owen. "You're not a parent. You don't know what it's like." She grips Owen by his shirt and lifts him up. God, no! NO! "None of you know what it's like!"

"Let him go!" I scream.

"None of you are prepared!" Diane doesn't hear me, even though I'm screaming at the top of my lungs.

Sam screams and kicks Diane hard. She lets go of Owen and he falls with a thud. Diane's head twists to Sam. She grabs Sam by her ponytail and tilts her head back. Sam cries out in pain as the gun touches her forehead.

"You want to try that again?" The gun lands on me, and Sam's eyes widen. Diane leans into her. "You try that shit again and I'll blow his brains out right here. I'm a sharpshooter. I won't miss." Sam sniffles. After a few moments, Diane lets her go.

"Please leave us alone." Pachi's voice cracks as he cries. "Please."

"Then you should've left my family alone," Diane scoffs.

Christina stomps her foot. "Mom, stop it! Please, stop!"

Diane finally listens. She turns away from my friends and faces her children. Her voice shakes. "I'm doing this for you. All of this is for you. I will do anything for you, and I want to give all of you the world." Diane pauses. She gestures around the room. "If this is what I have to do for a little ounce of respect, THEN SO BE IT!" Diane's yell echoes and rings in my ears. She takes a deep breath. "Please, let's go home."

Diane steps toward her kids, but Theodore jumps in front. He holds his arms out, blocking her from Olive and Christina.

"Theodore, be a good boy. Move."

"No. And don't call me that, when you have another son right there!" Theodore wails. "He's just as much as your son as I am!"

"He's lost to that man. You're not. You're my precious babies."

"Then I am not your son," Theodore says firmly.

Diane freezes. She takes a sharp breath. "D-don't say that." She has the gun in one hand, and her other hand pulling her hair. "Don't *ever* say that!"

She's lost it. She's really lost it. She pulls at her hair and leans forward, sobs racking her body. For a minute or two, all we hear are her sobs. Then she chuckles, then laughs.

"You are just like your father." Olive and her siblings turn pale as Diane continues. "Traitors, backstabbers. All of you!"

"No. Mom, no!" Christina cries.

"Did you even love me? Did any of you love me?"

"Of course we do!" Theodore stammers.

"Don't lie to me! I thought you weren't my son!" Theodore steps back, and Diane yells out, "I knew it. I knew I should've left crying in your crib. I didn't even want you. You just had to wake up, didn't you? I knew I should've picked Leonardo over you!"

Leo's jaw is on the floor and Theodore bursts into tears. "I've done everything you've asked of me! You're the one who lied! You told me I was your only son. Well, I'm not! You have no sons!" Theodore screams, straining his voice.

"You are my son. And I will do whatever it takes for our happiness and safety. All of you are coming with me, and we are going home."

"Leave them alone!" I yell. "Can't you see they're terrified of you?"

Diane clenches her jaw. "And whose fault is that?"

"Yours!"

"No. It's yours. All of this, it's because of you!" Diane stomps toward me, putting the gun back on my head. "I am tired of you ruining everything!"

"Leave him alone!" Olive cries.

She can't. They can't go back. "Olive, don't do it." I plead. She looks at me, and through my tears I whisper, "I'm not worth it."

"Not worth it?" Diane scoffs. Her eyes widen, almost with glee. "You're a brave one, aren't you?" I'm seething with anger. I want to tell her off. I want to wipe that smirk off her damn face. But that smirk only grows as she cocks the gun.

My soul leaves my body. The yelling only gets louder, and the pleading grows stronger. Diane's grip around the gun tightens.

"Ten." Fuck.

"Nine." Fuck! No! Not like this! I don't want to die!

"Eight." I shut my eyes tight. All I can do is listen to Diane counting down as my life flashes before my eyes.

"Seven." My friends' voices are begging for Diane to put the gun down. I start praying in Spanish. If this is really it, please just let it be me.

"Six." *Olive, I'm so sorry I couldn't save you.*

"Five. Four. Three. Two. One!"

19

— · —

"I'll go! I'll go with you!" Olive cries and my eyes pop open. I look at Olive. Tears stream down her red face. She sniffles. "Just don't hurt him. Don't hurt anyone," she pleads.

The gun tilts to my left, just enough where I can see Diane's face. She holds it there. Time is frozen. My pounding heart is all I hear. Olive steps forward. "I'm coming with you. Please, don't hurt him."

Diane sighs, her smirk softening to a smile. "All right then," she says as she lowers the gun. "I'm so glad you've come to your senses."

Diane turns away from me. My body falls forward. I can't catch my breath with all my sobs. Olive takes a step away from her mom. Diane holds her face. "My little Olive, I'm so happy you're coming home." Diane brushes her thumb over Olive's tears.

Olive cries. Her eyes flicker at the gun. Diane notices. "Oh, don't worry anymore." Diane tosses the gun across the room. "You're home now. That's all that matters. Don't cry sweetie, we're together again."

Diane grabs Olive's hand. Olive turns to me. *I'm sorry.* Her mouth moves, but nothing comes out.

"Y-you won't get away with this!" I yell, my voice hoarse.

"I already have." Diane grins. She turns to her children. "Now, let's go home."

Theodore and Christina follow their mother. They walk into the darkness and open the door. But I hear yelling, screaming, then silence. The door closes with a soft thud.

No. No. Dammit! I can't stop shaking. Tears pour down my face, no matter how hard I try to hold them in. I want to scream. I want to cry. I want to throw up. I want to go home. I can't look at my friends. God, why did I have to drag them into this? Why couldn't it just be me? And after everything we did, after all the shit I put them through, Diane still took the tuplets away.

"Not worth it?" My head turns. Sam glares at me. "Not worth it? Are you fucking kidding me?"

"It slipped out." Even I know that's a lie. I meant it. And honestly, I'm surprised I'm alive. My heart is beating against my chest, and I'm breathing so fast I might pass out.

"You thought about it. You meant it," Sam says. She's angry, so angry. Everyone must be so angry at me.

I can't hold back anymore. My voice cracks and more tears fall. "I'm sorry. I'm so sorry. I-I didn't mean for this to happen!"

"Don't," Sam says with a groan. "Let's get out of here first."

"How the hell do we do that?" Pachi asks. "I can't get this off."

"Is Yann okay?" Owen asks. I look at Yann while the room spins. My eyes can't focus in the darkness, but Yann's still on the floor.

I call his name a few times, and Yann finally moves. He groans as he sits up, holding a hand on his head. He looks at me and sighs in relief. "Oh, thank God. You're alive."

"I thought you were dead!" Sam cries. "Are you okay?"

"Felt like it. I was in and out. And yeah, I'll be fine." Yann slowly stands, using a chair as support. He scans the room and finds the pair of scissors. He grabs them and frees Leo.

Leo rubs his wrists. "She wanted to get me," Leo mumbles out of breath. "If it had gone how she wanted, I would've been with her. I would've been..." Leo can't finish the sentence. He wipes his eyes and stands.

"Go get help. I'll get everyone else out," Yann says. Leo nods, grabs his phone off the floor, and runs out of the yacht club.

Yann frees Owen next. Then Sam, then Pachi. They all stand up, stretch, and take off any excess duct tape. Then they look at me. I look down at the ground. I can't face them without knowing I'm the reason they're here. If they want to leave me in here, I won't even blame them.

My heart aches when Sam and Yann go behind me. Why aren't they leaving me behind? Pachi grabs the lantern off the table, and Owen holds up his flashlight. They shine the light on me while Sam and Yann take off the duct tape. Owen's bright flashlight goes over my face, and he gasps.

"Holy shit. Y-you're bleeding," Owen stammers.

"What?" I ask. The room goes silent.

"That shot must've grazed you," Pachi says, his lip quivering. He turns to Owen. "Stay here. I'll try to find something," he says before running off.

"Hold on, she shot you?" Yann questions.

"What? I-I didn't feel anything, and the glass shattered behind me." I look at Owen. "Is it bad?" His face is pale. Owen's not the best with blood.

Pachi runs over with some napkins from the bar. "There wasn't shit. The first aid kit only had tiny Band-Aids." He holds the napkins on the left side of my head. I don't feel any pain, but I'm dizzy, so I lean into Pachi's hand. His body tenses. "Get him out of there!" Pachi yells.

"Working on it! They used half of the duct tape on him!" Sam groans. The scissors struggle against the tape. Sam curses under her breath.

"Go without me," I say, the dizziness getting worse. "I'll only slow you down. You guys can get help."

"Shut up! We're not leaving you!" Sam shouts. The scissors finally cut the duct tape. Sam and Yann yank the rest off.

The room spins when I stand up. Sam and Yann catch me before I lose my balance. I put a hand on my head. When I take it off, it's covered in blood.

The sight of it makes me want to puke. All this blood from one bullet. Knowing it could've been a lot more than this, and knowing it could've been on their hands, or their blood on mine, it makes me want to...

"Are you okay?" Owen asks.

I snap out of my thoughts. My friends look at me. Tears roll down some of their faces. I nod. "I-I'm okay." I pause, trying to catch my breath. "Let's get out of here."

Owen leads us through the yacht club with his flashlight. Pachi gives me all the napkins and I hold them against my head as we move forward. Sam helps me walk and we all hold on to each other, trying not to get lost in the darkness. We reach the front door, and Owen swings it open.

The dizziness goes away, and I run down the stairs, shoving the red napkins into my pocket. Fireworks are the only thing lighting the sky. There are so many bright colors. I look around. The pink cat we won for Christina is on the ground nearby, and I pick it up. Only two cars are in the parking lot. One is a blue Ford, and one is a gray Honda.

I dash to the Honda with my friends following behind. The driver's window is open, and Pachi sticks his hand through the window and fiddles with the buttons. The trunk pops open, revealing four suitcases inside. Did they abandon everything?

Yann takes a suitcase out and opens it. He pulls out a laptop and taps the keyboard, showing the same lock screen we saw weeks ago.

"She wouldn't leave that! Hell, she wouldn't leave her car!" Sam says.

She wouldn't. Of course she wouldn't, but their stuff is still there.

They're still here. They haven't left. There's still time.

There's still time!

I fumble for my phone and open it. Olive's at the fair, and her icon is moving. I give the cat to Sam, shove my phone in my pocket, and start running.

"Where the hell are you going?" Pachi shouts.

"I'm going after Olive!" I announce. "You guys get to safety. Find Logan, find help!"

"What about you?" Yann catches up to me. "You're still bleeding!"

"I don't matter! Go!"

"No!" Yann yells. He grabs my arm and pulls back hard, nearly taking me to the ground. "You're out of your damn mind!"

I pull my arm, but Yann clenches harder. "Yann, come on, we're running out of time!"

"I am not letting you get yourself killed!" The world stops moving. My eyes widen and Yann grips my arm even harder. "We're coming with you."

"Someone has to go get help! We're running out of—!"

"That doesn't mean you do this on your own!" Yann pulls my arm again. Tears fall from his eyes and my eyes widen. He inhales sharply. "We're right here, dammit! We want to help just as much as you do!" Yann pauses. "You're not doing this by yourself. Say it!"

I gasp for air. Yann stares at me, still holding my arm. He won't let go. I sigh. "I'm not doing this by myself."

Yann lets go of my arm. Part of me wants to take off running. Run fast and far. But Yann will tackle me in a heartbeat. His eyes don't leave me until our friends catch up. We stand in silence for a moment. "So, what do we do?" he asks.

I take a breath. "Someone has to call Logan and give him an update. Maybe someone should keep an eye on the car in case she comes back."

Pachi looks at his phone and gasps. "Helen spotted one of the kids. They just ran past the ice cream stall, heading in the direction of the yacht club."

"Okay, let's go." I take another breath. "Let's go kick this bitch's ass."

Sam, Yann, and Pachi stay near the car, while Owen and I take off running. The fireworks and our heavy breathing are all I hear. We keep running for a few minutes, and Owen keeps falling behind. Owen's on the track team. He has no problems running long distances, and he's the fastest one out of all of us. I look back at him. He staggers to catch up and limps.

"Why are you limping?" I question.

"Diane messed up my leg when she grabbed me." I stare at him, full of worry. Owen shakes his head. "Don't worry. I've run injured before, and I can do it again."

The closer we get to the fair, the more people we see. Blood drips onto my shirt. People look, but we run past the crowd so fast, it takes too long for them to tell if it's real. The fireworks continue going off, and some people brought their own. They light them on the street. "The hell?" Owen says as he hops around one. "Are they trying to burn the town down?"

Sparks fly and children laugh. Fourth of July music plays and people cheer. The fireworks boom brightly in the sky. People surround the stalls. We slow down to a stop.

"Olive!" I yell. "Where are you?" I'm completely out of breath, but I don't care. My ears start to ring as we shout her name.

Where is she? I shove past people and keep yelling. I sound like a madman. I check her location again. It's gone. Her location's off. Shit! Shit!

"Olive!" I scream, and Owen does too. "Where are you?"

"Paco!" she finally answers. I find her at the other end of the crowd. I push past them and grab her hand. We start running when I realize she's alone.

"Where are Theodore and Christina?" I question.

"We attacked Mom as we were leaving. They got away, but she's after me now." Olive turns around. Her mother is behind us. She looks at me with tears in her eyes. "Please don't let her catch me. I don't want to go back."

"She won't, I swear on my life." For some reason, Olive tenses when I say that.

Diane pushes through the crowd to keep up. They stare at her in disgust. I look at Owen. He keeps having to hop as he runs. If we can't get out of here soon, he's going to fall. I need to get them out of here.

My head spins around, trying to find anyone that we know. Logan, Mom, Dad, even the cops will do at this point!

"Paco! Rose is over there!" Owen yells. I look to my left. Rose is there with Katie and Lucy. I call Rose's name. She smiles, but then her face falls. She motions to herself and points at Olive.

"Olive! Go to Rose!" I yell.

Olive's eyes fill with worry. "What about you?"

"We'll be fine! Go!" Owen yells, and I push Olive to Rose. Rose catches her, and the girls hide her from view. It works. When I turn around, Diane is still chasing us.

I turn to Owen. "How are you doing?" He doesn't answer. "Owen?"

"I'm fine!" His stance wobbles, and the fair lights shine on his bruised leg. There's blood on it too. Dammit. He always pushes himself. I scolded him for weeks after he ran that race freshman year. He collapsed as soon as he finished it.

I glance behind us once we get past most of the crowd. "I can't see her," I say. Owen slows down. Good, now he's ahead of me. Owen puts his hands on his knees and starts gasping for air. I look at the crowd again. A few seconds pass, and Diane comes into view. Owen and I make eye contact, and we take off.

I can only run so slowly to stay with him before it's impossible to do so. No matter what, tonight I'm faster. We're halfway between the yacht club and the marina. She has to get tired at some point. It's over for her. She's already lost.

"Shit!" Owen falls to the ground. I turn around, and Diane is running toward him.

No more. No fucking more.

I run to Owen first and push Diane back with all my strength. I throw a right hook, and she falls to the ground. Owen backs away, and I circle Diane. Making sure she won't lose sight of me.

"Is that all you got, bitch? Come and get me!" If Yann's taunts taught me anything, it's that they'll focus on you. Diane gets up, and when I take off running, so does she.

"Paco! Paco, goddammit! Stop!" Owen yells. He tries to catch up, but it doesn't matter. He can get away. He's safe. Everyone's safe. She's after me now.

Everything hurts. My head, my legs, my chest. My body is screaming at me to stop running, but I can't let her catch me. I make it back to the fair. I run through the stalls on the grass and reach the fence by the boats. I don't look back. It takes too much energy, and if she's close, I will throw up. I need to find someone. I need to find someone before...

SLAM!

"Fuck!" My body scrapes across the concrete and I hit the fence. I push myself up with my back against the fence. Diane stands over me, trapping me in a box. She raises her fists and starts punching.

"You asshole!" She yells between punches. "Leave my family alone!"

Yann's boxing tips can't save me now. My heart pounds in my ears while I block what punches I can. All I can do is wait for an opening or wait until she knocks me out. Fight, dammit, fight!

There it is! I punch her in the face. She backs off to assess the damage. It's all the time I need to get up and start running. I can only get so far before I have to hold on to the fence. My body is in so much pain, and I'm so exhausted.

We go at it again when Diane catches up to me. In the few seconds where she doesn't hit me, she's reaching for something in her pocket. I hit her in the side, and whatever she grabbed falls onto the floor. She rises. I swing. She ducks. I miss. She comes back up and socks me in the stomach. She pushes me against the fence, and I fall to the floor.

I can barely keep my eyes open. There's something sparking to life in front of me. My eyes focus on a firework pointing right at me. My life flashes before my eyes again. No. God, no!

"Run!" Owen screams. I don't know where he is, but he's nearby. "Run! Paco, run!"

I push myself off the ground and Diane races to keep me down. I fist her shirt and slam her against the fence. I hop over the firework and fall to the ground, rolling away as far as I can. Diane struggles to get up, knowing the predicament she's in. But it's too late. The firework hits her in the leg. It burns right through her pants and onto her skin. The crowd finally turns, alerted by her blood-curdling screams.

The sheer look on Diane's face as it hit her, watching the fear go to agonizing pain. I want to throw up on the spot. That was supposed to be for me.

She really wanted me dead. Or out of her way. Or that was her answer to getting me out of her way.

I stare at the crowd as they run to Diane. People shout at each other to call 911. Then someone actually calls 911. Jesus Christ. I can't look anymore. She's moaning and groaning in pain. It makes me want to shrivel up and rot into pieces. That doesn't even make sense, but it's making me sick.

My arms feel weak, and they give out. I fall onto the concrete with a thud.

"Paco!" Owen yells. I can't move. *I can't move.* I'm stuck on the ground. Owen reaches me. His face comes into view, and he turns paler, if that's even possible. His hands pick up my head and hold it off the ground. "H-hold on! We're going to get help!"

I cough. "Are you okay?"

"Yes! Jesus Christ, I'm fine! Paco, hold on! Don't fucking die on me!"

Die?

Die...

Oh, god. I'm going to die, aren't I?

"Paco! Hold on!" Owen yells again. His tears fall off his face and onto me. His head whips around, giving me whiplash with how fast he's moving. My eyes flutter shut, but Owen shakes me hard. "No, don't you dare!"

My vision blurs. Owen cries harder. His pleas for me to stay awake go in and out. "What..." I mutter, "what's happening?"

"Help! Somebody, help!" Owen's voice sounds so frail. He digs his hand into my pocket and pulls out the bloody napkins. He holds the napkins against my head, his hand trembling the entire time. Owen looks around again and screams, "*¡Ayudame! ¡Ayudame!*"

Oh, god. I must look like a mess if Owen's calling for help in Spanish. I can't feel anything at all. I can't move. I can't speak. My eyes look around. Owen's still yelling for help, and my eyes fall shut.

"Rose! Oh, thank God. I can't get anyone over here. No one's helping!"

"What happened to him?" Rose cries. Her hand reaches down. "Paco? Paco!"

My eyes open again. One of her hands is cupping my cheek, turning me toward her. Her other hand is holding mine. I drift my thumb over her hand, tracing the words *I love you*. Rose gasps. "He's awake. He's awake!"

"Oh, thank God." Owen sighs. Rose and Owen stop talking, looking in a different direction. Owen looks at me again. "They're almost here. You're going to be okay," he says as my eyes close again.

Every time I open my eyes, something's different. My ears are ringing, the voices around me are fuzzy, and I can't understand what they're saying. Someone shines a flashlight on my face.

"Can you hear me?" a voice calls. "Can you hear me?"

"What's your friend's name?" another voice asks, and another light shines on me. "Paco, can you hear me? Do you know where you are?"

"Pittsburg, California?" I answer with a weak voice. It hurts to breathe. My ears stop ringing. Sirens wail nearby, and fireworks are still going off.

It's like I've been burned a thousand times. I scream as my hand flies to the side of my head. My body feels like it's on fire. Everything hurts. Everything fucking hurts. The medics push Rose and Owen to the side and crowd around me. Their voices fade away, and the only thing I hear is my pounding heart getting weaker and weaker.

As I'm watching the fireworks burn brightly in the sky, my vision fades to black.

20

WHEN I WAKE UP, I'm not downtown. I don't know where I am, but the light on the ceiling is so bright that it hurts my head. The walls and ceiling are various shades of white, and there's a faint beeping in the background. I jump up and immediately regret it. I fall back down with a groan, placing a hand on my head.

"Don't get up so fast!" It's Rose. She puts a hand on my cheek. I lean into her hand as she brushes her thumb over my cheek.

"He's awake?" Footsteps stomp toward me. Owen hops into the chair on my left. He sighs in relief. "I thought you fell into a coma or something. Diane beat the shit out of you."

"What happened?" I ask, sitting up a lot slower this time. "When did I get here? I don't remember anything."

"You passed out after fighting with Diane," Owen says. "You were in and out, and your head was still bleeding, so they brought you to the hospital."

"My head hurts like hell." I groan. I look around the room. "Where's everyone else? Are they okay? The tuplets?"

The nickname I gave the kids throws him off, but he answers, "Everyone's fine. Calm down, man. It'll make your head hurt more." I look at Owen's wrist. He has a hospital band on. I point to it. Owen sighs. "It was for my leg. I'm okay though, it's not sprained or any-thing."

Rose leans toward me. "Hey, I'm going to go find a doctor, and I have to use the bathroom. I'll be back, okay?" I nod. Rose kisses my head before leaving. Owen and I sit in silence for a few minutes. I'm laying down when Owen opens a bag of chips. Where did he even get those?

"How are you feeling?" Owen asks, popping a chip into his mouth.

"Everything hurts, but I'll be okay." I look away and sigh. "I'm sorry."

"For what?"

"Everything. This wasn't how it was supposed to go."

"It's not your fault," he answers, but I don't believe him.

I sit up slowly. My arms are holding onto my body, as if it's the only thing keeping me together. I feel like a child. A stupid child. I glance at Owen. My jaw drops slightly. There's blood all over his shirt. "W-whose blood is that?"

There's a pause before he answers. "Yours."

Dammit. *Change the subject!* "Did anyone else see the firework?" I ask quickly.

Owen's face falls. His green eyes are dark. "No. I was the only one who saw," he says, a bit bitter.

"C-could we keep it that way?" I ask. Tears threaten to roll down my face. "I don't want to worry anyone."

"Everyone's already worried sick," Owen says. "I thought you fucking died, man. I thought my best friend just died right in front of me." Owen takes a deep breath. "There was so much blood. Your head, your face... God."

"Shit. I'm so sorry."

Owen sighs. "Don't be. I'm just glad you're okay."

"Paco!" I look up, and Sam runs inside. Oh no. I think she's still mad at me. I think all of them are mad at me. My mouth quivers, trying to find words to say.

Sam runs to me, leans over, and pulls me into a hug. My thoughts disappear when I hear her cry, "You're okay. I'm so happy you're okay."

I nearly burst into tears right then and there. Sam squeezes tighter until I finally hug her back. It takes everything in me not to sob on her shoulder.

Sam lets me go. Pachi and Yann are behind her. Yann's holding an ice pack on his head. Sam and Pachi have scratches and cuts on their face and wrists. My eyes land on the red stains on Sam's shirt. My blood. That's my blood.

"Are you okay?" Pachi asks.

"My head hurts, but yeah, I'm fine." I am going to have nightmares about Diane killing me for the rest of my life, but I'm fine. Maybe I deserve it.

My friends pull up chairs and sit by my bed. Yann puts his ice pack on the hospital nightstand and looks at me. "There's news reporters everywhere. They're outside the hospital."

"For what?"

"They found out about the sextuplets. Everyone is losing their shit." Yann plays a news broadcast on his phone. Ironically, it's his dad reporting outside the hospital.

Mr. Torre goes on about how the sextuplets were kidnapped and reported missing, how they were never found, and how the police ruled them deceased. After that, they show a video. It's downtown, and when they zoom in on the video, it shows me. Oh, great. Someone recorded Diane beating my ass. Thanks for the help. The video stops as the firework sparks to life. I'm praying that my friends don't notice.

Pachi points to the spark. "What the hell is that?" *Shit.*

Yann rewinds the broadcast and screenshots the fight. His eyes squint as he zooms into the picture. My heart pounds against my chest, and the heart monitor picks it up. My friends look at the machine and back at me.

"How long have I been out for?" I ask, hoping they drop it.

"About two hours now," Owen answers.

Two hours? If I've been out for two hours, why is everyone still here?

"We were worried about you! Of course we'd be here!" Sam answers, and I realize I've asked that out loud. My face heats up and I lie down with a groan.

"This is all my fault. You guys wouldn't be in this mess if it wasn't for me."

Sam would slap the side of my head if it wasn't for my head wound. "Don't even start. We all knew what we were getting into."

"Didn't think she'd kidnap us at a public event, let alone in the bathroom." Pachi shivers.

"In the bathroom? What happened?"

Diane's attack started the moment Olive and Owen went to the bathroom. That's where Diane and the kids were hiding. She grabbed Olive in the girl's bathroom, and Owen went to save her, only to get captured. That's when Christina took Olive's place. Sam called Owen when they made it to the yacht club and heard his phone ringing in the girl's bathroom. She and Pachi charged in. Sam went after Diane, and Pachi tried to free Owen, but Diane forced Theodore to tie them up. Sam's on the wrestling team too, but Diane overpowered her.

When I texted Owen, Diane forced him to respond. She watched him type every word.

After the power went out and everyone left, Theodore slammed a roll of duct tape into Diane's head, and they escaped. But Diane pulled out her gun, and it all ended there. We charged in, and she knocked Yann out. I feel so guilty. How can I not?

"I'm so sorry," I say, putting my head in my hands. "Honestly, I don't get why you guys are still here. I thought you were pissed at me," I mumble.

"How hard did she hit your head?" Sam questions. "I'm only pissed at what you said."

"What I said? What did I say?"

They all stare at me, but Pachi speaks first, "Not being worth it." He hisses. Oh. *Oh.* I forgot I even said that. But after all that I put them through, they're mad at that?

"I thought I was going to die," I whisper. The moments replay in my head. She tried to kill me. Not once, but twice.

"I thought you *did* die," Yann says, and I freeze. "The last thing I heard before passing out was her counting down. I woke up thinking you were dead." He hits my arm. "Never scare me like that again."

The scenes play through my head over and over. The screams, the yelling, the crying. *Deep breaths. Deep breaths.* "My life flashed before my eyes... twice..." I mumble.

"Twice?" Pachi questions.

I can bullshit it. She put the gun on me twice after all. I can lie my way through it. But seeing all their faces... I can't lie to them anymore.

"The thing in the video... it's a firework." I pause. "She tried to kill me with a firework."

Yann's eyes go wide. "She tried to kill you twice?"

Owen looks at me. "You don't have to talk about it, but we're here for you. You know that, don't you?"

The dam shatters, and I burst into tears. "You guys are the best." I bury my face in my hands so they can't see me. I must look like a mess. Bloody, bruised, a black eye definitely forming. "I'm so sorry."

"Stop, man. Stop," Owen says. I look at him, confused.

"None of this is your fault." Yann's voice is firm. "Don't blame yourself for Diane kidnapping us. Do you know how stupid that sounds?"

I chuckle. "I find that very hard to believe."

"You just wanted to help, and you did. All the kids are home now. You did stupid shit, but they're home." Yann sighs. "That's what you do. Hell, that's how we met. I was the new kid, and you helped me out. All of you did." Yann pauses and smiles. "I'm glad you guys are my friends."

"You guys are the best. I've never would've been able to do this without you." I sigh. "Thanks for putting up with my bullshit."

"We wouldn't have it any other way," Sam says, and my friends smile. My friends. God, I'm so happy they're not mad at me. It makes my head hurt a lot less.

Rose finally returns with a doctor. My parents and Paula are running behind them. The doctor tells us that I'm staying overnight for observation and that I'll be free to go in the morning. They want to keep an eye on my head wound for a little longer. Everyone stays as long as they can, but the doctor knocks on the door and says it's time to go. Mom and Dad can stay, and they sleep in the chairs next to me.

I fall asleep after midnight.

I'm right about the black eye. When I wake up in the morning, my left eye is swollen. My mom runs to a doctor, who comes back with an ice pack. The doctor changes my bandages before I leave. "You'll be able to take them off at home. This is so it doesn't get infected. Keep an eye on the wound, okay? It left a scar," the doctor says.

A scar? Oh, great. My mom and dad thank the doctors. A few minutes later, we get in the car and drive home, getting breakfast on the way. Dad opens the front door, and we sit at the table. We eat in silence for a bit. Mom and Dad haven't scolded me. I'm sure Paula told them everything, so why haven't they?

"*¿Están enojados conmigo?*" I ask.

My dad sighs. "*No, mijo. Estamos felices de que estés bien.*"

They're just happy I'm okay.

I go to bed after breakfast. About an hour later, someone rings the doorbell. Mom answers the door. She says something in a cheerful voice. The door shuts, and footsteps come up the stairs.

"*¿Quien es?*" I ask when they knock.

"It's Owen."

My eyes pop open. "Come in," I say as I sit up.

Owen opens the door and sits on the bed. "You all right, man?"

"Yeah, just a headache. A horrible headache." I groan.

Owen sighs. "I know you just got home, but have you looked at the news today at all?"

"No, why?"

"It's the top story. Everyone's talking about it." Owen pulls out his phone and shows me an article. *Missing triplets found alive. Suspect in custody.* I guess the burn wasn't that bad. She was released this morning too.

I get out of bed. "Really? Let's go watch it downstairs."

Owen and I spend the next few hours watching the news. Well, he does. It hurts to stare at the TV, so I listen instead. The first update is around noon. The police searched Diane's house and found Christina's diary. The police officer described it as "disturbing journal entries." The news reports that ripped-out entries were turned in to the police as well.

Olive sends me a message a few minutes later, asking me if I'm okay. She then tells me that everyone is finally reunited. From what it sounds like, it was a very tearful reunion. Christina is still shaken up, but she's doing okay.

"*Mijo*, we have to run to the store," Mom says. "Would you like us to get food? Owen, have you eaten yet?"

"Food would be nice. Thank you, Mama."

"You'll be all right on your own?" My dad asks, and I nod. They say goodbye and drive off.

We listen to commercials for a few minutes before Owen turns to me. "You still have the bandages on?"

I forgot about that. "Oh, yeah. I should take them off. I'll be back."

I get up from the couch and walk to the bathroom. I close the door behind me and look in the mirror. The bandages are clean. I guess it's time.

My hand touches the bandages. Sam's scream plays in my head. My body jolts back. I look in the mirror. Scratches and bruises run up and down my face. I turn my head and watch the scratches grow more and more. The bandages stop me from seeing any more skin. Maybe it's a good thing. I look horrible.

I grab the bandages again. Blood. All I see is blood. All I hear are screams. Tears fall down my face as last night plays through my head again. My friends' cries are so distinct. Pachi's voice cracks over and over, Owen screaming at the top of his lungs for help, Sam crying, Olive screaming. Their voices mash together, getting louder, and louder, and louder!

I catch myself on the counter. *Breathe. Breathe.* My heart's going to explode. Tears cloud my vision and my knees hit the floor. Why can't I do this? Why can't I take these stupid bandages off? It's not hard. It shouldn't be hard!

I lean against the sink and face the door. I gasp for air. "O-Owen?" I call out. "Owen?" My voice is barely louder than a whisper. I doubt he heard me. But his footsteps approach, stopping just outside the door.

"Yeah?"

"Could you... help with the bandages?" The words take all the air out of me. God, this is so embarrassing. I should be able to do this. I want to take it back, but the door's already open. He's helping me back on my feet, standing by my side.

I lean toward Owen so he can reach. My hand follows his, trembling the entire time. He pushes it back down. "I've got you, don't worry."

My hand clings to my shirt as Owen unwraps the bandages. I shut my eyes tight and try to focus on my breathing. Anxiety builds in my chest. The bandages fall to the ground, and Owen steps back. I look in the mirror.

It's a straight line on my left temple. Dried blood is around the edges, and some of my curls are frayed. Okay. This isn't bad. It doesn't look bad. It's just a reminder of one of the worst moments of my life. Just a reminder that I almost got everyone killed.

Just a reminder that I almost died.

I almost died... twice.

The sobs escape my throat. My breaths are shaky, and the sobs take everything out of me. I glance at Owen. He holds out his arms. I hug him tightly and cry on his shoulder. He hugs me back and lets me cry until I can't anymore.

The next days go by in a blur. As the police collect evidence for the case, they interview the tuplets. It's been two weeks since the fireworks show. I open the door to see a man in a suit holding an envelope. It's a subpoena, and that only means one thing.

I have to testify against Diane.

I run back inside the house, already in tears. I hate court, and I hated every minute of when I testified against that cop. I know it got him punished, but that shit is nerve-racking. Everyone is staring at you. The defendant stares at you like you're a monster, and worse, their lawyer. The defense lawyer was mean, and I couldn't stop crying.

I call Sam when I get back inside. She runs to the door, and I hear the interaction over the phone. "Paquito, it'll be okay," Sam says softly.

"I don't want to do this," I say through tears.

"I know. I know you don't." Sam pauses. "What day are you going?"

"Tuesday. You?"

"Tuesday too. I'll sit in the courtroom while you testify. Would that help?"

"It doesn't work like that. They kept me in a separate room while Mom was testifying." Sam curses in Spanish. I take another breath. "Will you go with me?"

"Of course I will. And hey, let's go to Logan's later. He might know something we don't."

Later that night, we pile into Pachi's van and drive to Logan's. All of us got subpoenas. The trial doesn't start until Monday, but Owen, Pachi, and Yann are going on Wednesday.

Logan lets us in, and we follow him to the couch. He's watching the news. The story stopped playing every day, but it started again once they announced her trial date. The TV flashes the headline, *Diane Page found fit to stand trial.* Apparently, she tried to appeal for insanity.

"How are all of you doing?" Logan asks.

"I don't know what day it is," I answer. I haven't been able to sleep since the fireworks show. And what's worse, I've been having nightmares almost every night. One was so bad that I called Rose, and she had to stay on a call with me until I fell back asleep.

"I'm surprised she's gotten a trial so quickly," Logan says, breaking the short silence. We look at the TV. It shows Diane's new mugshot. She looks like hell itself.

"Paco and I are going first. They want us on Tuesday," Sam says, placing her hand on my shoulder. The stress is visible on my face.

"I'm freaking the hell out," I mutter. "When I went up for my dad, it was terrifying."

Logan nods. "I remember hearing about it from your mother. I know it's stressful, but your testimonies will be very impactful. You are all close to Olive." He turns to me as he continues, "But you are the closest with Theodore. You were the one he talked to the most during this. Not only that, the kids said they talked about you a lot."

"I have the most leverage again." I sigh, looking at the ground.

"Sam is a close second. But, yes, I believe you do." Logan puts a hand on my shoulder, turning me to face him. "You can do it. I know you can."

"Do we have to testify?" We look at the stairs. It's Olive. She pokes her head around the wall. Christina and Theodore are behind her.

"If you don't want to, I'm sure I can talk to them about it," Logan says.

"No, don't do that. I want to," Olive answers.

"Okay then," Logan replies. The answer satisfies Olive, and she goes upstairs with her siblings. Logan turns back to me. "It's going to be okay."

I hope so.

"Please state your full name for the court."

"Paco Alejandro Cortez-Oliver." Chills run down my spine as I place my hand on the Bible in front of me.

"You do solemnly state that the testimony you may give in the case now pending before this court shall be the truth, the whole truth, and nothing but the truth, so help you God?"

"I do." They take the bible away, and it begins. My eyes search the crowd. There are a bunch of news reporters here. The trial is being broadcasted live. I was watching Sam's testimony in the bathroom. Witnesses aren't allowed to see other testimonies, but I had to watch it somehow. Because of that, Sam's waiting in her car.

My eyes find Diane. My body freezes as she looks at me, crossing her arms. Her face is stone cold, and yet she's trying to murder me with her eyes. I look away. I can do this, dammit. I can do this.

I've had two panic attacks since waking up. If I'm honest, they're not new to me, but these were painful. The other thing I hated about court was reliving my dad's assault. I feel like I'm eleven again. I have to do this. I have to do this for the tuplets, for my friends, for everyone. If this gets them their happy ending, I'll relive the fireworks show how many times they want.

"How did you meet Olive Page?" Ginger, the prosecution lawyer, asks.

"She broke into my house, and I found her in the laundry room. My friends were over, and we caught her."

"Your friend Sam said you faked a call to the police. Is that true?"

"Y-yes," I stammer, "I called Owen instead, hoping it would get Olive to say her reason for breaking into my house. She was avoiding my questions."

"What did she tell you?"

Ginger continues to ask me questions, and I answer them. Then it's the defense attorney's turn. His questions are cold, and Ginger has to step in a few times to tell him to knock it off. They question me about everything. As the questions go on, I look at Diane again. I tell them the truth without breaking eye contact. For a second, her facade breaks.

My testimony is over. Someone escorts outside the courtroom and to the parking lot. Sam's truck speeds around the parking lot and parks in front. She runs to me, pulling me into a hug. "It's over now. You did good," she says. Our suits wrinkle as I hug her tighter.

"I forgot how much this sucks." I groan, letting her go to get in the car. Sam drives out of the parking lot. I wipe my eyes. "She just... sits there. No emotion, no reaction, nothing!"

"I know." Sam sighs. "She was like that during mine."

"Do you know who's next?"

"Not sure. I think Diane's manager is speaking right now, but there's a recess afterward. Everyone else goes tomorrow."

"Aren't we saying the same things at this point?"

"Yann might remember something Pachi doesn't, and Owen might know something Yann doesn't. I don't know, I don't understand court shit."

"Owen saw Diane take out the firework. Maybe that's something."

Sam sighs. "Maybe." The rest of the ride is in silence. Sam drives up to my house and turns off the car. She gets out and walks me to the door.

I put the key inside the lock and turn it. The door opens, but I don't move. My body tenses, my hands are sweaty, and I just... can't.

"Are you okay?" Sam asks.

I look at her. "Could you stay with me? I don't want to be alone right now."

Sam locks her car. "Of course." We step inside, and Sam shuts the door while I turn on the TV. Sam joins me on the couch as I put on the trial. Sam sighs. "Hey, Paquito. You're the strongest person I know."

"Who are the other candidates?" I say, trying to get her to laugh.

"We're all here for you, okay? Don't forget that," Sam says, and I smile.

"The prosecution would like to call Christina Page to the stand."

Our heads whip toward the TV. Christina? The camera zooms in on Diane's face. It's the first visible reaction I've seen come out of her. She looks pale, and she grips her arm. Diane is squirming in her seat as Christina finishes the oath.

"How old are you, sweetie?" Ginger asks.

Christina responds quickly, "I'm fourteen."

"I know this is hard, but you are very brave for coming up here. Your words are very important." Ginger grabs her papers and organizes them. She takes a deep breath. "How would you say your relationship with your mother is?"

Christina looks at her mom, then back at Ginger. "It's not that bad. She's nice, sometimes."

"Why do you say sometimes?"

"She can be mean," Christina says as she fiddles with her hair. "One time she locked Olive in our room for going outside and saying hi to the mailman."

Whispers run through the crowd. Sam and I look at each other. It's still a bit shocking hearing the kids recall what their mom has done to them. Ginger is shocked as well. She stutters, trying to process what Christina said. "F-for saying hello? What was she in trouble for?"

"I don't know. Mom doesn't like Olive." Christina twirls her hair. "It's sad, I love Olive. I don't know why Mom doesn't."

Ginger stares at her papers for a second. She takes a deep breath and grabs a book off her table. I recognize it instantly. "Do you know what this is?"

Christina nods quickly. "My diary."

"And these?" Ginger swaps the diary for loose pieces of paper.

"The entries I ripped out..."

"Why did you do that?"

"I didn't want to read them."

"How come?" Ginger questions.

"Mom was being very mean." Christina looks at her mother and flinches. "We were bad kids, so Mom had to teach us a lesson."

I turn to Sam. This isn't good. Diane is manipulating Christina without saying anything. I think Ginger noticed, because she asks Christina to look at her.

"Christina, has your mother done anything that hurt you or your siblings?"

Christina tilts her head. "On purpose or on accident?"

"Just…" Ginger pauses, trying to figure out how to phrase it. "Can you name a time when your mother really hurt you? Or when she made you feel very sad?"

"There's been a few," Christina says. "Mom was mean after Olive ran away. She blamed me for it, even though it was Mom's fault."

"What do you mean?"

"Mom and Olive were fighting a lot, so Olive wanted to make dinner. She burned the whole pot of soup. Mom got really mad, knocked the pot off the stove, and it landed on Olive." Whispers swim through the crowd again. "Mom yelled at Olive. She said she was a mistake, she hated her, and that she should've left her with Dad and taken someone else. And if you don't believe me, the burns are there. They scarred on Olive's left arm."

This is it. Ginger steps forward. "Can you elaborate on what you meant by—?"

"Objection! Irrelevant!" Diane's lawyer shouts. When no one moves, he yells, "And the witness has been on the stand too long!"

"Overruled!" the judge bellows.

"It's okay, Christina," Ginger says in a soft voice. "I need you to explain. What do you mean by being left with Dad?"

"Mom took us away after we turned two." The tension thickens. "She said it was to save us, but I think she just wanted to hurt Dad."

She turns to her mother. "Mom likes hurting Dad. She hurt Leo to hurt him. She took us to hurt him."

Christina looks at her mom the entire time. "For years, she told me everything. She spilled every secret, shared every thought." Christina speaks fast, and her breathing picks up. But she doesn't stop. Tears fall down her face as she holds eye contact with Diane. "She did everything to hide us. She got a fake ID. She homeschooled us. But whenever she got drunk, she would tell me everything. How Dad had betrayed her even though he was trying to help, how she couldn't handle the idea of not having her kids even though she yelled at us the night before."

Sam and I lean closer to the TV as Christina takes a sharp breath. "How she hated him, how she hated us, how she wished she'd never gone through with the pregnancy, and how she wanted to take Leo instead of Theodore! There's even more stuff on her computer—!"

"You ungrateful bitch!" The camera lands on Diane, who is standing up. "After everything I've done for you!" The court goes ballistic. Diane's lawyer can't calm her down. The judge hits her gavel on the desk. Diane has to be escorted out by security, and she yells at Christina the entire time.

Christina finishes her testimony without further interruption. To top it off, the next witness is Olive, and she doesn't hold back. She tells the court everything, even the fight between Logan and Diane. She smiles as she gets off the stand. I know she can't see me, but I hope she knows how proud we are of her.

It's finally over.

21

— · —

GUILTY. DIANE IS RULED guilty on all charges. The moment they read the verdict, I sigh in so much relief. The camera flies to Diane. She puts her head in her hands, and she's crying. She's actually crying. My parents are home watching it with me. We jump for joy, watching the officers take Diane away. She somehow finds the camera and looks at it. That look in her eyes will haunt me for the rest of my life. They truly are *ojos del diablo.*

Owen, Pachi, and Yann text that they're on their way home. All of them testified today. We turn on the news once they stop showing the trial, and reporters surround the courthouse.

The verdict is trending on Twitter. *Diane Page: Guilty.* It's everywhere. I keep pinching myself to see if I'm dreaming. Mom changes the TV to music, and I head upstairs to my room to breathe. I still haven't been able to sleep, and Mom's suggesting I make a therapy appointment. I went for a bit after what happened with Dad, but I haven't gone since. Owen mentioned it too. He says it helps.

I collapse into bed. I stare at the ceiling fan above me. It's over. It's really over. Diane's in jail, Olive and her siblings are home, and it's over. It's not hitting. For the past two months, I've been worrying and stressing over it, and now it's over.

I feel like I've been squished.

My phone goes off a few seconds later. It's a text from Rose.

Rose: Hey, are you okay?

Me: Yeah, relieved she was found guilty.

Rose: Me too. But are you sure you're okay? I finally had time to watch it. You looked pale in your testimony.

I sigh in defeat and call Rose. She answers instantly. A moment passes before I speak. "She was staring at me the entire time." I shudder.

"I know. I don't understand how she was able to keep her composure. Have you seen the courtroom drawings of her? She looks like she's about to kill someone!"

"She tried," I reply, trying to joke. Rose's breathing halts. I freeze. "*¿Mi amor?*"

"I didn't want to believe it when you said it. I just..." Rose pauses. "I don't know what I would've done if she did."

"I'm still here. I kept our promise." I smile.

"Barely! You had a black eye and a head wound! That's not being safe, babe!"

"I'm sorry!" I stutter. "I was as safe as I could be."

"I'm glad you're okay," she says. We sit in silence for a while, just saying nothing. "Paco?" Rose says, breaking the silence.

"Yes?"

"I love you."

My heart soars into the sky, and I smile big. "I love you too."

We talk for hours. I hang up when Dad calls me down for dinner. We order food. No one wants to cook after such an eventful day. Paula comes over too. We turn the news on during dinner. It's the top story of the night.

The news shows clips of the testimonies that were given. They start with Logan's on Monday. His testimony hurts to watch. He tells the entire story of him and Diane and starts crying. Then it cuts to Sam's.

"Why did you surrender when she pulled out the gun?" the defense attorney asks. I remember that. He thought it would confuse Sam.

Sam stares at him, obviously irritated. "We're high school students in America. What high school student here isn't scared of a gun?"

It jumps to my testimony next. Rose is right. I look really pale.

"What happened after you said that?" Ginger asks. I know what part they're playing. Why does it have to be this part?

"She laughed and said I was brave. Then she pushed the gun harder on my forehead and cocked it. She started counting down…" I took a deep breath after that. It's weird watching myself. "I thought I was going to die."

It shows Christina's next. But it skips to the part everyone cares about. Diane's outburst looks even worse on the TV. The news has to censor all the swears she said. Next, the news shows small clips of my friends' testimonies and a clip of Theodore's. He was the last witness to testify.

"She told us for as long as I can remember that Dad was the monster," Theodore says through tears. He looks at his mother, who was let back into the courtroom today. "The only monster there's ever been is you."

The news cuts to something else outside the courtroom. It's Logan. I think this is right after they announced the verdict.

"I'm thankful that my children are all back together. I never stopped loving them. They have been my pride and joy since the moment I met them. We have many years to make up together, but I'm grateful I'm able to do it at all.

"I want to thank Paco, Owen, Sam, Pachi, and Yann for their help in bringing my family back together. Without them, this would just be a dream. A wish I would make for the rest of my life. But now it's reality. I will forever be in your guy's debt. And thank you to everyone who has supported me throughout this difficult journey. My family is home, and so am I."

Mom reaches for the napkins to dry her eyes. Even Dad has a tear rolling down his face. Paula looks at me with a smile. "Hell of a summer, huh?"

"Yeah, absolutely," I say.

When I go to bed, I have the best sleep I've had since the triplets knocked on my door.

The rest of the week goes by in a flash. I can't believe summer's practically over. Preseason starts Monday. Summer went by so fast, but it felt like the longest months of my life.

Diane was found guilty three days ago. Sentencing takes place in a few months, and it could be as much as life. Logan decided now was the time to throw the welcome home party. Since Paula was never able to throw that summer party, she opened up her home to celebrate. With her pool in tip-top shape, it'll be a big pool party. Olive, Theodore, and Christina haven't been to a pool in years, so they're ecstatic.

I arrive early to help set up decorations. Paula gives me a hug and hands me some balloons. After blowing up a few, I walk to the kitchen. Paula pulls on my shirt. "Nope, don't even think about cooking. I'll order food later. The only thing you have to worry about is having fun."

"*Gracias hermana,*" I say, picking up another balloon.

Sam shows up next, and Paula runs to her. "It's been so long!" Paula picks up Sam and swings her around. "You're so tall now!"

"Made sure I was finally free of this one." Sam laughs. Sam reaches into her tote bag and pulls out a...

My body freezes until Sam finishes taking it out. It's a water gun. Just a water gun. I sigh in relief. *Yeah, I will book that appointment.* "Get ready for the biggest ass-kicking of your life." Sam laughs, pointing it at me.

"Samantha!"

"*¡Lo siento, señora!*" Sam says to my mom, and I smirk. Sam pulls the trigger and splashes me with water. "Ha! It's been filled!"

"And you are cleaning that up," Paula says, taking the gun from Sam's hands. She then shoots both of us with it. Sam and I grab napkins and wipe up the puddles.

Owen arrives next. He's wearing his swimsuit, along with his glasses. He's also holding a water gun. Quickly, he puts his things down and runs to the snack table. "What?" he asks when we look at him. "I'm hungry!"

Yann and Pachi run through the front door. "Ha! I won!" Pachi cheers. He's dressed in his swimsuit, along with his green googles.. Yann denies the loss and pulls his hair into a bun.

"What've you guys been up to?" I ask, "Feels like time keeps flying. Summer's basically over too."

"Oh, I auditioned for section leader," Owen announces. He holds the suspense as we wait for him to answer. "You are now looking at the low brass section leader!"

We all cheer. "I told you that you'd make it!" Yann says. "You're one of the best players we've got."

"Do you know who the second one is?" I ask.

"Not yet. I found out directly. I think they'll tell everyone later."

"Are you going to swim or what?" Paula points to the backyard. "It's ready!"

Pachi and Owen dive into the pool as the rest of us go to change. Once we're all changed, we head outside. Sam's putting sunblock on whatever her one-piece isn't covering, and Yann takes off his shirt and cannonballs into the pool.

I jump into the pool just as Olive and her family show up. My parents and Yann's run to Logan, eager to catch up at last. With all the girls standing side by side, it's hard to tell who's who. That is until one of them jumps into the pool and lands right next to me.

I cough up the water that splashed into my mouth. "Olive!" I cough again. "Watch where you're jumping!"

"Ha! Sorry!" Olive smiles. She points to something underwater. "Did you know they make swim shorts?" she questions. "I've only seen girls wear one-pieces and bikinis! I've never seen shorts!"

I always forget how much she hasn't seen until she says something. Olive looks to the left. "Christina got a one-piece with strawberries on it." Olive points to her sister, who's putting sunblock on. "You should've seen her face. She was so excited."

"Oh, yeah. There are a lot of clothes that have fun prints. I have donuts on mine."

"That's sick." Olive looks around. Her eyes landed on the water gun behind me. "Pass me that gun. I'm going to get Sam."

I give her the gun. Sam is talking to Yann, completely distracted. "Good luck!" I tell her as she shoots Sam.

"What do you mean—?" Sam lunges at Olive and picks her up. "Ah! Shit! Put me down! Put me down!" Sam dunks her into the pool. I can't stop laughing.

When Olive comes back to the surface, she glares at me. "What?" I ask, still laughing. "I said good luck for a reason!"

More people show up, but the last people that I know are Katie, Helen, Rose, and her parents. I swim up to the edge of the pool and say hello to Rose. She's wearing a flower-printed one-piece, and her hair is pulled back into a ponytail. She gets more beautiful every time I see her.

"You can swim, right?" I ask as she steps into the pool.

"Yeah, why?" I pick her up and put her on my shoulder. She squeals. "Put me down! Put me down!" I dunk us underwater, but not for long. She splashes me as we rise to the surface.

I hold her close. Rose puts her hand on my face. Her fingers gloss over my scar, trailing down to my cheek. We lean in and kiss. I kiss her again. It doesn't matter that we're soaked and smell like chlorine. It's her, and I won't change it for the world.

The party continues. Rose and I start a chicken tournament with everyone else. We beat Owen and Katie, even if Rose falls off a few seconds after Katie. But Sam and Yann kick our asses. When Rose falls, so do I. The finale is between Pachi and Helen, and Yann and Sam. I don't know who won. They both fall into the pool at the same time.

Christina swims up to me sometime after. I don't know what to do. Technically, it's my first time meeting her. We've talked only once before, and that was when she was disguised as Olive. I know so much about her, but at the same time, I don't.

"I'm sorry I read your diary," I say, breaking the silence. I don't think it'll make her feel better, but I still feel bad about it. "I know it's not much, but I want you to know I'm sorry."

"Oh, it's okay. You weren't the only one." Christina looks down at the water and whispers, "I'm sorry I tricked you. Could we still be friends?"

"I already considered you one." Christina smiles and hugs me. After a few seconds, she swims after her brother.

Olive is at the deep end. I swim over and sit next to her. "What did Christina say?" she asks.

"She wanted to know if we could be friends. She was worried I was mad at her for tricking me."

Olive smiles, her eyes on her sister. "She's so sweet." Olive's eyes are filling with tears. She swallows and clears her throat. "Hey, you remember the promise you made me?"

I blink. "The swear?"

"Yeah. About that, no more swearing. Back to promises."

"How come?" I ask. Her eyes flicker to the side of my head. "Oh. Right. Well, I promise."

Olive jabs me with her elbow. "Good. Least I know you'll keep it."

A few seconds pass before I speak again. "So, what do you want to do now?"

"I don't know." Olive shrugs. "Theodore and Christina started a bucket list with me. It was Peter's idea."

"What's on it?"

"Eat a taco, have a sleepover, become an artist. You know, things like that."

I tilt my head. "Really? Christina said you wanted to be a nurse."

Olive shakes her head. Her face is full of disgust. "No way. That's all her. She's been wanting to be a nurse for as long as I can remember. The stuff they do on TV makes my stomach feel weird. I would not be able to do that for a living."

I look at Christina. She's tossing a beach ball back and forth with Rose. Theodore watches with a big smile on his face. For the past twelve years, he's been worrying about his sisters being with their mother, and now he never has to worry again.

"We're going to see her in jail." I look at Olive, confused. Olive frowns. "Christina wants to see her. Mom will be behind a window. I don't know why she wants to go."

"For closure maybe," I say. "Well, it's up to you if you want to talk to her."

"I'll go. Maybe just to insult her one last time." She shakes her fist, but puts it down with a groan. "I don't know. It's hard with her."

"That's okay. It's okay to feel what you feel. And don't forget, we've got your back, Olive."

"You mean that?"

"Of course. We're friends after all. All of us."

Sparkles shine in Olive's eyes, and she smiles. "Thanks, Paco. You're awesome."

"Hey, Paquito!" Paula calls from outside the pool. I tell Olive I'll be back, and I swim over to Paula. Owen follows behind. She scrolls through her phone. "What do you guys want to eat? I can get burgers, pizza, chicken..."

Owen and I look at each other. "Want to get chicken?" I ask.

"Let's get chicken," he says to Paula.

Paula gets two big baskets of fried chicken. We get out of the pool and rush for the towels. As we serve ourselves food, Logan hits a fork on his soda can, calling everyone's attention.

"I'd like to make a toast." He raises up his soda can. "To Paco, Owen, Sam, Pachi, and Yann. And their friends and families. There are no words to express my gratitude for what you've done for my family. This is something I thought I would only experience in dreams. Thank you!"

Everyone cheers, and we start eating. "Man, I feel special." Pachi jokes. "It feels like we're important."

"Feel like an actual council now." Owen smiles.

"Hell yeah!" Yann says, and we laugh.

"Any last-minute summer ideas?" I chuckle. "We only have tomorrow."

"It's worth it. Look at them." Sam points to the sextuplets. "I've never seen Olive this happy."

They sit around the table together and pile their plates with food. The tuplets tell stories and play games. Christina follows her siblings around all day, with a big smile on her face. Watching them be a happy family is one of the best things about the whole day.

A few minutes later, Olive walks over to us. She gives me a piece of paper, and I recognize it. It's the drawing I saw at Sam's house, only that it's finished. It's all five of us. My friends look over my shoulder.

"You drew this? Is that us?" Owen asks, and Olive nods.

"Holy shit! You got my skin tone right!" Sam smiles, pointing to her brown skin on the drawing. "This is amazing!"

Olive smiles big. "I made copies, so you guys can all have one." A tear rolls down her face. "Consider it a thank you for everything you've done for me."

I smile. "Of course, Ol. And I am going to frame this in my room." Olive walks away, and I turn to my friends. "This is going to be the best summer ever."

And we'll make sure of it. As the sun sets, we gather inside Paula's house. We watch movies, play games, and Mr. Torre brought a karaoke machine he got in high school. The tuplets sing their hearts out. My friends and I help Olive put more items on her bucket list. The night ends with a round of video games. As the night goes on, people head home.

I kiss Rose goodbye and go back inside. My friends are staying the night. Paula gives us her office, and Mom and Dad sleep in Paula's room. My friends and I go swimming again after getting our sleeping bags set up. The pool lights make the water turn different colors. After a while of swimming, and filming a video of a giant cannonball, we sit on the edge of the pool.

"What a summer, huh?" Owen says. He's sitting on my left, with Pachi between us.

Pachi stretches. "Yeah, for sure."

I look across the pool. "Thank you," I say, and they all turn to me. "Thanks for having my back these past two months, even though I was being a dumbass. You guys are the best friends I could ever ask for. I'm sorry that risking my life was the only way I knew how to show it."

"That's the best thing you've said all day." Sam smiles. She's sitting on my right. "But never do it again."

Yann is next to her. He pokes his head around. "You're alive. That's all that matters." He smiles. "We're all here, and we're not going anywhere."

Owen points up at the sky. "Shooting star!" We look up quickly, barely catching the star as it fades from view. I've never seen one before. "Make a wish, everyone."

"A good job!" Pachi yells.

Yann puts his hands around his mouth, making a tunnel. "Video games!" he shouts.

"A full night of sleep!" Owen yells.

"The second season of my favorite anime!" We look at Sam. "What? It ended on a cliffhanger!" She hits my arm. "What did you wish for?"

"More nights like these. You guys, Rose, family, having everyone over was nice." I put my arms around them, squeezing a little tight.

"When did you get so sentimental?" Pachi jokes.

"I think I always have been." I smile. "I love you guys."

"Love you too."

We stay up for the entire night. Swimming, horror stories, pillow fights—we do whatever we can think of. This is the best night of my life. Passing time with them just makes everything better.

And even though it started off as a different summer, that's what would make it the best. Maybe Pachi's right about me being sentimental, but it's true. These two months might have been hell, but it's worth it. Olive and her family are back together, Rose and I are together, and I have the best friends in the world. Despite everything, they stayed with me through it all. No matter how many times I messed up, they were there. They've been there. They truly feel like home.

And it's so good to be home.

ACKNOWLEDGMENTS

You know, for some reason I keep coming back to this. It feels like I haven't said enough, done enough, thanked enough. I never used to read the acknowledgments, but after writing a book, I read them every time.

I started writing this book when I was fifteen and a sophomore in high school. As I'm typing this, I'm eighteen and a freshman in college. I never thought I would make it this far. This was an untouched dream of mine for years, and to the ones who pushed me to go for it, thank you so much.

Before I continue thanking let me just... *deep breath* OH. MY. GOOOOOOOOOOSSSSSSSHHHHH!!!! The book is finished!!! I've been dreaming about this moment for years and it's finally here. Thank you God!!

Thank you Mom and Dad. You two have been so supportive of my dream since you found out about it. You've been there for me since the beginning. You're the best parents I can ever ask for! I love you two so much.

Next, I want to thank my siblings. Rudy, Bobby, Bri, Simone, and Dom. You're the best siblings I can ever ask for. Thank you for supporting me and being by my side. I love you guys.

Thank you Ernesto and Ella, the two gabagoons that helped this story come to life. If it wasn't for our plushies and joking about a council anime for them, this book wouldn't exist.

Ernesto, I can't thank you enough for being by my side and showing me endless support and love. Thank you for always listening to my story rants and cheering me up, no matter what I'm upset over, (even if it's a cookie). I love you so much.

Ella, you've been one of my biggest supporters from the start, and I can't thank you enough for your friendship and encouragement. Thank you for always wanting to read my late night lore snippets, for lowkey being another editor, and for always having my back. I love you.

To my many friends. I fear that if I try to name you all, I'll forget someone and cry myself to sleep forever. Thank you for your support and friendship. You guys are amazing and I wish you all nothing but success and happiness!!!

To my wonderful family, who have always been supportive of me despite how annoying I may be. Thank you for putting up with me.

To Makenna Albert, my wonderful editor. Thank you for answering my endless questions and your beautiful suggestions. You made my confidence shoot through the roof. I didn't know what to expect when I sent it off to you, but your support, encouragement, and excitement made me burst into tears. I can't thank you enough.

Thank you Ruhi Parikh, the author of the Subversion trilogy. I don't know if you'll ever read this, but your TikToks about you writing your books gave me so much confidence, especially since we're the same age. You made me feel like I could do it too. (Please go read her books!! They're so good!!)

To Dr. Glenn Keyser and Andrea Gonzalez. My college and senior year English teachers, respectively. You two were so supportive of me and I can't thank you enough. Thank you for being the amazing teachers that this world needs.

To my younger self. I can't deny that for a long time I hated you. But... it's not your fault. I thought you were weak and so many other things but you're not. You got through it. No matter how many times you fell, no matter how many times you wanted to quit, you got through it. We got through it. Thank you for not giving up on us. And to my current and future self, keep going. And to anyone else going through a tough time, please keep going. It'll get better, I promise.

Lastly, I want to thank YOU! You, who picked up this book, looked at it, and decided to get it! Whether you're reading it at home, on your phone, in school, (PAY ATTENTION! Or don't let the teacher catch you. Don't tell anyone I said that!), or browsing through it at the store, (because who hasn't done that?), thank you for giving this book at chance.

See you in the next one.